WRONGFUL DEATH

To Elin & Len
 Enjoy
 Walter J. Edwards M.D.

WRONGFUL DEATH

Walter T. Edwards, M.D.

Copyright © by Walter T. Edwards.

Library of Congress Number:		98-89883
ISBN#:	Hardcover:	0-7388-0317-0
	Softcover	0-7388-0318-9

All rights reserved. No part of this book may be reproduced or transmitted in any form or by any means, electronic or mechanical, including photocopying, recording, or by any information storage and retrieval system, without permission in writing from the copyright owner.

This is a work of fiction. Names, characters, places and incidents either are the product of the author's imagination or are used fictitiously, and any resemblance to any actual persons, living or dead, events, or locales is entirely coincidental.

This book was printed in the United States of America.

To order additional copies of this book, contact:
Xlibris Corporation
PO Box 2199
Princeton, NJ 08543-2199
USA

1-888-7-XLIBRIS
1-609-278-0075
www.Xlibris.com
Orders@Xlibris.com

PREFACE

No area in all of medicine creates as much fascination by the public as the Emergency Room. Many human dramas begin and end there, as did this one which resulted in the death of a patient, a malpractice case, and multiple murders.

Because of shoddy care by a primary care HMO physician, a young executive died unnecessarily, his family was shattered, and his company was bankrupted.

The resulting wrongful death suit was disrupted by the brutal murder of three witnesses. The primary physician became entangled in an affair which ended tragically for both him and his mistress and the HMO was destroyed due to its unethical medical care and criminal attempt to cover it up.

CHAPTER 1

Alex Boomer sat near the head of the table in the luxurious conference room of Acme Electronics. He nervously fingered his coffee cup and chain smoked Benson & Hedges cigarettes. He had arrived earlier than usual in order to be prompt for a 7:30 a.m. meeting of the Board of Directors, the most important meeting of his life.

In a few minutes he would be introduced as the new CEO of the company he had spent ten years of his life building and nurturing.

As he sat there listening to the chairman drone on about the growth of the company and Alex' contribution to that growth, he thought of all the previous meetings, travels, late nights, weekends and holidays he had spent reaching this goal. He thought about how he had neglected his wife, Elizabeth and his children to reach this pinnacle of success. The chairman interrupted his revelry by introducing him as the new CEO.

As he rose to respond, he noticed a slight twinge of pain in his chest and left arm. This had become more familiar to him in recent days and he had sought medical consultation. It was too late to take a nitro glycerine now. There was no time to display weakness.

"Thank you for the generous introduction, Mr. Chairman, and thanks to my fellow board members for the confidence you have expressed in me."

He had prepared a lengthy recitation of his plans for the company changes, taking it public and expanding its markets both domestic and foreign. His chest pain was growing more severe and more constant. He could feel perspiration on his forehead and upper lip, and he felt slightly dizzy. What an awkward time for this to occur, he thought. With that, he collapsed and fell to the floor.

The chairman rushed to his side and noted that he was covered in perspiration. His skin was gray and no pulse was palpable.

"Call the paramedics. Does anyone know CPR?"

Two board members quickly responded and one started mouth to mouth breathing after the other administered a blow to the chest. There was no response and he then started chest compressions along with the breathing. Someone else called 911 as the CPR continued.

It seemed like an eternity to the assemblage before the paramedics arrived. They immediately took over CPR, started an IV, and after contact with the hospital base station, administered electric shock and started IV medications.

There was no response and the decision was made to "load and go."

Suddenly a scream rang out through the emergency room bringing all activity to a halt and focusing the attention of everyone on its source. Just inside the door there was a well-dressed, attractive lady who was wringing her hands, crying and continuing to scream, "No, no, no, can't be." Those of us in the department immediately knew what was happening. We had just given up resuscitation on a 45-year-old man who had been brought in from his office following a "fainting episode." When he arrived in the emergency room, he was obviously in cardiac arrest. There was no pulse, no blood pressure, no respiration and his skin was a deep blue. He was moderately overweight and appeared to be a person of means and responsibility.

The paramedics had given a history which indicated that suddenly, in the middle of a meeting, this man had fainted and fallen to the floor. One of his colleagues immediately started CPR and someone else had called 911. The paramedics were at his office in approximately five minutes and had continued CPR, started an

IV, administered electric shock and had given the usual medications for cardiac arrest. None of this had caused any response and the cardiac monitor was flatline. The patient was immediately transported to our emergency room and taken into the resuscitation area. He was intubated and then ventilated by the respiratory therapist. Epinephrin and calcium carbonate and other cardiac stimulants were given intermittently through the IV, and he was shocked several more times, but there was no response to any of these measures. Nearly an hour passed with continuing efforts by the resuscitation team, but to no avail. The monitor remained flatline and the patient made no response as far as pulse, respiration and blood pressure was concerned. Finally, he was pronounced dead at 9:55 a.m.

In the meantime, his wife had been called and summoned to the hospital. Apparently, upon entering the door, she immediately discerned the situation and became semi-hysterical. She was then escorted to the privacy of the social workers office where the physician, the nurse and the social worker were faced with dealing with one of the most dreaded chores in all emergency medicine, notifying the wife of the sudden, unexpected death of her loved one.

Dr. Williams introduced himself and told Mrs. Boomer what had happened at the office, the CPR by his colleagues, the paramedic efforts at resuscitation and his treatment in the E.R.

"Your husband had the best of emergency care from the time he fainted until we realized that further efforts were fruitless. We gave up a few minutes ago."

"Was there nothing that could have been done to save him? We see it every day on television, and the media tells us all about the wonderful progress being made in emergency treatment of heart attack victims."

Dr. Williams explained, "This is the real world, not the media. They don't tell you about that. I am so sorry about your husband. Has he had heart trouble before or any type of serious illness?"

"No, but he just had a physical."

With that Dr. Williams excused himself to return to the other patients who had accumulated during the resuscitation efforts.

Elizabeth wanted to talk to the other doctor and asked the nurse to get him. Williams had been matter-of-fact, and she wanted to talk to someone with whom she could feel more confident, someone older. Jackie sought out Dr. Evans and found him in the minor suture room repairing a small chin laceration on a five-year-old boy.

"The wife of the cardiac patient wants to talk to you. She is very distraught and has little rapport with Dr. Williams."

"Okay, I am finished here. Put on a dressing, give him a booster and appointment at the outpatient clinic for three days from now to get his sutures removed. Get Dr. Williams working on the backup of patients and tell him I'll pitch in as soon as I've talked to the wife. Jackie, tell me the story of this patient. You heard the paramedic call and helped with the resuscitation, didn't you?"

"Yes," she said and furnished the details.

Dr. Evans entered the consultation room and introduced himself to Elizabeth Boomer. He extended his sympathy at her loss and gave her the details of her husband's sudden collapse including the CPR by his colleagues, resuscitation efforts by the paramedics and ER personnel.

"He just did not respond to anything. His heart stopped in that office and all the best efforts of everyone were in vain. I am so sorry. Is there anything I can do for you?"

"You can explain how this can happen. He had his routine physical by Dr. Lawrence, a primary care physician at the company HMO. The physical was a requirement for his promotion. He was told he was in excellent health, but needed to quit smoking, lose weight and start exercising regularly. Subsequently, while on a treadmill, he developed chest and arm pain and became sweaty. When he stopped walking, the pain disappeared and he returned to normal. The next day he saw Dr. Lawrence again, told him the story and was given a prescription for nitroglycerin. Reassured and told to exercise in a more leisurely fashion, he was to report the effects of the nitroglycerin if he had another episode. He did, took the nitroglycerin and was promptly relieved. He called the doctor and was reassured again. I then called and asked if Alex should not be referred to a cardiologist and have more tests. I was told it was unnecessary. Now, two days later, he is dead of a presumed heart attack. What do you think?"

"I think we should get an autopsy before you jump to any conclusions."

"Can that be done here?"

"Yes, but there will be a fee. If, on the other hand we make it a coroner's case, a post may not even be done, and we may not know any more than we do right now."

"Don't you think Dr. Lawrence was negligent?"

"I really cannot comment on that until we have the results of the post, and I have more facts concerning his previous care."

"Okay, let's get the autopsy," Mrs. Boomer requested.

Shortly thereafter she left, after signing permission for the post-mortem exam.

Elizabeth Boomer was a 38-year-old former beauty queen who became a professional golfer after graduating from the University of Houston. She had been successful, winning two tour events and placing in the top ten in many others.

On one of her trips across country, she happened to sit next to Alex Boomer in the first class section of the plane. By this time, she could afford herself this one luxury to make up for her grueling schedule.

He recognized her immediately since golf was his only avocation at the time. He was gregarious and outgoing and struck up a conversation with this beautiful lady. Though she was reserved by nature and background, she felt she had to maintain a hospitable public image. Soon they were engrossed in conversation about golf and his business career and eventually they moved to personal aspects of their respective backgrounds.

The long cross country flight passed in what seemed like record time and both realized if something wasn't done quickly, this relationship would end with the flight. She gave him a pass to the tournament she was playing in the next day and made him promise to come and follow her on the course and then have dinner afterwards.

This chance meeting and the subsequent weekend led to a relationship which included daily phone conversations, long trips by one or the other for brief times of togetherness stolen from their extremely busy and conflicting schedules.

Soon it became obvious her love for Alex was more important than her career and she knew she couldn't have both. At his urging, she gave up her golfing career and they were married.

Their marriage had been blissfully happy and they eventually had two children, a boy and a girl. His business career had been her only rival, but their love overcame the restriction on their time together. Every day they were together was like a honeymoon all over again.

And now it was all over. She had lost him as suddenly and as unexpectedly as she had found him.

Dr. Evans then called Dr. Lawrence and told him of the death. His response was one of shock and dismay. Evans questioned him about EKG findings and other lab and physical findings. His response was quite vague and defensive. The conversation ended abruptly when Dr. Evans told him there would be a post mortem.

CHAPTER 2

The Cardiac Care Registered Nurse and Dr. Evans discussed the case and both felt the patient had an acute M.I. which possibly could have been prevented. About that time there was a commotion outside the office and a loud voice shouted, "Just give me a reason, you son-of-a-bitch, and I'll blow your head off." On peering cautiously out the door into the corridor, there was a policeman with his gun drawn and a prisoner on the floor. It turned out the prisoner had tried to escape while the officers were getting a cup of coffee, and one of the waiting patients had tripped him. The officer had pinned him to the floor with his knee in his back and had his gun to the man's head. Needless-to-say, everyone took cover until the matter was resolved and the prisoner was in handcuffs and being lead to the patrol car by two burly policemen.

Shortly after the conversation with Dr. Evans, Dr. Lawrence called his malpractice company and was referred to a malpractice defense lawyer. The clinic clerk came to Dr. Lawrence's office to tell him he was getting behind and he needed to get off the phone and see patients. His response was that his phone calls at the moment were more important than seeing patients. He called the lawyer and filled him in on the Boomer case. The defense lawyer, Dennis McAllen, said he would obtain the clinic records, the autopsy results and the ER records, as well as some personal and financial information. Lawrence returned to seeing patients but seemed both distracted and upset.

Jackie called Dr. Evans to see a patient in Medical Room Three. The patient was a double amputee at hip level who had been living on the street for several years supporting himself by begging to supplement his Social Security Disability benefits. He moved about on a wooden platform mounted on four skate wheels. He had an indwelling catheter. His complaint today was fever and chills for two days. On exam, he was found to have a temperature of 105 degrees and was extremely anxious. He had no pain and no sensation from the waist down. There were no abrasions on the stumps of his legs. His blood pressure was 100 over 50. His catheter was draining cloudy urine and was leaking around it. Lab work was significant for pus in the urine with white cells too many to count and a white blood count of 22,000 with 90% polys indicating a severe urinary infection. Dr. Evans said, "This patient must be admitted stat and started on antibiotics and fluids." Shortly, the director of admissions called and said the patient was ineligible for admission to this hospital for financial reasons. He was a California medical financial aid plan patient. He would have to be transferred to the county hospital.

Dr. Evans replied, "This patient is not transferrable. He is in toxic shock and the delay might result in his death. "

He was given IV antibiotics and transferred anyhow. Six hours later he arrived at County Hospital in critical condition. The county doctor called and promised to file a protest with the Department of Health and Health Care Financing Administration. The rest of the day in the ER was routine with lacerations, fractures and a few elderly patients with medical problems.

Next morning Dr. Evans received a call from the administrator to report to his office.

"What now?"

The Administrator did not appear to be happy. He stated that there were several problems in the ER. Colin Bradford was a rather brusk individual and he was no friend of the ER. He was concerned with "bean counting." The problems he referred to at this time were, first of all, the police scuffle with their prisoners.

"One of the medical staff members complained to me that his patients do not feel safe in the Emergency Department and wanted a separate space and staff to care for all the private medical staff patients. He plans to bring it to the Medical Executive Committee."

Secondly, there was a call from the Health Department about the transfer of the kidney patient. They were also expecting action by HCFA, the Federal Health care Financing Administration. Thirdly, I got a call from a plaintiff lawyer about a Mr. Alex Boomer. He wants to discuss this case with you and Dr. Williams and the CCRN."

Dr. Evans stated, "The police matter was out of our hands except we could file a protest with the police chief about the officer's conduct. Secondly, we do not have either the space or personnel to dedicate a separate area for private patients of the medical staff. That would mean two cardiac rooms, two trauma rooms, two of everything as well as doubling the staff to take care of perhaps 300 patients a month. As to the Department of Health and HCFA, the regulations are clear about transfers and we violated them on the orders of your nursing director, and I assume with your approval. As to the lawyer, he will have to subpena our personnel and each of us will need a separate council provided by our respective malpractice insurance companies in order for us to talk to the lawyer. I suggest you notify the hospital insurance carrier of a potential lawsuit."

The meeting ended with the exchange of few pleasantries.

On return to the ER, there was a call from the pathology department about Mr. Boomer. He died of an acute Myocardial Occlusion involving the left anterior descending artery, nicknamed "the Widow Maker". The findings were otherwise normal. Dr. Evans called Dr. Lawrence to inform him of the pathology report and suggested that he notify his malpractice carrier. Again, Lawrence was defensive and insisted that this was not a preventable death. Evans did not argue with him and the call ended.

Jackie Hart, the day charge nurse, chastised Dr. Evans for the time spent out the Emergency Room with patients stacking up. Probably as retribution, she had saved a particularly unpleasant patient encounter for him. The patient was a 15-year old retarded female who had been raped and sodomized on the front steps of the local Catholic Church in broad view of the street and the sidewalk at 11:00 a.m. She was dirty, bruised and hysterical and had feces all over her buttocks, thighs and perineum. It was necessary to take slides for semen from the vagina and rectum before cleansing the patient, an extremely unpleasant task. After the nurse's aides cleaned the patient, she was carefully examined for bruises, abrasions and tears, especially about the perineum and rectum. The vaginal orifice and the rectum were stretched as well as lacerated. It was obvious that this episode was not wholly responsible for the distortion of both orifices. History from the police confirmed this conclusion. It seems that the patient had been abused for years by her father as well as neighborhood teenagers.

The rapists had been captured at the scene during the assault. The father will also be arrested and charged. The child was transferred to the County Pediatric Unit.

CHAPTER 3

Dr. Lawrence was somewhat shaken by the pathology report and called his malpractice insurance company and was transferred to the investigator. Lawrence informed him of the visits to his office, the death and the pathology report. The investigator inquired whether he had been served or put on notice. He indicated that he had not. The investigator assured him that in all likelihood he would be served and asked him to supply copies of the office records and pathology report. He stated he would obtain hospital and paramedic records, interview the personnel involved and attempt to interview the widow as well as the co-workers. Dr. Lawrence asked about the defense lawyer and was assured he would get the best available. All of this made the doctor even more apprehensive and he examined the office records of Mr. Boomer which contained little information which would be helpful in court. He silently cursed the system under which he was forced to practice.

He'd been well-trained in one of the better medical centers and was accustomed to appropriate tests and consultations, spending adequate time with patients, and being very conscientious in his medical practice. All that ended when the medical group became affiliated with an HMO and an MBA had taken over management of the group from the founding physician, who retired on signing the contract with the HMO. Management strategy changed rapidly soon thereafter. The ten doctors (four internists, two surgeons, two OB-Gyns, an ENT and a dermatologist) were called in for a meeting with the new manager and given a set of guidelines which included seeing more patients per day, ordering only the most necessary and least expensive tests, avoiding referrals to outside specialists, avoiding ER referrals, keeping patients out of the hospital whenever possible and avoiding expensive therapies if a less expensive one was possible. They were told they would work longer hours for less pay and that their level of income would depend upon how well they adhered to the above procedures. The above recommendations were against everything he had been taught and believed in.

This system had been in place only six months and already there had developed hostility of the patients and among the doctors themselves. The manager was universally hated with the exception of the senior surgeon, who was the other founding partner, not only for his suggestions about medical practice, but also his general attitude. He was brusk, domineering, curt with the personnel and developed a spy system with two of the nurses. Dr. Lawrence dreaded the encounter with him when he became aware of the suit, almost as much as he dreaded the suit itself.

After the discussion with the investigator, Dr. Lawrence was brought back to reality by Melissa Haley, his office nurse, who began to chastise him for spending so much time on the phone and letting patients stack up. He told her that his calls were related to the death of Mr. Boomer. He resumed seeing his patients, now more carefully and ignoring some of the directives of the administrator.

At noon he was directed to meet with Alex Garrison, the Clinic Administrator, after office hours. The meeting started off on a very disagreeable note. Mr. Garrison said, "I understand you are about to be sued. I also understand you have resumed some of your old practice habits. Tell me about the possible suit."

Dr. Lawrence explained that he had not yet been put on notice but had been told that a suit was almost inevitable. He explained the facts and then asked what was meant by returning to old practice habits. He was reminded that he had been warned about expensive tests, referrals and hospitalizations, but was ignoring these admonisitions. Dr. Lawrence said that had he followed his inclinations about medical practice, Alex Boomer would be alive and there would not be a lawsuit.

Garrison said, "You have malpractice insurance. Settle if necessary and get the best defense lawyer available."

Dr. Lawrence inquired, "Are you not the slightest bit concerned about the death of the patient?"

"My business is to see to the financial bottom-line, yours is to care for the patients as best you can following our guidelines. You are to continue to practice as you have been told or you will be unemployed."

On that note the meeting ended.

Dr. Lawrence returned to his office and found Melissa waiting for him. He was surprised and asked why she had not gone home.

"I was waiting to talk to you," she said. "I know what the meeting was about."

"So you're spying on me and reporting everything to Garrison."

"Yes, but I could be persuaded to stop and help you."

"And what would it take for you to do that, Melissa?" asked Dr. Lawrence.

"If you were willing to resume our affair, I could be very helpful in showing my appreciation in many ways."

Michael Lawrence was somewhat shocked. He thought that episode in his life was behind him, even though there had been an obvious tension between the two of them since the breakup.

The affair had started shortly after he joined the clinic two years ago. His wife had remained behind after he finished his residency until he could get settled in his new job and find a suitable place to live. He was lonesome, had no friends here and had more free time than at anytime during the three years of his residency. Melissa was bright, attractive and very helpful in orientating him to the clinic, the patients and the community. As often happens, one thing lead to another and they were soon involved in a torrid affair, which soon became the talk of the clinic. He was eventually given an ultimatum by the then Physician Director of the Clinic to break off the relationship and move his wife to the city, or find another job. He complied and was assured that Melissa would be replaced. However, the HMO took over before that could occur and Melissa remained in her position. She took the breakup hard, but continued to do her job and make his life as unpleasant as possible. Despite this he was surprised she would betray him in this fashion. What could he do? He loved his wife and did not want to lose her. The relationship with Garrison was such that he did not expect help from him. He could not face a scandal, especially now. And he had no idea how far Melissa would go to get even with him. "A woman scorned."

He decided to try to defer a decision and hope she would reconsider and accept the inevitable.

Dr. Lawrence, "Let me think about it. This comes as a complete surprise to me, and I have too many other problems right now to give this one proper consideration."

Melissa, "I give you one week." With that she flounced out of his office, giving him reason to recall the pleasure she had once provided him.

CHAPTER 4

It was a busy day in the emergency room, starting with a patient brought in from the airport in status epileptic seizures. He had been given IV Valium by paramedics and on arrival was free of seizures, awake, slightly drowsy but oriented times three. He was very pale and sweaty. His history was that he and his girlfriend had arrived at LAX from Alaska and were boarding a flight to Houston. Suddenly he started convulsing in the airport waiting room and had one seizure after another. The paramedics were called and gave him IV Valium which stopped his seizures. He was questioned as to previous seizures, diabetes, head injury, drugs and other things which might cause seizures. He denied everything. Exam revealed a thirty-year old, well-developed, well-nourished white male, conscious and oriented, but drowsy, and presently in no acute distress, but pale and drenched with perspiration. His blood pressure was 170 over 90 and pulse was 100. Further history and the exam by Dr. Evans was non-contributory. Lytes, blood sugar, CBC and a drug screen was ordered. Chest and abdominal x-rays and EKG weren't done in the emergency department. Dr. Rex Albright, the internist on call, was called in and he instructed Dr. Evans to admit the patient into the ICU and he would see him shortly. Evans suggested the patient should be seen before leaving the emergency department, but the internist insisted. Shortly after arrival in ICU, the patient again started seizing. This time Valium did not stop the seizures. Dr. Evans was called to see the patient in ICU. He arrived just as the patient expired. CPR was to no avail. Lab and x-ray were only partially complete and the drug screen had not been finished. However, the x-rays of the abdomen revealed multiple balloon-like objects in the colon. Obviously, this was a case of body packing to transport drugs into the United States. Most likely the drug was cocaine and a balloon had ruptured releasing a massive amount of cocaine into the bloodstream. Dr. Albright was informed of the death as well as a report to the coroner.

Dr. Evans returned to the emergency department somewhat chagrined. He was aware of this type of intoxication but had never seen it before. The patient had been in the hospital less than an hour and in all likelihood, could not have been salvaged. He was apparently more afraid of the drug dealers than his illness, and therefore refused to give medical personnel any information concerning the drugs.

The rest of the day was consumed with multiple patients with lacerations, fractures, abdominal pain and the usual gunshot and rape victims. At the end of his shift, Dr. Evans wanted to go home and relax, but he had to prepare for a meeting with the Medical Executive Committee about the proposed private patient area in the emergency department. The only thing the Administration would pay any attention to was cost/profit statistics so he had to be ready for tomorrow's meeting. He figured an extra physician for the twelve hours not presently covered by the out-patient clinic would be fifty to seventy thousand dollars a year. In addition, it would require at least four nurse equivalents, for instance, $165,000 and $100,000 in equipment. The income from the private patients would be offset by loss from the emergency department. In addition, the care of these patients would be less than optimal.

The next day Dr. Evans was contacted by the insurance investigator for his malpractice company to discuss the Boomer case. They met in the Administrator's office and the administrator and the hospital lawyer were also present. The crux of the investigator's report was as follows: Everybody, including the paramedics, the city, the hospital, the cardiac nurse, Dr. Williams who saw the patient in the Emergency Department, and Dr. Evans, as director of the department, plus Dr. Lawrence would be sued. The claim would be a high dollar amount since Boomer had a very large earning potential for the next fifteen to twenty years. Part of the objective in suing everyone would be to try to find the deep pockets, to obtain shared responsibility, and to try and develop dissension and finger pointing among the various and sundry defendants. This always guaranteed a plaintiffs verdict. This analysis produced stunned silence in the room since everyone involved believed Dr. Lawrence was solely responsible and he alone would be sued.

"So, what do we do now?" Evans asked the investigator.

"Each of you needs to meet with the lawyer assigned to the case by the insurance companies involved. Do not discuss the case with anyone else especially the plaintiff's lawyer or investigator. They like to con unweary doctors and/or nurses by stating, 'We are just trying to find out what really happened. We are suing someone else and you're not going to be involved.' The next thing you know you have a subpena and the statement you made will appear in the proceedings against you." The Administrator was to discuss the matter with the cardiac nurse and Dr. Evans with Dr. Williams and all the parties agreed to meet with their respective lawyers. On this sobering note, the meeting ended.

Dr. Evans returned to the emergency department quite depressed. In addition to this lawsuit and the potential of a similar one every time a patient presented to the Emergency Department, he was tired of fending off proposals like the one for separate space and staff for a handful of patients, increasing violence and the increasing problem with managed care which meant more problems providing the proper care for patients, and decreasing fees.

He had taken the position of the Director of the Emergency Department with the instructions to, "Clean up the mess and get it out of my hair. I don't care how much money you make." That statement had come from the previous Administrator twenty-five years ago when there was no such thing as Emergency Department Specialists or Emergency Departments. The ER was just that, a room at the back entrance of the hospital staffed by a nurse who couldn't get along with the director of nurses and medical staff physicians who took turns covering the place. These doctors included all specialties, radiologists, dermatologists, allergists, as well as surgeons and internists. The delivery of medical care was changing and doctors no longer made house calls and there was an ever increasing number of patients seeking care at the Emergency Room after hours. Their problems varied from cuts, bruises, and fractures to life-threatening problems such as heart attacks.

Dr. Evans was a natural to staff the ED, he'd had two years surgical residency before he was obliged to start making a living. In those days, residents made $10 to $100 a month and had no time to moonlight. Being married, even though his wife was working, there was not enough money to survive. He joined a clinic in a small town and was so competent and popular with patients that he soon left the clinic and developed a solo, private practice. This was successful but he eventually was offered the ED position in a large, metropolitan area. His experience in general medicine and surgery qualified him to deal with any type of patient presenting to the Emergency Department. He also had the experience of dealing with the financial aspects of medicine, hospital politics and personnel management. His personal background was that of middle-class upbringing, athletic prowess leading to a college football scholarship, and eventually a professional football career. He was an above-average student and he combined a pro football career with medical school. Unfortunately, an injury ended his athletic career in his senior year of medical school leading to the financial necessity to leave his residency after two years. He had married his college sweetheart in his senior year at college and had two young children. He was now fifty-eight years of age and all of this had taken a toll on him. The idea of retirement in the face of all the negative changes in medical practice was increasingly attractive. Perhaps it was time to discuss it with his wife.

CHAPTER 5

Dr. Lawrence was depressed for an entirely different reason. His marriage was in jeopardy, his career was dangling by a thread, the possibility of a lawsuit was hanging over his head and he had to deal with a jealous, vindictive woman for whom he still had feelings. At home he was short-tempered with his wife, Nancy, complaining about her spending and shopping habits. She was hurt but was offered no explanation. He must resolve the matter with Melissa who had the power to cause the loss of his position at the clinic and to be a hostile witness in the malpractice trial, if it came to that. He decided he would have to play along with her demands, at least for the time being. Besides, the thought of rekindling the passion of a romance with her might be a welcome diversion from his other problems.

The next day he made a date with her for dinner in a romantic, out-of-the-way restaurant they had frequented before, allegedly to discuss the relationship between them. Melissa was delighted and went shopping for the sexiest outfit she could find.

He called his wife and told her he had to have dinner with his lawyer about a potential problem at the clinic and might be late. The day dragged by, seeing his quota of patients. He was both excited and frightened by the prospect of being with her again and was not sure just how he would approach the deception.

When he arrived at her apartment, his doubts disappeared on seeing her. She was even more beautiful and desirable than he remembered. She was a twenty-eight year old blond with a voluptuous figure which was well displayed by the black mini-dress she wore. Rather than the bitchy, vindictive nurse he had become used to in the office, she was pleasant, happy, affectionate and desirable.

Over the course of the evening with good wine and good food, deception was replaced by desire and he knew how this evening was going to end. Their lovemaking temporarily blotted out all of his problems, he would worry about that tomorrow and probably many other tomorrows.

CHAPTER 6

Dr. Evans presentation at the Medical Executive Committee was smooth and convincing to most committee members. However, Dr. Albright had supporters who clung to the idea of the old type of ER which was for their convenience to allow them to see their private patients after hours. The hospital should not be in the business of supporting a group of doctors in the practice of medicine in the hospital emergency department. They also were concerned about the type of patients brought into the hospital and admitted to them as on-call specialists. Dr. Evans pointed out the change in the neighborhood and the change in the delivery of health care. Because of Medi-cal and the lack of medical insurance of a significant segment of the population, the ED is the only source of medical care for a large segment of the population. The hospital has a moral and legal responsibility to provide emergency care for these patients as well as the private patients. In addition, many private patients are seen in the Emergency Department for acute emergencies. The hospital does not have the funds or personnel to provide separate facilities for this group of private patients. The vote was close, but the proposal was voted down. No doubt Dr. Evans and the Emergency Department lost several friends and back-up specialists due to this very divisive proposal.

The police matter was also brought up by the Administrator. It was pointed out to him that five police agencies depend on this emergency department for all their emergency care and it would be disastrous to the hospital to anger them or try to bar them from bringing prisoners and injured officers to the department. It was decided again, with some dissension, to allow the Emergency Department Director to deal with the problem by informal discussions with the Chief of Police.

The meeting was adjourned after wrangling about several non-emergency matters. It seemed that each month a different department was singled out for criticism. With the advent of managed care and increasing government intervention in the practice of medicine, doctors were attacking each other like a pack of hungry wolves.

CHAPTER 7

On arrival at the clinic the next morning, Dr. Lawrence found a bubbly, pleasant office nurse waiting for him with a cup of coffee. Melissa kissed him on the cheek and obviously wanted to reminisce about the previous night. He was embarrassed and apprehensive about such displays in the office and told her that they must be very discrete, especially at the office. She looked a little hurt and pouted for a few minutes until she considered the wisdom of the matter.

The secretary brought in a return receipt letter from the attorney's office. He opened it with sweaty palms and hurriedly scanned the contents. It was a notice of intent to sue for medical malpractice, medical negligence causing the death of Mr. Alex Boomer.

He called his malpractice insurance company and notified the clinic investigator. The individual at the insurance company told him he would notify their defense attorney and someone from the firm would contact him shortly.

Meanwhile at the emergency department, Dr. Evans was summoned to the Administrator's office. There he received a similar letter notifying him of intention to sue. Garrison told him the hospital and the cardiac nurse and Dr. Williams were also put on notice. As expected, each entity would need to be defended by their own separate malpractice carrier and separate attorney. What a donnybrook this was going to be. It would be necessary for all attorneys to meet and plan strategy. Meanwhile all records pertaining to this case needed to be reviewed by each individual and his or her attorney. Dr. Evans returned to the Emergency Department to find the nursing personnel preparing to receive a major, multiple trauma. Jackie told him that the paramedics had called to alert the department that a car full of kids had been hit by a train and would be bringing multiple victims to the Emergency Department.

"What is their ETA?"

"Unknown, they had not reached the scene when they called."

"How long ago did they call?"

"About 10 minutes ago."

By now all was in readiness. The x-ray and lab techs had arrived. The trauma surgeon was on his way. Respiratory therapy was in the Emergency Department and both physicians were freed from other patients. Another twenty minutes went by and no ambulance or radio contact had occurred. About that time, the paramedics had appeared with one conscious, alert female on a gurney with a bandage on her right knee. Three teenage males and two females walked in behind the gurney, none of whom appeared injured. All seemed somewhat chagrined. The doctor asked the paramedics, "What is this? We are expecting major, multiple trauma. Is this it?"

"The kids car stalled on the track while they were playing chicken with the train. When they realized the car wouldn't start again, they all scrambled out and the only casualties are the car, which was demolished, and Susie here, who fell and skinned her knee. The ED staff was both annoyed and relieved. Susie's knee was examined, x-rayed, cleaned and dressed, and she was given a tetanus booster. The parents were notified to come after their kids, hoping they would point out the error of their ways to these kids.

The episode broke the tension of being notified of the impending lawsuit.

CHAPTER 8

No such event to ease Dr. Lawrence's tension. The Administrator abraded him for allowing such a disaster to occur and instructed him to settle, if possible, and avoid publicity that might reflect on the clinic and to keep the HMO out of it. Otherwise he would find himself without a job and significant difficulty in finding another. This lack of support was not unexpected.

Dr. Lawrence entered the downtown offices of the most prestigious malpractice defense firm in Southern California. The receptionist was a well-dressed, attractive young lady who smiled and asked him if she could help him. In a feeble attempt at humor, he replied that nobody could help him but she might direct him to the defense lawyer's office. He was ushered into an imposing paneled office in which every flat surface was covered with medical files. Dennis McAllen was an imposing man with grey hair and a beard to match. He was friendly and pleasant, but all business. He selected the appropriate file from the floor behind his desk and a fresh yellow legal pad and began his interrogation.

"Tell me briefly about your medical training and experience and later be prepared to assemble the most flattering and detailed curriculum vitae possible, especially with emphasis on cardiovascular disease."

Dr. Lawrence briefly recounted his premed education at Bradley University, the University of Illinois Medical School, internship and residency at Cook County Hospital in Chicago. He specialized in internal medicine with emphasis on cardiology.

McAllen interrupted, "What is the difference between training in internal medicine and cardiology?"

"Cardiology is a subspecialty of internal medicine, which requires three years of additional training with an emphasis on cardiac catherization, angiography and angioplasty."

"All right, what about your practice experience after residency?"

"I applied for a job with this clinic in Los Angeles and was accepted. I have practiced there for two years, the last six months as a part of an HMO."

"Has that change in management changed the way you diagnose and treat patients in any way?"

"Yes, we are encouraged to see more patients daily, to order fewer tests, to avoid consultations if possible, to avoid sending patients to the emergency department, to avoid expensive procedures such as MRIs, Cat Scans, cardiac caths, and surgery that is not urgent. We are to prescribe generic drugs and we are not to discuss alternative treatments with patients or criticize the HMO in any way."

"Is that not quite a change from your training and the way you practiced when you first became associated with the clinic?"

"Yes, it's dramatically different."

"Do your colleagues abide by these rules?"

"Yes."

"Do you?"

"As nearly as possible within confines of my conscience."

"Judging by this chart, you ignored your conscience in your care of the deceased."

Dr. Lawrence was somewhat taken aback by such a comment from his own lawyer. Though he knew that he was right, it seemed inappropriate for his legal representative to be indirectly criticizing his patient care.

"If you believe I was negligent, how do you propose to defend me?"

"It doesn't make any difference what I believe, it's what the jury believes that matters."

"You believe this will go to court then?"

"Yes, there is no way to settle. The economic loss alone will be several million dollars and your policy's limit is one million. It will depend on how much the city, the hospital and the emergency physicians will add to their share of a proposed settlement. Based on the records I have seen none of them has any responsibility and will add little or nothing. That being the case, you will spend the rest of your career paying off the balance of the judgment."

"What can I do then?"

"We will try to settle for policy limits, we can try the "devil-made-me-do-it defense", or after the judgment, countersue the HMO."

"What kind of defense is that?"

"You admit your negligence, offer your policy limits and state that the HMO, as a result of its policies, forced you to practice in a negligent manner."

"What are the chances of success?"

"I don't know, it's never been tried. If it works not only will it get you off the hook, but will force every HMO in the country to change its policies drastically. I would like to try it, but it is your decision."

"It sounds like you're gambling with my life to explore an unproven legal theory. Perhaps I ought to seek another legal opinion. "

"You are welcome to do that, but your insurance company does not pay for second opinions. I am sure you will want to consider your options. Think about it, talk it over with your wife. Seek another legal opinion, if you must, but do not discuss the case or the options I have outlined with anyone else."

On that depressing note, he shook hands with the attorney and promised to get back to him within a week.

How could he have gotten into such a mess? He knew better than to practice in such a slipshod matter. He had considered the alternatives and risks when he saw Mr. Boomer, but was more concerned with his position at the clinic than the welfare of the patient. Not only had he destroyed his career and life, but he had also been responsible for the death of an innocent patient and the grief of his family. How could the best system of medical care the world has ever known be sacrificed on the altar of political expedience, government interference and questionable economic savings and bureaucratic incompetence?

It was now three in the afternoon of his day off, and he wanted to see Melissa but she was still at the clinic and would be for at least three more hours. He briefly considered stopping at the bar in the office building where he had spent the early afternoon, but he didn't want to risk getting on the freeways after drinking what may turn out to be way too many scotch and waters. So he decided to go home to contemplate his predicament and drown his sorrows.

He opened his garage door and was surprised to see Nancy's car. She normally didn't get home from school until five thirty.

She greeted him rather coolly and inquired, "Where've you been?"

"I just spent a depressing two hours with my lawyer."

"What did he say this time?"

He had used evening dinners and appointments with his lawyer as an excuse for times he had spent with Melissa.

"He was very discouraging."

Dr. Lawrence then recounted the substance of his conversation with McAllen.

"Why has his opinion changed so much since your other conferences?"

"He's gotten more information about the patient's job status, and therefore, he expects a demand that would be greater than my insurance policy limits."

"What are you going to do?"

"I haven't decided. We could be destroyed financially and professionally if we lose."

"Nancy, let's get dressed and go to the club for some drinks and dinner. We can worry about this in the morning."

That was one of their problems with their marriage. She was a great procrastinator and very impractical. He, on the other hand, had been regimented all his life, especially in medical school and residency. Their personality differences led to many conflicts, increasingly so since the beginning of his affair. Melissa, on the other hand, was very practical, serious, regimented and had good business sense in addition to being the most sexually attractive woman he had ever known. He really wanted to be with her especially now, but he opted for dinner at the club with Nancy to avoid suspicion.

CHAPTER 9

Dr. Evans also spent the afternoon of his day off with his attorney. Fortunately his malpractice carrier assigned him to a firm and an attorney with whom he had worked as an expert witness. Mr. Jim Bishop was an affable man in his late forties, alert, handsome, and immaculately dressed.

"So now you are going to be on the other side of the bench."

"Afraid so, though I can't understand why."

"Have you ever seen a doctor who felt he should be sued?"

"Come to think of it, no."

"However, in this case I agree with you. From the records I've seen, Dr. Lawrence is solely responsible and should be the only party to this suit. The plaintiff lawyer is sharp and he knows the jury will have the option of assessing percentage blame to each of the defendants so we will have to prepare for trial anyhow. I will meet with Mr. Sloanberg and try to convince him to dismiss you and Dr. Williams, subtly suggesting that your testimony as an expert for his client might be more valuable than any settlement he might obtain from your insurance company. This is going to be a very high-dollar case and he might want to keep everybody in, hoping all the defendants might engage in finger-pointing. I'd rather have you out of the suit and serving as a plaintiff's expert."

"How would that work out for the hospital and the paramedics?"

"There would have to be an agreement that you would testify that they were blameless also and Dr. Lawrence is solely and completely responsible for the wrongful death. I'm sure I won't be able to make such a deal until you have been deposed. If you can convince him that your testimony will be very damaging to

Lawrence, he might be amenable to such a deal. Don't discuss this with anyone else. Remember, your answers are separate and distinct from each and everyone involved. You have no friends in this matter except me."

They exchanged small talk about families and mutual friends in both medical and legal professions. Bishop again admonished him about not discussing the case. He indicated that the suit would move through the court system more rapidly than usual because of the prominence of the victim and the publicity surrounding his death.

Alex Boomer was well-known in both social and business circles. He had been a man on the rise in the local business community. He was vice-president of a well known electronics firm and rumored to be the next president. In addition, he had been active in local charities and had received significant publicity because of that. He was personable, handsome and a natural for the media. His wife was beautiful and very active in the country club and golfing circles, having been a professional golfer before her marriage. Because of all this, their pictures and publicity concerning their activities appeared frequently in the local newspapers and on television. Their image was of success and money which made the public interested in them. When the news of his death first appeared, people were shocked and concerned. The account of Boomer's death was anything but flattering to the medical community and hinted at medical negligence.

Dr. Evans arrived home two hours earlier than usual and his wife was surprised to see him at this hour. He decided that this was as good a time as any to tell her about the lawsuit.

"I spent part of the afternoon with Jim Bishop."

"What is this about? Do you have another case with him?"

"Well, yes, but this one involves me. Do you remember I told you about a cardiac patient that came in DOA about a month ago? I thought that the suit would be against his primary physician only, but the family's lawyer is Eric Sloanberg, the most ruthless and successful plaintiff's lawyer in Southern California, and he is suing everybody who came near the patient hoping to get a little money out of each party and a lot out of the primary physician."

"Do we have anything to worry about?"

"Just the annoyance of being sued, the time spent and the notoriety. My lawyer is Jim Bishop who I have worked with, as you know, the best malpractice defense attorney in the business. He seemed pretty confident. Let's relax tonight. I have tomorrow off and work the weekend."

Relaxation to them meant a bottle of wine, dinner and a rare evening of lovemaking. However, he was unable to concentrate on the prospect of any of this. He was somewhat worried about the suit and he was thinking of retiring and wanted to discuss it with Ann. Now was not the time, however. He couldn't seriously consider retirement until the suit was settled and there was no point in bringing it up until then.

They decided to eat at one of their favorite French restaurants in the suburbs. It was a small inland place located in a converted house just off of a busy thoroughfare. The lighting was subdued and there were no more than a dozen tables, two middle aged male waiters with French accents, a large bar and the menus were on chalkboard brought to each individual table. After ordering a bottle of chardonney, Dr. Evans looked around the room and was surprised to see one of his old friends from County Hospital, a urologist. Dr. Jim Rose recognized him and came over, shook hands and introduced his wife. After the usual small talk, he asked Evans if it was not him who had sent a double amputee with septic shock due to a urinary infection to his service. Evans admitted it and was ready to be very defensive.

Rose said, "Don't be perturbed. The resident who threatened you has been disciplined not only for his unprofessional conduct with you but also for his care of the patient. "

"Why?"

"First of all, the transportation system screwed up and made this a routine transport rather than stat. It took six hours to get this man to our hospital rather than thirty minutes. The poor guy was nearly moribund when he arrived. Then, on his own initiative without consulting the staff, the resident took him to O.R. and inserted a supra pubic catheter. This was done without anesthesia since the patient had no sensation below his waist. The drainage helped his immediate problem and the patients infection and shock improved dramatically. However, since he has been up on his cart, he is still leaking urine through his penis and passing none from the catheter. The resident, in his zeal to solve this problem, forgot gravity, that the outlet to the penis is lower than that of the catheter. Both the doctor and the administrators are so chagrined and concerned about a suit they do not dare go after you for transferring the patient. Just imagine if the newspapers and a plaintiff's attorney got hold of this story."

He then realized that both wives were slightly pale and apologized for telling the story at the dinner table. Such is the lives of doctor's wives. They exchanged pleasantries and returned to their respective tables.

Dr. Evans usually spared Ann the gory details of his patient encounters and she only heard about them from the news media. She had been a college English teacher after graduation. They had met during their college years and had married shortly after graduation. She'd had to work while he was in medical school and residency, despite his athletic income. She was really not prepared to deal with all the gore of his profession and he respected that. The story of this unfortunate incident put a damper on their night out.

CHAPTER 10

Although their evening seemed doomed from the beginning because of Nancy's bad humor and Michael's depression, it turned out to be more pleasant than either had anticipated. Nancy dressed very seductively and attractively. That alone raised her spirits and improved her disposition. After all it had been weeks since he had taken her out and she had felt deprived and lonesome. Tonight must be special.

When he saw her, he was again impressed with her beauty and felt some of the emotions and sensations that brought them together originally. He also felt guilty about his love and passion for Melissa. How could he have gotten himself into such a predicament? As the evening passed, his depression about his career, the lawsuit and his affair was replaced by his desire for Nancy. None of this was discussed. They finally cut short their evening out and returned home to a fabulous evening of lovemaking. He would worry about his problems in the morning.

CHAPTER 11

Dr. Evans' weekend at the ED was horrendous. It started Friday at 3:00 p.m. and ended Saturday at 7:00 a.m. and continued the same shifts both Saturday and Sunday. These were normally the busiest shifts of the week, with the exception of holidays. Children were home and fell off trampolines, bicycles and were hit by baseballs, bats, cars and parents. Adults drank too much beer, beat their wives or girlfriends, shot their friends or neighbors, got into auto accidents and tried to rob the nearest liquor store. And, of course, there were some medical ailments both minor and serious.

    This Friday evening was no exception. When he arrived, the place was backed up at least two hours with the walking wounded and the noise from the paramedic radio crackling continuously requiring the full service of the cardiac nurse. His first case was that of two narcotic officers who had busted a PCP lab and inhaled some of the product as well as the ether used in its manufacture. They were both dizzy, pale and sweaty, confused and moderately hypertensive and agitated. They wanted to go home but he felt they should be sedated with haldol and kept in the Emergency Department observation area. The police sargent arrived and wanted them admitted. Soon four other colleagues came into the ED and were concerned that all of the personnel had not stopped what they were doing to concentrate on the officers. This was always the case. Police became semi-hysterical when one of their own was sick or injured. They could be very disruptive, but were reasonable when handled with firmness and compassion. This episode was no exception. After about four hours of observation and sedation, the officers symptoms abated and they were sent home. Dr. Evans felt like he had put in a hundred yards of sutures in various areas of the body of both kids and adults. All resulted from minor trauma and were not serious, except one.

Police brought in a black man who had been cut three ways: long, deep and frequently. The lacerations were about the face, neck, arms and hands. There had been significant blood loss although the wielder of the knife had missed all major arteries. It was almost as if he was punishing or torturing the victim.

Dr. Evans asked, "How did you get cut?"

"My friend and I got into an argument over a bottle of beer. He had a knife and I didn't," explained the patient.

The officer stated, "He insists that is what happened and I don't know any different."

Dr. Evans set about repairing the wounds which required over a hundred stitches in one and a half hours. Fortunately, there was a second doctor in the department who kept the place cleared out of other patients. Ordinarily lacerations such as this would go to the OR and be sutured by a plastic surgeon. Since this was a police case and compensation was minimal, Evans decided to repair the wounds in the Emergency Department.

He had just finished when a second policeman entered and said to the patient, "Did you know that your girlfriend was found dead in the garage behind your house?

She was shot in the back of the head in a kneeling position with her hands tied behind her."

The patient, "You're kidding me."

"No, she's in another room of this department. Do you want to come and see her?"

He was escorted into the morgue room and there was a young girl on the gurney with a small hole in the back of her head and part of her face blown away by the exit wounds. Her hands were still tied behind her back with a telephone cord. At that sight, the patient broke down crying and cursing alternately.

When he finally got his emotions under control, he said to the officer, "I'll tell you everything. I'm a runner for a local dope dealer by the name of Moses Johnson. Two days ago I was boosted by one of his rivals and lost $10,000 worth of coke. I tried to tell him that but he didn't believe me so he went to work on me with his blade. He finally stopped and took Dorsey out of the room because she was screaming and begging him to leave me be. The police came and brought me here before I could look for Dorsey. That MF cut me and shot her. If you don't get him first, I will."

Policeman, "Will you testify to all this if we arrest Moses?"

"You bet I will."

After he was bandaged, he was taken to the station to formally make that statement. The rest of the night was fairly routine with an assortment of drunks, minor auto accidents, sick kids and rape victims.

Saturday night was also busy. Summer brought on an increase of both minor and major emergencies. People were doing more activities outside, performing physical work and athletics they were not used to, which exposed them to accidents both minor and major and stress on their cardiovascular system beyond their capability. One such case was particularly tragic. A twenty-seven year old man was in the park with his wife and two young children. He became involved with a pickup basketball game with some of his friends. He had been an athlete in high school and college, but for the last four or five years, had been an office manager in a real estate firm and had been almost completely sedentary. He suddenly collapsed, fainted and became pale and sweaty. On falling to the ground he came to but was still weak, pale and sweaty and had pain in his left shoulder. He rested for a few minutes and began feeling somewhat better. His pain disappeared and his color improved. He wanted to return to the game but his wife prevailed on him to continue to rest. He still did not feel up to par and the pain in his arm returned. His wife insisted he, "go to the ER for a check up." He finally consented but refused to allow her to call the paramedics and he drove himself to the hospital. He went to the front door rather than the Emergency Department entrance. He walked through the endless corridors of the hospital until he finally found the Emergency Department. By this time he was short of breath, his pain was worse and he was perspiring despite the air conditioning. He was seen by the triage nurse and immediately taken into the cardiac room and monitored. He told Dr. Evans his story and suddenly he collapsed, convulsed and became pulseless. The monitor was straight line. CPR was started immediately, an IV was established and the patient was given medication. He was given epinephrin and calcium and he was intubated. He was shocked repeatedly. This was continued for an hour without any resulting establishment of heart rhythm and he was pronounced dead. The wife was inconsolable and the children couldn't understand why daddy couldn't go home with them. On questioning, after his wife had somewhat regained her composure, it was ascertained that the patient had no history of heart trouble by name or symptom. However, his father had died of a heart attack at age 40. Needless to say, a sense of gloom hung over the ER personnel like fog on a early June morning in Southern California. Not only was there a sincere feeling of compassion for the patient and his family but also a sense of defeat by their ever present arch enemy, death.

Sunday night was extremely quiet. After a minor flurry of routine patients in the afternoon and early evening, patient flow decreased to a trickle. So much so that Evans decided to go to bed about 11:30 p.m. The weekend had been both physically and mentally draining. About 2:00 a.m. he was aroused by the nurse to see an auto accident victim. The patient was a nineteen year old, clean cut male who was lying motionless on the gurney complaining of neck pain. He stated that he had no feeling below the neck and could not move any of his extremities. He was returning home from a church outing when his car ran out of gas. He stepped out of the driver's side and fell into a ditch. It was dark and he didn't realize that his car was on the edge of a ten-foot deep cliff. He had no chance to break his fall and landed very awkwardly on the side of his head. He remembered nothing else until he was lifted out of the ditch by paramedics. His head, neck and extremities were immobilized and he was on a gurney.

Exam revealed a well-developed, well-nourished white male lying quietly on the gurney strapped to a backboard. He was complaining of pain in his neck and that he had no feeling below his neck and could not move his extremities. He had priopism and a positive babinski bilaterally. His pulse was 50 and regular and his blood pressure was 100/50. His neck was very tender near the mid-point. He was asking what was wrong, "why can't I feel anything, why can't I move my arms and my legs. "

Dr. Evans, "We are not sure. We'll have to take x-rays to see."

A cross-table lateral c spine was ordered and there was a fracture dislocation at C 4 and 5. The patient's parents arrived and wanted to know what had happened to their son and how he was.

Dr. Evans, "Your son was in an unusual accident and has broken his neck. At present he is paralyzed from the neck down and has no sensation below his shoulders. I have a call in to a neurosurgeon to come and see him and possibly operate. Sometimes when a fracture is reduced and stabilized, motion and sensation will return."

Parents, "You say sometimes. That doesn't sound very optimistic."

Doctor, "Optimism in a case like this is somewhat misplaced. The neurosurgeon will be more qualified to discuss the prognosis with you but only after surgery will we be sure."

Nurse, "I called Dr. Gibson and he sounded quite drowsy and apparently dropped the phone because I kept getting a busy signal. He frequently is very difficult to arouse."

Evans, "Send the police out to get him. We can't transfer this patient and eliminate any possibility of restoring his function. Besides I've already told the parents that he would be here."

The police arrived at Dr. Gibson's home and were unable to arouse anyone. They called the ER to ask for instructions. Knowing this had happened before, there was some question whether or not to break in. Dr. Evans made the decision for the police to break in and check on the doctor's well-being or just arouse him to come to the ER to see this patient. The police, after conferring with their sergeant, broke into the house only to find Gibson dead drunk. They reported back to the ER. Evans decided this was the responsibility of the chief of staff who was an anesthesiologist, named Casper, who went to Gibson's home and poured coffee down him until he produced a wide-awake drunk. Since there was no other neurosurgeon available, Dr. Caspar brought Gibson to the hospital, but carefully avoided his having any contact with the boy's family. He reviewed the x-rays, however, but was unable to see a fracture which everyone else was able to see from across the room. Dr. Caspar met with the family and told them their son would be admitted, observed and possibly operated on at 8:00 a.m. (It was now 4:00 a.m.) In the meantime, he continued his efforts to sober up Dr. Gibson. This was eventually successful and Gibson took the patient to the OR and applied sugar tone traction to the head and neck. After twenty-four hours of traction, the patient was taken back to the OR by Gibson's associate who performed a debriedmont and stabilization of the fracture. The cord damage was permanent and the patient was permanently quadriplegic.

At 7:00 a.m. Dr. Evans, weary from lack of sleep, tension and frustration, ended his weekend marathon and returned home to recover. He slept away Monday and Monday night from pure exhaustion.

CHAPTER 12

Monday morning brought Dr. Lawrence a return to reality. His weekend had been like old times and he had been able to forget his problems at the clinic, the lawsuit and even Melissa. On his arrival, Melissa was anxiously waiting in his office somewhat perturbed that a whole weekend had passed without a phone call from him, but ectatic to be with him again. She knew this was one of the penalties she must pay for the privilege of loving him. Despite the deja vu he had felt with Nancy, he was excited to be with Melissa again, and he was again under her spell.

Their tet-a-tet was interrupted by a call from the Administrator notifying him that a subpena had been served for him to appear Wednesday for a deposition. This was a hell of a way to start a new week. He hurriedly called his lawyer to notify him only to find it had already been arranged between the two opposing attorneys.

The CEO of the HMO also had been notified even thought it was not named in the suit. However, William Blake felt that the HMO must be represented as an observer only and he notified the house council to be present.

CHAPTER 13

On arrival at his lawyer's office, Dr. Lawrence found himself confronted by five hostile attorneys, one each from the hospital, the city, Evans' ER Group, the HMO and the plaintiff. He had never been in this situation before and was petrified. He was sworn and then asked by the plaintiff's attorney if there was any reason why he could not give accurate and truthful testimony today because of illness, medication, drugs or for any other reason. He answered in the negative. Eric Sloanberg, the plaintiff's attorney, introduced himself and stated that he represented the Boomer family in a wrongful death suit against him. He then introduced the other attorneys and stated who they represented. Each one had a long yellow pad and was poised to take notes. The court reporter with her little machine was already typing furiously and sitting across the table from him. The questioning began with inquiry about his name, address and profession. That was followed by extensive questioning about his education, starting with college, medical school, and continuing with residency and present occupation. He was then asked about his qualifications to diagnose and treat cardiac patients. Dennis McAllen, Lawrence's defense attorney, objected on the grounds that when Dr. Lawrence first saw Boomer, it was not known that he was a cardiac patient. Sloanberg then modified his question to reflect cardiac patients in general, not the deceased in particular. He then produced Boomer's office records and asked Dr. Lawrence to identify them. McAllen again objected, stating the suit pertained to what happened in the Emergency Department rather than the office. Sloanberg was becoming frustrated and a prolonged argument ensued between the two attorneys with threats to take it to the judge for a ruling. Finally McAllen withdrew his objection and the records were accepted as Exibit 1. The questioning began again as to whether the handwriting was that of Dr. Lawrence. McAllen corrected his adversary stating that these were copies and Lawrence had not written or made the copies, but only the original. Another heated exchange between attorneys ensued. Lawrence was becoming upset by all the wrangling. He was visably nervous.

McAllen noted this and asked to go off the record and step outside and speak privately with client.

Dr. Lawrence, "All of this arguing seems pointless. Why don't we get on with this and get it over with."

McAllen, "You don't understand. It is my job to upset the opposing council as much as possible and try to disrupt this deposition. I want him to get as little information as possible from you. So, relax and let me do my job."

They returned and went back on the record.

Sloanberg, "This first record is a copy of your physical exam of Boomer, is it not?"

"Yes."

"Your findings were that he was in normal health except that he was overweight, smoked and didn't get enough exercise."

McAllen, "Those were not findings, they were medical advice like any physician might give to almost any middle-aged American male."

Sloanberg, "Those comments are part of Boomer's medical record, yes or no?"

McAllen, "They are not findings."

Sloanberg, "Overweight is."

McAllen, "Where is overweight mentioned in this record?"

Sloanberg, "You're nitpicking, trying to disrupt my deposition. If you don't stop it, I'm going to stop and go to the court for sanctions."

McAllen, "I just want this record to be accurate."

Sloanberg, "The fact that you made these suggestions after

the physical indicates that you did not think the deceased was in good health and his lifestyle was compatible with heart trouble."

McAllen, "Don't answer that. It calls for a conclusion that is not based on any facts in the medical records."

Sloanberg, "Does the medical record indicate that your examination found anything that would lead you to believe that Boomer had heart disease?"

Lawrence, "No."

Sloanberg, "There was no treatment that should have been recommended at that visit?"

Lawrence, "No."

Sloanberg, "The fact that the records are rather skimpy does not indicate that you did a skimpy exam, or does it?"

McAllen, "This record reflects only pertainent, positive findings and not negatives and I resent your inference that the doctor gave a poor quality examination. You may answer, doctor."

"No, I did my usual complete exam including blood pressure, blood count, EKG and chest x-ray and all were within normal limits."

McAllen, "You've answered the question."

"It's twelve o'clock. Let's take a lunch break and resume at two p.m."

All this wrangling had encompassed two hours and little had been accomplished. Just as McAllen had desired. He and his client had lunch together as he had wanted to discuss the other records and phone calls.

"When Boomer returned and told you the story about exercise-induced pain, were you not concerned about heart disease?"

"It had to be considered. I thought the nitro might serve as a diagnostic test. If he was relieved by the nitro, I would be more concerned about angina and would order further tests."

"According to the patient's wife, he was relieved by nitro and you were notified and did nothing."

"I never received those calls. If they were answered by another doctor or nurse, I was not informed. With that history I certainly would have sent the patient to a cardiologist for further testing despite the admonitions of the HMO."

"That is a good answer to the most damaging part of the case. Stick to it and don't let him shake you."

Lunch break concluded and they returned to the office and the depo resumed.

Sloanberg, "Back on the record. The second copy of the alleged chart from your office is in your handwriting. Correct?"

"Yes."

"It states that ten days after the physical exam, the deceased returned to your office with a chief complaint of chest pain on exertion."

"Yes."

"Did you examine him?"

"Yes."

"Did you do an EKG?"

"No."

"Did you do any blood work?"

"No."

"Did you refer him to a cardiologist?"

"No."

"You did give him a prescription for nitroglycerin."

"Yes."

"Does that not mean that you thought he had heart disease?"

Lawrence, "It was part of my differential diagnosis."

Sloanberg, "In this day and time, is nitro adequate for a young, vigorous man with heart disease?"

McAllen, "At that time there was no evidence that this patient had heart disease. Don't answer that."

"Chest pains on exercise in a middle-aged obese male who smokes and has a very stressful job is very suggestive of heart disease, is it not?"

McAllen, "Don't answer that. Sloanberg has just asked you a hypothetical question, which does not specifically refer to this patient. You do not have to answer it."

"He is a doctor, isn't he?"

"Yes, but he is not here as an expert witness to help you make your case with a hypothetical."

"Boomer was a middle-aged, slightly obese male who smoked, had a tension-filled job and had chest pain on exercise, was he not?"

"Yes."

"Was it not suggestive to you that he had heart disease?"

"It was one of the possibilities."

"Did you think nitro was adequate treatment for such an individual who might have heart disease?"

"As a test for heart disease, it was reasonable."

"Are there not more specific and well-recognized tests, such as a stress test, blood test and angiography?"

"You're again asking a hypothetical question, but he may answer."

"Yes."

"Why did you not order one or more of these tests?"

"I felt that heart disease was only one of several conditions which could be causing his pain and if nitro relieved it, other tests would be indicated."

"Did nitro relieve his pain?"

"I don't know."

"Mr. Boomer called the office and reported that the nitro did relieve his pain, did he not?"

"I never received such a call."

Mr. Sloanberg, "At this point, I want to suspend this depo and resume it at a later time."

McAllen, "I object to that. You have covered all that this witness knows about this case."

Sloanberg, "I have other witnesses who may dispute your last statement, and I want their testimony under oath in order to clarify the doctor's last answer."

After much wrangling between attorneys, it was decided that

a continuation of this depo would be scheduled at a future date convenient to all parties.

Dr. Lawrence and Mr. McAllen went back to his office to discuss the depo.

Lawrence, "What was the reason for that?"

"He wants the depo of Mrs. Boomer that her husband did indeed call you and report the results of the nitroglycerin. Did you not receive such a call?"

"No, I did not."

"Do you know if anybody else in the clinic did?"

"No."

"You will have to question everyone to see if such a call was received. If not, it's your word against the widow."

Lawrence, "No one at the clinic is going to admit such a breach of protocol."

McAllen, "If we could prove that, we would have a more specific cause of action against the HMO."

It was almost 4:00 p.m. when Dr. Lawrence returned to the office. Melissa had been on pins and needles all day because of the deposition. She had fallen so deeply in love with him that she was extremely sensitive to his feelings and he was visibly upset . She was also confused by the slight change of attitude towards her after the weekend. She knew he still lived with Nancy and possibly slept with her, but she tried to put that out of her mind. She was able to when they were together, but it had been nearly a week since they had seen each other away from the office. She was feeling all the insecurities of a mistress but rationalized his detachment on the basis of the office problems and the deposition.

Melissa, "How was it?"

"Terrible. I was made to feel very incompetant. Besides, apparently Boomer called the office to report that the nitro relieved his pain and was reassured. The wife thinks he talked to me and that really makes me look incompetant. You didn't talk to her, did you?"

"Of course not. You know I am too professional to do something like that. I may have been mad at you then, but I certainly would not have done something like that to hurt you."

"Then, who could have? Who is so stupid or unprofessional as to violate medical protocol in such a manner?"

"I can't imagine, but I'll make some discrete inquiries."

"Finding the source may be the only way to get me out of this mess. My lawyer is very pessimistic. Be careful about discussing this whole, unpleasant mess."

Melissa, "Enough shop talk for today. Let me take you home, feed you some wine and take advantage of you."

He wasn't in the mood, but how could he resist such an offer from so beautiful a woman.

CHAPTER 14

The HMO attorney reported back to his CEO about the depo. He indicated Dr. Lawrence had done reasonably well at the depo but his lawyer was a formidable opponent.

"Can he win?"

"At this stage it's hard to say. The most important point that developed out of this depo was the question whether Lawrence received a phone call from the deceased about his relief from nitro. It may come down to who the jury believes, the doctor or the plaintiff. The other problem is whether someone else at the clinic took that call. If that should surface, the HMO would be brought into the suit, at least as a co-defendant."

"That must not happen. Meet with the personnel and point out the legal and professional ramifications of medical advice by anyone except a physician. Also meet with the doctors separately, emphasize the medical/legal perils to them of giving advice to someone else's patient without reviewing patient records. Do not refer to this incident or the malpractice case."

Dr. Lawrence returned home just before midnight disheveled and drunk. He had given little thought as to his excuse. Nancy was awake and both alarmed and hostile.

"Where have you been? No deposition lasts this long."

"My lawyer and I had dinner and a few bottles of wine after the depo."

"You two are becoming drinking buddies because of this case." She was skeptical, but had no real reason to suspect him especially after last weekend. There was not further discussion but she resolved to be more observant.

At breakfast he recounted the details of the deposition and its implications despite his hangover. She was more sympathetic this time, even though she did not understand the potential consequences.

Melissa began her inquiries with the telephone operator. She did not remember a specific call but checked her phone records for the date in question, and found a notation of a call which fit the description given her. The call at 4:45 pm., March 2nd and was referred to Sue, the nurse of Dr. Shepard, the founding partner. Melissa went directly to Sue and inquired about the call. She was told, yes, she took such a call and referred it to Dr. Shepard after being told that Dr. Lawrence had already left for the day. Obviously Melissa could not quiz Shepard about his disposition of the phone message. She reported this to Michael Lawrence. He was relieved by the news but did not know how to proceed. He called his lawyer and reported the findings. McAllen indicated the only way to deal with this information was through a deposition of Dr. Shepard, which he would schedule forthwith.

In the meantime, John Bailey, the HMO attorney, scheduled a meeting with the clinic employees, nurses, secretaries, etc. This was highly unusual. The only similar meeting occurred after the HMO contracted with the clinic. There was a buzz of rumors ranging from closure of the clinic to speculation concerning the malpractice suit. The HMO management style was arbitrary, inflexible and militaristic and was totally unsympathetic to the welfare of employees as well as patients so the scheduled meeting generated both fear and apprehension.

Everyone was assembled in the waiting room an hour before office hours since attendance was compulsory. Bailey was friendly and affable and put his audience at ease almost immediately. After a bad joke, he assured the group that this was just a routine review of the HMO and clinic policies and procedures. He emphasized courtesy to the patients both in the office and on the phone as well as the accuracy of handling phone calls. He also indicated that it was both contrary to policy and illegal for anyone except physicians to dispense medical advice, including prescription refills, whether or not to see the doctor about any problem and comment about the merit of any treatment or procedure. Finally, they were not to discuss patient problems or treatment outside of the office or among themselves.

Because of the publicity of the Boomer malpractice suit, the motivation behind the topics discussed was clear, especially to Sue. She had already breached the policy by revealing the details of the handling of the Boomer call. If her action became known, she would most assuredly lose her job and she certainly could not afford that. So, immediately after the meeting adjourned, she called Melissa and invited her for a drink after hours. Melissa knew what this was about but had no choice but to comply.

Between patients Melissa found Dr. Lawrence in his office and told him of Sue's call.

"What will I tell her?"

"Just tell her I was surprised when told of Boomer's claim that he called. I wanted to know if it actually happened or if Mrs. Boomer's attorney was making it up to strengthen her case. Ask her to keep your conversation in confidence and assure her that you will do the same."

Melissa and Sue met at a small bar a block from the clinic and the adjoining hospital, a bar called the "Annex" by the medical personnel who frequented it. Sue came right to the point.

"Why did you inquire about that telephone call?"

"Dr. Lawrence was surprised by questions about it and wondered if it actually occurred."

"I already told Shepard about your interest in it and he said he took care of it. So now I guess we're both in trouble."

"I don't think there's any reason to worry. The incident is just among personnel."

Of course she knew better. As soon as Shepard was subpoenaed, both she and Sue would be in trouble. Both left the bar uneasy, but for different reasons.

The next day Bailey met with the clinic doctors and reviewed with them his discussion with the personnel. He also emphasized that they must be the only source of medical advice in the clinic and that they too must keep patient information confidential. He also reiterated the rules about ordering tests, outside consults, hospitalization, ER referrals, etcetera. After the meeting was adjourned, he requested to speak to Dr. Lawrence privately.

The conversation was friendly and light. He asked about Lawrence's reaction to the depo and how he likes his lawyer and if there has been any change in his relationship with the other doctors and the clinic personnel. He assured him that the clinic and the HMO were behind him one hundred percent and felt he had acted properly in his care of Alex Boomer. He did, however, suggest that the doctor avoid any reference to the HMO policies in depositions or court testimony. There was a thinly veiled threat that he should not invoke such policies in his defense. This conversation left Lawrence with misgivings about his support from the HMO and the eventual outcome of the suit.

CHAPTER 15

Dr. Evans received a call from his attorney who informed him that the opposing attorney would not consider dismissing anyone from the suit. He was also informed that his depo was scheduled for next week. They agreed to meet an hour before the depo to prepare for his testimony. Eric Sloanberg's offices encompassed the forty-sixth floor of the most prestigious office building in downtown Los Angeles. The view was magnificent stretching from the ocean on the west to the mountains on the east and the valley on the north. The elevators open directly into the waiting room and the receptionist area. In back of her desk was a large glass enclosed conference area furnished by a long marble conference table surrounded by approximately twenty chairs. Beyond the table and chairs was a glass wall exposing the western view. The lighting in the reception area was subdued and the furnishing was contemporary. There were several paintings of modern art. It was all awe-inspiring.

In the midst of all this splendor, it was comforting to find Jim Bishop waiting for him. They were ushered into an equally imposing office adjoining the conference room. Dr. Evans, "Crime does pay after all. We can't think of these people as criminals just because they exploit the legal system and take from the rich doctors to give to the poor patients while lining their own pockets in the meantime."

"Forget your hostility towards the opposing attorney and be as objective and calculating as possible. Remember, you are the defendant rather than the expert and answer the questions accordingly. That is the only advice I have for you now. Just the facts, man. No opinions today. Do you have any questions?"

"No."

"Okay, let's get started."

They were ushered into the previously described conference room by one of the many secretaries. The court reporter was already seated and loaded the paper spool into her machine. A chair near the end of the table across from the recorder was reserved for Dr. Evans. Five individuals, each with a briefcase and a legal pad, were seated around the table. There was an empty chair at the end, nearest Dr. Evans and the reporter, obviously for the plaintiff's attorney. Bishop was next to his client. When all was in readiness, Eric Sloanberg made his entrance and took his seat without so much as a nod to the assemblage.

"Is everyone here? Please introduce yourselves to the doctor and state who you represent."

The names meant nothing to Evans but he did take note of the entities represented, the city, the paramedics, the hospital, Dr. Lawrence and the HMO. The latter was somewhat of a surprise as was the absence of a representative for Dr. Williams. He wondered if Bishop was to represent them both.

"Please swear in the defendant."

Dr. Evans was startled by the reference to him as was his attorney.

Jim Bishop, "I believe you should have more respect for my client. He is a respected member of the medical community and not a criminal."

"My other depo on this matter was very contentious. Are we going to have the same atmosphere today?"

"Only if you want to make it that way."

"All right, I apologize to the doctor and ask that the court reporter swear him. Is that better?"

"Yes."

"Then proceed."

"Do you solemnly swear that the testimony you are about to give in this matter is the truth, the whole truth and nothing but the truth, so help you God?"

"I do."

"Please state your name for the record."

Sloanberg asked for Dr. Evans C.V. and spent several minutes perusing it.

"Is this document up to date and complete?"

"To the best of my knowledge."

"In the interest of time, I will accept it as is and mark it as Exhibit 1. Your hospital training was primarily surgical, was it not?"

"Yes."

"Do you feel that training prepared you to diagnose and treat medical conditions, especially cardiac patients?"

"My overall training, including medical school, clinical experience and post-graduate education prepared me for all conditions I might see in the emergency department."

"What kind of post graduate education have you taken?"

"It's in the C.V. but…"

Jim Bishop, "You've answered his question."

"From your C.V., please point out those courses you believe prepared you to take care of medical patients as opposed to surgical patients in the E.R."

Evans listed, marked and briefly described emergency department post graduate courses he attended at Massachusetts General, Johns Hopkins, Baylor and Tulane Medical Centers that emphasized diagnosis and treatment of medical illnesses in the emergency department.

"Do you feel that you are as competent to diagnose and treat a cardiac patient as a cardiologist would be?"

"More competent in the Emergency Department."

"Really, why do you say that?"

"Because I see more such patients at that stage of their disease than cardiologists."

Mr. Bishop, "I'm going to have to object to this line of questioning since my client did not examine or treat Mr. Boomer. His knowledge of this case is purely from the medical records and any testimony he might give would be opinions based on his review of records. That would be expert testimony and that is not his role here."

"Okay, I only have a few other questions. You hold the contract to provide emergency services to the Southwest Hospital and Medical Center, do you not?"

"Yes."

"In that capacity, you are responsible for the professional conduct and competence of the staff in the emergency department."

"Only the physicians. The hospital is responsible for the nursing and clerical staff."

"That is all I have at the present time, but this witness will be subject to re-examination at a future time.

Mr. Bishop, "That is not acceptable. He did not see the patient and he cannot give medical opinions unless you dismiss the suit against him and his group and call him as an expert."

"I'm not about to do that at this stage."

With that Sloanberg picked up his notes and strolled out of the room after instructing the court clerk concerning the deposition.

In the elevator, Dr. Evans and Mr. Bishop considered the results of the depo.

"He's a real hard-ass."

"He is, but we won that round and he left the door open for your dismissal with the provision that you testify as his expert. He is aware of your reputation in the medical-legal field."

"So we just wait and see what happens?"

"That's all we can do now."

CHAPTER 16

Melissa was called in to Dr. Shepard's office.

"Sue tells me you were inquiring about the call from Mr. Boomer."

"Yes."

"What is your interest in this matter?"

"Dr. Lawrence asked me if I had received such a call and forgotten to mention it to him so I asked Sue if the call had actually come into the clinic. She told me that it had and she referred it to you since you were the only doctor in at the time. I relayed the information to Dr. Lawrence. That is the only interest I have. Is there a problem?"

"No, I just wondered what your interest was."

"Is that all?"

"Yes, for the time being."

Melissa was very upset, particularly by the last comment. Her job could be on the line. Financially that was no problem. She was the only child of a very wealthy couple who had been killed in a car accident during her sophomore year in college.

She had dropped out of college and gone though a severe emotional crisis which resulted in alcohol abuse and an ill-advised marriage which lasted only six months. The divorce was bitter but actually resulted in her being able to cope with her problems. She enrolled in nursing college more to fill the emptiness in her life than out of dedication. After graduation, she found employment at the clinic and there met and fell in love with Dr. Lawrence. She was shattered when her affair ended and became bitter and depressed. With the recent resumption of the affair, her love and happiness was boundless. She would do anything for him and knew he needed her help desperately now.

She reported her conversation with Dr. Shepard to Michael. He was quite upset that she had breached the confidence and wondered when the next shoe would drop. His life was a mess. He was being sued for more than his insurance covered, his job and career was on the line, he was in love with two women and unfaithful to both, and eventually would be unmasked and face a divorce. He could only react to these problems and keep on juggling them.

He had sought his second legal opinion and was dismayed to find it more pessimistic than the first. He was advised to remain with his original lawyer and hope for the best. He seriously considered suicide, but decided that that was a permanent solution to what he hoped was a temporary problem. Besides, he could not bear the thought of hurting both women.

His life dragged on with a very dull and unsatisfying medical practice. Many of his patients were hypochondriacs who neither got well or died, but just kept on coming to see him. Others were executive physicals, which he could do in his sleep. The occasional patient who was a diagnostic or therapeutic challenge was complicated by the restrictions placed on him by the HMO. Because of the publicity associated with the lawsuit, the relationships with his colleagues and the clinic employees were strained. It was sort of like a cancer patient who was politely shunned by his friends who thought that "there but the grace of God go I". All physicians were constantly looking over their shoulder to see if the lawyers were gaining on them and thinking of patients as adversaries. Such was the practice of medicine in the decade of managed care. The only person he could communicate with was Melissa. She was aware of all his problems and familiar with present day medical care and the politics of the clinic. Besides, he deeply loved her and wanted just to be with her and ignore all the rest. They discussed the bad things only when it was necessary and this was one of those times. He told her of the consultation with the second attorney, Barry Sherwood, and his pessimistic outlook.

Melissa, "You must return to your original attorney, weigh your options and reach a decision as to how to proceed. You cannot continue to vascilate and be increasingly unsure of yourself and what to do next. I love you too much to see you this way."

This advice made sense to him and gave at least temporary relief from his uncertainty and apprehension. It was a goal to strive for.

It seemed all of his free time was spent in attorney's offices now. Mr. McAllen greeted him cordially, but coolly. He really wished he was someone else's client.

Maybe the second opinion would make that possible. Not so. Dr. Lawrence was here to again discuss his opinions and evaluate them. Mr. McAllen again pointed out the potential courses they could follow and the merits and pitfalls of each. The first and least attractive was to offer policy limits and settle the case. No chance for that because of the economic loss to the family by the death. The second and only slightly more reasonable was to go to trial and let the jury decide. The third was to try the case and if lost, an award greater than the policy limits was mandated, countersue the HMO. This would be a long, drawn-out process and he would have to bear the expense of the countersuit. Finally, "the-devil-made-me-do-it" defense, which Dr. Lawrence accepted his share of the blame, but asserted that he was forced to follow the policies of the HMO. This was risky. It had never been tried before and the HMO would do whatever was necessary to win because it would set a precedent that would destroy managed care as we know it today.

Dr. Lawrence, "Incidently, Mr. Boomer did call the clinic. I had left for the day and the call was referred to Dr. Shepard, the senior partner of the clinic. He was made aware of my nurses's inquiry and she was called in and asked why she was interested. She told him I was questioned about it and wondered if such a call ever was made."

"Smart girl, how loyal is she to you?"

"Completely."

"Are you involved with her?"

He looked stunned and didn't answer immediately.

"I need to know because she could be a valuable witness to that incident as well as the policies and principles of the clinic."

"Yes, I am. That would bring her credibility into question."

"Who all knows?"

"No one that I'm aware of."

"I doubt that. People are very observant of such things, especially of their fellow workers. We'll just have to deal with it if it comes up. That call could be very significant in bringing the HMO into the suit.

"How do you want to proceed?"

"It seems the only reasonable choice I have is to blame the HMO."

"I think that is the best of our options. I don't want to tip our hand yet, so I won't depose your Dr. Shepard until the last possible moment. Warn your girlfriend that she will be the star witness, besides you, and to keep her mouth shut. You keep her happy, whatever it takes."

He resented the inference, but let it pass.

"What about Dr. Evans' depo?"

"It was a non-event as far as we're concerned. His lawyer would not let him give any medical opinions since he did not have any direct contact with the patient. He is only being sued as the contractor for the emergency department with responsibilities for the actions of the associate physicians. His lawyer did make a pitch to trade him as an expert in the case for a dismissal of the suit against him. That could hurt us because he has had significant experience as a medical expert and is very court-wise. Sloanberg turned him down, at least for the moment. If he made that deal, he would lose all his other defendants. If that should happen, we might offer the HMO, with its almost limitless resources as a substitute. In the meantime, go about your normal activities, keep your mouth shut and your girlfriend satisfied and let me do the worrying and make the decisions. Okay?"

CHAPTER 17

In a nearby office downtown, another strategy session was taking place. Michael Epstein, the temporary chairman of APEX Electronics chaired a meeting of the board of directors in an emergency session to try to develop contingency plans for the survival of the company. Alex Boomer had been one of the founders and executive director and was totally responsible for its success. He had developed plans and finances to take the company public as an IPO (initial public offering) this month. With the news of his death, the stock plummeted and the planned IPO was dead in the water. No one on the board had enough business clout to manage the company, keep it afloat, much less shepard an IPO. There was also no takeover interest by any of the corporate raiders without Boomer as its president.

Since his death, Boomer's office and files had been sealed to prevent the piracy of anything which might be of value to any potential corporate raiders. Eric Sloanberg had engaged an economist to evaluate the potential worth and earning power of Alex Boomer. He was demanding access to the office and files, as well as the books of the company. So far that access had been denied. Finally, with the consent of Elizabeth Boomer, Sloanberg had obtained a subpena for access to the office, files and company records. Hence, the emergency board meeting to decide, among other things, if they would go to court to try to quash the subpena. The board with one decenting vote decided against that strategy and to cooperate as long as any sensitive company secrets would remain confidential and members of the board would have equal access to the material and decide what should remain confidential. Besides this action, the board named Epstein as temporary chairman and CEO. The board recessed until the next day, when the economist, auditor and corporate attorney were scheduled to arrive. Promptly at 9:00 a.m., the financial team arrived almost like an occupying army. Kenneth Brock, the economist, introduced the other two and each was assigned to his area of expertise. The auditor to the company books and the attorney and Brock to the office and the files. Epstein accompanied them to the office suit, unlocked the doors and stood by as a silent observer. His job was to examine any material they wanted to copy and decide whether or not allow it. He soon realized that his access to this area of the company had been limited to sitting across the desk and being informed of Boomer's decisions. Boomer ran the company with an iron hand and sought rubber stamp approval from the board, not advice. Nobody cared much until now. Epstein asked Sherry Parker, Boomer's Executive Secretary, to join him in locating the material requested. She had been his confidant and knew almost as much about the business as he did. On entering the office, she noted that the answering machine on his private phone was blinking. She ran the tape back and listened to about one week's worth of messages. All but one was of no interest. However, that one message was from a Dr. Ronald Shepard indicating that he was returning a call made to the clinic concerning the use of nitroglycerin. He stated that it was good that it relieved Boomer's pain and to continue to use it when necessary. She had heard that message, relayed it to Boomer, and he had acknowledged it stating he would call the doctor. She was aware of the malpractice suit and decided to remove the tape from the machine and secret it for safekeeping. She was able to produce the requested files. They were only interested in those concerning company stock, Boomer's stock options and the files on the IPO. These documents were copied and surrendered to Brock. He and the attorney left, while the auditor continued to pour over the books. Epstein and the other board members milled around and drank coffee, not really understanding what was happening. Sherry took the tape and put it in her purse for future reference.

CHAPTER 18

It was time for Elizabeth Boomer to find out what it was like to file a malpractice lawsuit in Southern California. So far, she had only discussed the matter with her children, her attorney and briefly with Dr. Evans at the emergency department. In the meantime, she had been immersed in arranging Alex's funeral, notifying friends and relatives and all the other things that temporarily delays grief. Now it was reality time.

As she entered the conference room of Dennis McAllen, Esq., she was amazed and taken aback to see a room full of men with briefcases and long yellow pads waiting for her like a cage full of hungry tigers. Of course, they were all polite, but appeared intent on tearing her to shreds. Even though she was terrified, she retained her poise and composure. McAllen was a young fifty-five, tall, lean and mean. He was known in legal circles as the person who stole from widows and children to give to the rich doctors and hospitals. A sort of Robin Hood in reverse. He was the most successful malpractice defense attorney in Southern California and possibly the nation. He would go to any lengths to win acquittal for his medical clients. This case was to be a classic contest between the top plaintiff's attorney and the most renowned defense attorney. The stage was set. The first victim was in his lair.

The depo began in a most polite and benign manner. After Elizabeth Boomer was sworn, McAllen extended his sympathy on the loss of her husband and assured her that this was a mandatory, legal process to get the facts concerning her lawsuit. He introduced her to the other individuals in the room and explained what their function was and who each represented. Her attorney, Eric Sloanberg, was seated next to her and appeared ready to shield her from McAllen's onslaught. It came sooner than anyone expected. After a few general questions about her husband, their life together, his general heath and their standard of living, he asked her if she was aware of the affair between her husband and Sherry Parker. Sloanberg leaped to his feet and screamed that there was no basis in fact for such an accusation and even so, it had no relevance to this procedure.

McAllen, "I withdraw the question."

However, it had completely shattered the victim's composure and reduced her to tears. Sloanberg noted the effect on his client and demanded that this depo be concluded and he would go to the court to demand sanctions for unprofessional conduct. A heated argument ensued between the two attorneys but it finally ended with McAllen agreeing to question her on the facts of the case only, and Sloanberg agreed to allow the depo to continue and not pursue the sanctions.

McAllen, "Mrs. Boomer, how long were you and your husband married?"

"Eighteen years." She had partially regained her composure, but her face was tear-stained and her voice was little more than a whisper.

McAllen, "Mrs. Boomer, you must speak up so all the folks can hear you, especially the court reporter."

"Eighteen years," she repeated in almost a shout.

"When did your husband join Acme Electric?"

"Twelve years ago."

"In what capacity?"

"Sales Manager."

"And he rose rapidly until he was on the verge of becoming President and CEO at the time of his death? During that time did he put in long hours in job and travel frequently?"

"Yes."

"Did he get adequate rest?"

"He didn't require as much rest as most people."

"Unresponsive, yes or no?"

"No."

"Was his diet meticulous, or did he survive on junk food and large amounts of fatty food?

"Taste governed his diet."

"Was he overweight?"

"Yes."

"How much?"

"Twenty pounds."

"Did he exercise?"

"He played golf when he had time."

"Did he smoke?"

"Yes."

"How much?"

"Two packs a day."

"Was his job stressful?"

Sloanberg, "This line of questioning sounds like the history portion of a routine physical and is irrelevant to this case."

"Don't be naive, Eric, even lawyers know that a lifestyle such as this is conducive to heart disease and early death. I'm sure you will get one of your well worn experts to testify on this matter."

"This suit is not about lifestyle, it's about a group of health professional who failed to recognize all these risk factors and an impending heart attack, which could have been prevented with appropriate diagnosis and treatment."

"All right, enough pontificating. Let's get to the facts. Mrs. Boomer, when did your husband first complain of chest pain?"

"About ten days before his death."

"What were the circumstances?"

"He'd had a physical and was told to exercise and he was running on the treadmill."

"How long did the pain last?"

"It stopped when he stopped exercising, almost immediately."

"Did he call his doctor?"

"Yes."

"What was he told?"

"He was sent a prescription for nitroglycerin and told to use it if he had a recurrence of pain and report back as to the results."

"Did that happen?"

"Yes. Three days later he was again on the treadmill, developed chest pain, dissolved a nitro under his tongue and the pain disappeared within five minutes."

"Did he call his doctor?"

"Yes."

"What was he told?"

"The doctor was not in and he was told he would call back."

"Did he?"

"Yes. The doctor called back at his office and told him that was good and he should continue to use nitro when he had pain."

"Which doctor returned his call?"

"I presume it was Dr. Lawrence."

"You don't know?"

"The call went to the office and Alex told me that he had been contacted by the doctor about the nitro."

"You do not have personal knowledge of which doctor he talked to."

"No. I presume — "

"You have answered the question."

"I'm finished with this witness. Does anyone else have any questions?"

Sloanberg, "Mrs. Boomer, I have only one question. I don't want to keep you any longer than is absolutely necessary. Did the doctor give your husband any advice, such as returning to his office, scheduling further tests or referring him to a cardiologist?"

"No."

McAllen, "Is that a firm no or you just don't have any knowledge of such advice?"

"Alex didn't mention any other instructions."

The court reporter was instructed about getting the depo signed and copies to all those attending and the session ended.

Sloanberg and Mrs. Boomer returned to his office to discuss

the depo.

"I don't want to upset you any more than Dennis did, but I don't want to be blind sided by anything. So, did Alex have an affair with his secretary?"

"Not to my knowledge. She was his right hand in his business. He was very dependent on her and she occasionally traveled with him. She has been in our home many times and our relationship has always been cordial. He never gave me reason to doubt him though he was busy with his career and I was busy with the children and our social obligations. Sherry's an intelligent and attractive woman. What else can I say?"

"Okay, you stated that Alex did not tell you who he talked to about the nitro or whether he was advised to have other tests or consultations."

"That is correct."

"Would he have told you if he had been advised to have further tests?"

"I'm sure he would have. We always discuss such things."

"You did very well considering the way you were treated."

After she left, Sloanberg called his private investigator for an appointment. He wanted to find out everything possible about Sherry Parker and the relationship between her and Alex Boomer. He could see his case unraveling if the public, (including a possible jury pool) should find Alex Boomer was not the knight in shining amour, American success story and loving family man he had been portrayed in the media. He was also concerned about Elizabeth's lack of direct knowledge about who Alex spoke with at the clinic and what he was told.

CHAPTER 19

Maria Gonzales was a reporter for the Daily Telegram who had a nose for scandal, especially involving individuals painted as above reproach. She had followed this case since the unexpected death of Alex Boomer and wondered if there had been some precipitating factor in his business, family or personal life that had not been exposed to the light of day. She also wondered about the clinic and the hospital and the doctors involved in his death. She decided to investigate each person and each entity involved knowing that the trial potential had all the glitz of the Simpson case, even though this was rarely true of a civil trial. However, this one had the unexpected death of a business tycoon and media darling, the pitting of the two most prominent L.A. malpractice attorneys against one another, the question of competence of the busiest hospital ER and trauma center in the city and one of the most prestigious medical clinics in Southern California.

The autopsy proved that the death was from a heart attack, natural causes rather than something more sinister. The attorneys were not commenting for the press yet so if there was a story here, it had to either involve the lack of competence of the medical people or some personal scandal or both.

She had been assigned to cover the case and decided to approach it as a potential expose rather than a routine story of an interesting trial. She decided to present herself to the clinic as a patient hoping to uncover some flaw in the system or someone who would gossip with her. She checked out "Cecil's Practice of Medicine" and poured through the index in hopes of finding some rare disease that was potentially deadly but extremely difficult to diagnose. It so happened that the newspaper's employee's heath coverage was with the HMO so it was no problem to get an appointment with Dr. Lawrence.

At 2:15 p.m. Wednesday, Maria presented herself at the clinic, gave the receptionist her insurance card and filled out the mandatory forms. She noted that the reception area was filled and there seemed to be a rapid turnover of patients. Promptly at 2:30 p.m., her name was called and she was ushered into the small treatment area which was furnished with a treatment table, a stool and a straight chair. There was a cabinet built in with several bottles of liquid, tongue blades, a flashlight, stethoscope and blood pressure gauge.

A very pretty nurse came in, greeted her, asked her symptoms, took her temperature, and told her to get undressed. She handed her a paper gown and left the room. Shortly the doctor appeared, introduced himself as Dr. Michael Lawrence and asked what her problem was.

Maria said, "For several weeks I have had brief episodes with my heart beating too fast. There's also been some chest pain on occasions."

Doctor, "Is this new or have you had it before?"

"It's started about three weeks ago and I've never had anything like this before."

"Has your health been good prior to this problem?"

"I haven't had anything more serious than colds since childhood."

"Did you have any serious illnesses as a child?"

"I was told that when I was five, I had some kind of infection that lasted three months."

"Do you know what it was called?"

"Something like Chagas Disease."

"Was that here in Southern California?"

"No, I was born and raised in the Rio Grande Valley of Texas."

"Did the local doctors make that diagnosis?"

"No, they sent specimens to the CDC."

"After you got well. Until now, have you had anything resembling that illness?"

"I don't remember the symptoms but I have not been sick since then."

At that point, he did a rather complete exam on her with the exception of a pelvic. He listened to her heart, with her sitting, lying and on left side, and again after exercise.

"I don't hear any murmurs, unusual sounds or abnormal breath sounds. The rate is within normal range. Your blood pressure is also normal. Have you been under stress in your job or in your private life?"

"No, there is no stress at all."

"Do you take any drugs, either medicine or recreational drugs?"

"No."

"At this time I find no evidence or heart disease or anything else abnormal. I'm going to prescribe a small dose of Valium for the next month and see if that will stop your symptoms."

"Doctor, aren't you going to do a chest x-ray or an EKG or any kind of blood work to find out what is causing my problem?"

"No, insurance companies frown on extensive testing in the face of vague symptoms."

Melissa, the pretty nurse, returned just in time to hear the last comment and seemed to become somewhat ill at ease. She touched him on the arm and asked if she could see him in the hall. They seemed slightly more familiar than one might expect.

Doctor Lawrence reassured Maria, gave her a prescription and instructed her to make an appointment in three weeks, but to return promptly if the symptoms persisted or grew worse. With that, both doctor and nurse left the room. Maria had only been with the doctor about ten minutes and she became part of the rapid patient turnover. She dressed, made her appointment and left the clinic. As she headed back to her office, she felt her suspicion somewhat justified. Patients seemed to be on an assembly line. The comment about the insurance company frowning on tests and just the hint of familiarity between doctor and nurse. Yes, this clinic needs further scrutiny.

CHAPTER 20

On returning home from work, Melissa noted her backdoor was unlocked and the alarm was off. She entered, expecting Michael to be in the apartment and called his name. She heard a commotion in the front of the apartment and a door slammed. She still thought it was Michael. She called his name again, but there was no response and she was suddenly afraid, but continued through the apartment. Finding no one, she began to notice subtle evidence of her belongings out of place. It became obvious that someone invaded her home. As she continued the search, she found nothing missing, just misplaced. She suddenly panicked and desperately wanted to speak with Michael but dared not call him. She debated whether or not to call the police but decided against it. She relocked both outside doors and turned the alarm on. She felt both violated and vulnerable and spent a long, restless night anxious to tell Michael.

Melissa was at the clinic bright and early, waiting impatiently for Michael to appear. He finally arrived and she lead him into the privacy of his office and threw herself into his arms and began to cry.

"What is the matter?"

"Someone broke into my apartment yesterday," she sobbed.

"Did you call the police?"

"No, I didn't know what to do and I didn't dare call you."

"I would have told you to report a break-in. That is a common event in this city. Is there anything missing?"

"No, but he was still in the apartment when I got home."

"Did you see someone?"

"No, but I heard them leave."

"I'm just glad you're all right. Have your alarm changed and at least report it to your security company."

"Just hold me for a few moments. I need you so bad."

CHAPTER 21

Maria was still shaking when she reached her car. She was not accustomed to breaking into someone's home and had been very clumsy. If she had been caught, there would have been some serious explaining to do to her boss. There was no authorization to pry into the private lives of the principles of the lawsuit. Besides she had learned very little by her adventure. Only that there was a male part-time occupant of the apartment.

Maria's next project was to visit the ED to see what she could learn there. It was a Friday night, a party night for the citizens and a working night for the perps, which frequently produced the busiest time of the week in the ED. This was a terrible early evening shift, so much so that Dr. Evans had been called in to help. The place was full of police because of the gang war with five gunshot victims and a critically injured cop who had been run down by an auto full of juveniles who were trying to escape from the shooting scene. He had been knocked down and run over by the car. His partner unloaded his shotgun at the car as it backed up to take another run at the downed officer. The driver lost his head to the double o buck and the others had assorted wounds. With a headless driver, the car plowed into a cement light pole, further dismembering the remaining occupants. The car exploded in flames and there were no survivors. The injured officer was picked up by two of his fellow officers, put in the back of the police car and taken Code 3 to the ED. Whatever chance of useful life he might have had ended with that maneuver.

He was lying still on the gurney, fully conscious, barely breathing and moving none of his extremities, but complaining of neck pain. The exam and x-rays revealed a fracture dislocation of the cervical spine at the four five level producing quadriplegia. There was also evidence of fractured ribs and pneumothorax bilaterally. Chest tubes were immediately inserted in both sides of the thorax and the lungs reexpanded. This improved his respiration but he was still in shock, presumably from blood in the abdomen. A CAT scan revealed a large volume of blood in the abdominal cavity. O negative uncrossed matched blood was started in both arms and the patient was taken to the OR where he died. The other gunshot wound victims were cared for by the trauma team and all but one was discharged to the jail ward.

The ED was filled with hysterical officers as was usually the case when a fellow cop was shot. They could only console themselves and each other with the knowledge that street justice had been swift and sure for the perps. No court room opportunity for the bleeding hearts and the high-profile defense attorneys to make a reputation and fortune from this case.

Maria observed part of this scene from the waiting room for the past three hours. Her name was finally called about midnight. She was ushered into the inner sanctum of the Emergency Room to a curtained off cubicle. A nurse with a blood-stained uniform and shoes apologized for her appearance and took her temperature, blood pressure, pulse and asked for a brief description of her complaints. She could hear the cops discussing the activities of the evening and the moaning of several patients.

Dr. Evans entered the cubicle shortly, introducing himself and asking what her problem was. She told him the same story she had told Dr. Lawrence yesterday at the clinic, but added that earlier this evening her palpations had started again and she had some pain despite the Valium. He asked about her visit to the clinic, what exam and tests had been done and what she had been told. She enumerated the whole thing in detail.

Dr. Evans, "He didn't do an EKG, x-rays, blood tests or anything other than a short history and physical?"

"No, he said it was probably just tension and the Valium should relieve it."

Evans, "Without further tests he had no basis for that conclusion. Your symptoms could be a result of your previous infection, causing damage to your heart muscle. Simply listening to your heart is not going to answer that question. It is not practical to do these things at midnight in the ED so I can either admit you to the hospital or refer you to a cardiologist. However, your insurance might not pay for all you need to rule out myocarditis. That's why a clinic doctor did not order it."

"I can't go into the hospital tonight, I'll see a cardiologist whenever you say. Just give me a referral."

"I can give you a name but a referral must come from your doctor if the insurance company is to pay for it. He is sort of a gatekeeper for the HMO."

She left the ED with another bit of information. She'd never understood what an HMO was or how it differed from her previous health insurance. If she was really totally dependent on the capriciousness of one doctor for her health care, it was frightening. She decided to research managed care systems in the computer to see what effect they really could have on an individual such as she had pretended to be.

In a nutshell, she learned that all managed care systems, while differing in minor details, depended on signing up primarily the young, healthy adults for a fixed fee and limiting the health care provided as much as possible. In addition, they contracted with physicians, clinics, hospitals, pharmacies and other ancillary health services to provide care for their clients. The physicians, etcetera were pressured into contracting for as large a discount as could be negotiated thus decreasing their income and compromising their incentive. In addition, the HMO's paid only a discounted percentage of fees. Tests, x-rays, consultations, hospitalizations and elective surgeries were discouraged and controlled by a physician gatekeeper and a utilization committee. The result was that patients either became disgusted with the process and gave up trying to get proper care or died while waiting. Managed care was dismantling the finest medical system that had ever been devised. A few physicians were prostitutes and the rest were victims. The HMOs were extremely profitable for their owners and executives. Recently it was found that even the Mafia was taking a cut of some HMOs. The other source of huge profit was the leverage buy-outs of smaller HMOs by larger and richer ones. With more patients and medical organizations signed up, the greater the profit. This whole process was legalized larceny spawned by the government and corporate America desperate to decrease their health care costs at the expense of the public health.

Maria was aghast at the implications of her findings after her only experience at the clinic. She wondered if Alex Boomer's life had been sacrificed on the altar of managed care. She committed all this to her PC, printed it and decided to take it to her editor for his approval for an expose. Bright and early Monday morning she was in Tom Dougherty's office with a summary of her experiences, suspicions and research. He read it carefully. When he finished, he asked what she proposed to do with this.

"I want your permission to write an article based on this and what other facts I can uncover concerning the trial."

"What you have is only speculation."

Maria, "What if Alex Boomer was a victim of his own health insurance HMO?"

"Is the HMO a party to this lawsuit? And, if not, why not? You know we can't publish something as inflammatory as this on the basis of a collection of isolated and possibly unrelated facts. It would destroy any possibility of an impartial trial and whoever lost would most assuredly sue the paper."

"Can I at least pursue this and see where it leads?"

"Yes, but on your own time and without harassing any of the principles of the case."

CHAPTER 22

Eric Sloanberg entered one of the older office buildings in the lower south end of Los Angeles, went up an ancient, self-service elevator to the third floor and made his way to a frosted glass door with the number 311 above block lettering (Legal Investigative Services). The reception room was small and empty and furnished somewhat shabbily. No one was at the desk so he rang the bell. A somewhat obese man in his sixties dressed in slacks, shirt and tie slipped down from the open collar appeared.

"Eric, what brings you to the low-rent district?"

"Don't poor mouth me, you have money you haven't counted yet." Tim Carlton was an ex-FBI agent who had retired fifteen years ago and established the most honorable and successful private investigative service in Los Angeles. The majority of the most prestigious law firms in L.A. used his services. He employed ten agents and kept them busy.

"What can I do for you?"

"I want to know if the deceased husband of one of my clients was screwing his secretary."

"I didn't know you did divorce cases on the side."

"You know better than that. This is a med/mal case and my opposing council sprung that on me in the deposition this week. While you're at it, you might do a reality check on the wife, the defendant doctor and nurse and a potential medical expert. I want you to do this yourself. This is a high-profile case and potentially very lucrative. I do not want any surprises when I get to the courthouse and as always, I expect complete confidentiality. They discussed fees and a time frame and Eric gave him the basic facts on Sherry and Alex Boomer, Dr. Lawrence and Melissa and Dr. Evans.

Eric retraced his steps, caught a cab and returned to his office hoping he had not been recognized. Private investigators were essential but usually an anonymous tool for all trial lawyers, hence the low profile office.

Checking infidelity was the most frequent and easiest task for investigators, however, the fact that one of the parties was dead made it infinitely more difficult, especially with the need for confidentiality. He could start by checking Sherry's bank account, home and work habits, credit cards, telephone records and personal habits. To invade computers for bank and credit cards, he needed a social security number, a bank account number and credit card numbers. He would have to start by breaking into her home to hopefully find credit card receipts, bank deposit slips, etcetera.

First he needed to know her schedule. Starting with her home address he staked out her home for several days, following her to work, to lunch, to home. Her schedule didn't vary. She left home at 8:15 each morning and arrived at the office at approximately 9:00. The commute was direct and uninterrupted except for stopping at cleaners, eating breakfast or any other errands. Promptly at 4:15 p.m. she left the office and went directly home. The schedule was unchanged for one week and gave him the information he needed as to when to enter her home. The house was modest but tasteful and moderately expensive in an upper middle class West Los Angeles neighborhood. She lived alone and had no visitors. Access without observation by neighbors would be easy since there was no one home during the day. He decided to continue his observation through the weekend to ascertain whether she had any social life. She did not go out and had no visitors. In addition to the bank and cards, he would have to install a telephone tap.

On Tuesday of the next week he easily disarmed the alarm and entered the house through an unlocked window. The home was neat, modest and tastefully furnished. A small room near the bedroom served as a home office and he found everything he needed in the way of receipts, bank statements, etcetera. He carefully copied the numbers he needed and replaced everything as neatly as he had found it. He carefully searched the house for anything that would suggest either a male or female companion. Nothing was found and there were no personal letters. If this lady had a personal life she kept it completely separate from her home. He rearmed the alarm after exiting through the same window he had entered.

The computer checks revealed modest checking and saving accounts, no record of brokerage investments, and no bank vault or no evidence of offshore accounts. Her credit cards were used for gasoline, department stores and occasional restaurants and there was no travel for one year. Telephone records were no more revealing. There was no number that she either called or received calls from frequently. So far, she was pristine.

He met with Sloanberg and reported his findings. Neither could believe that a very pretty, thirty-five year old, single female executive secretary living in Los Angeles could have such a dull life. He asked Eric if he had access to Boomer's personal and business expenditures.

"Sure, we just obtained those from the company last week and they're being audited now."

"I need to see the results of that, especially travel records, unusual expenditures for apartment rent checks for large sums of cash, etcetera. If he was involved with this girl, he was very careful."

"Have you done anything about the other parties?"

"No."

"You can be a little less secretive about the others."

CHAPTER 23

Dr. Evans was disturbed by what Maria had told him. She had seen the same doctor who had taken care of Alex Boomer and was given the same, incomplete care for a potentially serious or even fatal disease in a young girl. He had been disturbed about the quality of medicine being practiced by the clinic physicians even before he saw either of these patients. He was convinced that neglect was directly responsible for Boomer's death. He had difficulty getting past the gatekeeper to admit seriously ill patients to the hospital, ever since management had changed. He decided to follow up on Maria to see if she actually got a work up for the possible myocarditis. He called Dr. Lawrence the next morning ostensively to report seeing Ms. Rodriguez. Dr. Lawrence listened to Evans report. At the conclusion, he thanked Evans and was prepared to hang up.

Evans, "Do you plan to admit her and finish your workup or refer her to a cardiologist?"

"Are you trying to tell me how to practice medicine? I do not report to you and since we are both involved as defendants in the same lawsuit, we should not be discussing patient care." With that, he hung up.

Evans, "I hope I get a chance to nail that incompetent son-of-a-bitch in court."

Melissa had heard the tail end of that conversation and asked, "what's that all about?".

"The doctor at the ED is harassing me about another patient, the girl who was in here Friday complaining about chest pain and palpitations. She was in the ER Friday night with the same symptoms and the doctor thought she needed a cardiac workup."

"Did she?"

"Probably, but if I ordered it, the Utilization Committee would harass me and I can't afford a confrontation with them about a questionable workup."

"You've got to practice good medicine, regardless of what they think."

"And get fired.?"

"Call her and get her back in here for a recheck and do what you think is best."

Maria had learned what she needed to know from both medical facilities and had not planned to pursue further fruitless testing. However, when she got the call to return to the clinic, to seem credible, she felt she must comply and made the appointment.

She was again seen by Lawrence and again asked to repeat the history and an inquiry was made concerning her ED visit, why she went and what she was told. A more detailed exam was performed and Dr. Lawrence indicated he would order the tests Evans had suggested. However, he stated that his orders would have to be passed on by Utilization Review Committee and he would call her as soon as they met.

"In the meantime, continue your Valium, try to decrease your physical activity and stress."

Utilization Committee was another piece of information for Maria's computer summary.

Despite her admonition to Michael, Melissa was vaguely suspicious of Maria. Since the invasion of her home, her apprehension had been raised. Why would someone rummage through her belongings and take nothing? Was it because of Michael? Had she and Michael been too careless or was it something concerning the suit? Why would an apparently healthy twenty six year old woman come in with such a patently unlikely group of symptoms and then go to the ED without consulting the on- call clinic doctor. She remembered the comment Michael had made about the insurance concerning tests and winced. She had admonished him about that after Maria had left but had been brushed off.

CHAPTER 24

Tim Charleton had been in the investigative business too long to believe that Boomer and Sherry's relationship had been as pristine as it appeared. Consequently he obtained credit card receipts, bank receipts and hotel receipts from the Boomer office and spent a full day going through them entry by entry. Still nothing. He had shadowed Sherry, invaded her home and gone through her papers and personal effects, checked her business records and Boomer's business records and found nothing. It was unbelievable that this young woman not only had no relationship with her boss, but had no personal relationship with anyone. He called Sloanberg on his private phone and reported the result of his investigation.

"She's too clean. I can't believe it, but I found nothing. McAllen just wanted to upset your witness. Has the wife any suspicions?"

"She says not. Perhaps she should have a conversation with Sherry Parker herself. It couldn't hurt anything with the exception of Elizabeth's pride."

"I'll approach her on the subject. In the meantime, check out Lawrence, Dr. Evans and Melissa, and see if anyone else is nosing around."

Elizabeth Boomer was elated to know that Sherry and Alex had been found innocent by the investigator. However, she was somewhat reluctant to quiz Sherry directly.

"Is it necessary?"

"Yes, we must do everything possible to eliminate any surprises at trial. Do you have any real hesitancy about approaching her?"

"It will be awkward at best, but if it's necessary, I'll do it."

"Okay then, as soon as possible."

When she got home, Elizabeth did all sorts of meaningless chores, delaying the inevitable as long as possible. Finally, at 2:45 in the afternoon, she made the call.

"Sherry Parker, please. This is Elizabeth Boomer."

"This is Sherry, Elizabeth. What can I do for you?"

"Could you stop by the house on your way home?"

"Yes. I can be there about 5:00."

"Thank you."

There had been a hint of surprise and apprehension in her voice at the unexpected call. She had not seen Elizabeth since the funeral.

Elizabeth had her maid prepare coffee and a light snack, then sent her home. She wanted this meeting to be completely private. Promptly at 4:55, Sherry rang the doorbell and was admitted to the den. The meeting was awkward for both of them, but after some small talk, Elizabeth came right to the point.

"At my depo, one of the first questions I was asked was whether I had any knowledge concerning an affair between you and my husband. Needless to say I was rendered speechless and totally devastated. I have never been given any indication that Alex was unfaithful to me, with you or anyone, but I must know."

Sherry could hardly believe her ears and broke into tears.

After she regained her composure, she looked into Elizabeth's eyes and said, "Absolutely not. There was never any romantic or sexual element to our relationship. I loved your husband, but like a father or an older brother."

Elizabeth looked somewhat skeptical and asked, "Are you sure? We have been friends for years and I have never before entertained any jealousy of the time you spent with him, traveled with him, of his dependence on you until now."

Sherry lost her composure momentarily. When she regained it, she said, "perhaps this is the time to tell you the whole truth. I did love Alex because he helped me to regain my sanity and emotional stability at a time when I was on the verge of suicide. I confided things in him that I have never until this moment told anyone else. It's a long story but you must hear it all now in order to understand. My childhood and adolescence was a disaster. My father began molesting me when I was ten. That progressed to incest during my adolescence. My mother was aware of it but did nothing to put a stop to it. I learned later that my father could only be stimulated by having sex with me in order to be able to have sex with my mother. This went on regularly until I was sixteen. I finally was so devastated by learning of their kinky relationship that was spurred by a strange mixture of disgust and jealousy, I went to the authorities. This eventually resulted in the arrest, trial and imprisonment of my father and the suicide of my mother. I was left alone, wealthy and suicidal. At this point I went to college just to get away from the scene of my shame. During my freshman year, I tried sex with every boy that appealed to me, all to no avail. There was no satisfaction either sexually or emotionally. Finally I gave up on boys and decided to try girls. This proved equally unsatisfying until I met a girl who I will call Anita, who had a similarly abnormal childhood. We fell in love and my life became deliriously happy for the first time. This lasted through college and two years afterwards. At that time, she became ill and rapidly deteriorated. She died of AIDS, which she had contracted in her search for love before we met. This again brought me to the brink of suicide. My psychiatrist suggested that I must find something to occupy my mind and my time in order to save my sanity. I found employment as Alex's private secretary when the company and his career was just beginning. We became friends and there was more free time than work. He detected the sadness in my life and gradually we began to talk. I finally told him this story. His sympathic ear and wise counsel got me through this crisis. I was completely loyal and devoted to him without any romantic or sexual overtones on the part of either of us. He loved you completely and never strayed with anyone. His death was just as much a blow to me as to you but in a much different way. It is like the loss of my parents and my lover all over again."

Elizabeth was sobbing openly and she embraced Sherry. "I'm

so sorry I put you through this, but I had to know."

"I understand. The story gets less painful with the telling."

"I will keep your confidence, but assure my lawyer that there was no affair between you and Alex."

Sherry was reminded of the tape and it seemed an appropriate time to tell Elizabeth of its existence and the story surrounding it. She opened her purse, removed the tape and presented it to Elizabeth explaining how and why she found it, the circumstances surrounding the recording, and the fact that she had been present when Alex returned the call.

"He talked to a Dr. Shepard who assured him that it was good that the nitro relieved his pain and to continue to use it when necessary."

"Did he say anything else?"

"No. Did he mention the call to you?"

"Yes, he said the doctor called him back and said everything was all right. I'll give this to my lawyer, if that's okay with you."

"Oh, yes, anything that might be of help. I must go now."

Elizabeth was left with her thoughts and felt an overwhelming sadness for her loss and Sherry's life. She was relieved that Alex had been true to her. She would make an appointment with Sloanberg to give him the tape and tell him of Sherry's assurance of Alex's fidelity.

Sloanberg listened to the tape.

"Did Sherry overhear the conversation between Alex and Dr. Shepard?"

"Yes, it was on the speaker phone. The doctor assured Alex everything was all right and to just keep taking the nitro. Alex told me the same thing and seemed quite relieved."

"Are you convinced of Alex's innocence?"

"Yes."

"Who is Dr. Shepard and why did he return the call?"

"I don't know."

He realized these facts would make Lawrence's plight a little less desperate, but it might add another defendant. He would have to depose Dr. Shepard. Perhaps Shepard could clarify the relationship between himself, the clinic and the HMO.

CHAPTER 25

When Ronald Shepard received the summons, he was quite surprised and upset. What could he tell them about the Boomer case? He called his attorney and the HMO attorney. They both assured him that Sloanberg wanted to establish the contractual relationship between Dr. Lawrence, the clinic and the HMO.

"Why do they want telephone records, too?"

Neither lawyer could answer that question and seemed unconcerned.

Sloanberg called Tim Charleton again and told him to add Dr. Shepard to his list of people to be investigated.

"You're going to use up all your fee paying me," Charleton said with glee.

"Not quite. The potential dollar amount of this case is horrendous, especially if we can tie the HMO in as a co-defendant. Shepard might be that link."

"What do you want to know about him?"

"I want the details of the contract with the HMO, his financial relationship with his former partner, his personal relation with the HMO, official position as well as any character defects."

"That's a tall order. I do have a report on Dr. Evans. He's clean financially and socially. He is a conscientious doctor, well respected by the hospital administration, his colleagues and the ED staff. In addition, he has an excellent reputation with the legal community as an expert witness. He is honorable, sharp, and medically competent in his testimony. He will not take a case unless he is convinced the position of his client is valid. He will work with either defense or plaintiff attorneys if he can conscientiously support the claims of the suit."

"It sounds like you've unmasked the original Mr. Clean. You're batting a thousand so far, as usual."

"You're too cynical. Which one of this cast of characters do you want me to do next?"

"I think the defendant, Dr. Lawrence. Okay?"

Tim decided to start at the clinic and follow Dr. Lawrence to see what he does after hours. He hit the jackpot on the first try. The doctor went straight to the condo in the upscale West L.A. area and used the key to enter one of the units. Tim had the doctor's address and it was not this complex. The address had a familiar ring and when he checked, bingo, Melissa. Two birds with one stone possibly. He could be legit, but the key made that unlikely. He noticed the occupant of another car seemed unduly interested in that same condo. Perhaps he should follow that car and see where it leads. The only thing he could learn here was how long Lawrence stayed and whether he went home from here. It seemed the other individual was going to wait for just that information. The hours dragged on and nothing changed. At 10:45 p.m., Dr. Lawrence emerged alone and left the scene. The other car followed rather obviously and appeared not to be skilled at surveillance. The doctor arrived home shortly after 11:00 p.m. The other observer left the area hurriedly with Tim following at a discrete distance until they reached a high rise apartment complex in Santa Monica. The person in the car turned out to be a young woman who entered the lobby by means of a card key after parking her car in the underground. Apparently she was home for the night. Tim wondered who else is shadowing Sloanberg's subjects. He decided to have one of his investigators try to identify this person while he concentrated on Lawrence and Melissa.

Maria was so ecstatic to have her suspicions about Lawrence and his nurse verified that she did not notice the car which followed her home. She would add this bit of information into her computer and tell Tom Dougherty in the morning. Identifying her was easy enough. Betty Carnell, the other investigator, simply waited in the garage early the next morning until Melissa entered her car, the description of which and the space number having been provided her by Tim. With a license number, Betty's source at the DMV provided, Maria Gonzalez' name and address and car loan information from the bank revealed her employment. Her interest in Michael Lawrence and Melissa Hailey was going to be more difficult. Maria went directly to Tom's office. She told him of Michael's visit to Melissa's condo confirming her suspicions.

Tom, "I can't see the relationship between the trial and a possible liaison involving a young doctor and his pretty nurse."

"Neither can I but it lends itself to the intrigue of this case."

"Such relationships are quite common between doctors and nurses. If this comes out during the trial, it will not help Lawrence's image with the jury, but it is not our responsibility to disclose it now. We are not a tabloid."

Maria was somewhat disappointed with his lack of enthusiasm for her discovery, but she could see the logic. She was unaware that she too was under surveillance. On arriving home that evening, she noticed that several objects seemed out of place and the papers on her desk appeared to have been disturbed. She was a meticulous housekeeper and any slight deviation would be noticeable to her. She frantically checked her computer and her files and was relieved to find everything intact. Perhaps she was overly suspicious because of this case.

CHAPTER 26

Tim's background check on Michael Lawrence was benign. He'd been a good student in college and med school. His work as a resident had been above average, his marriage and financial history were above reproach until he came to L.A. Within a short time he became involved in an extra marital relationship with Melissa Haley, the nurse assigned to him at the clinic. This became a hot topic of gossip at the clinic until they were both threatened with dismissal. He broke it off and brought his wife to L.A. and everything calmed down about the time the clinic entered into the contract with the HMO. From his findings, it would appear the spark was rekindled. He decided to secrete a bug and a camera in Melissa's condo to confirm the nature of the doctor's visits to his nurse.

He entered the condo with ease, placing his bug and camera in a strategic location. Dirty old man that he was, he hoped the film would reveal what he expected. Before leaving he examined the condo's contents. The only things of interest were men's toiletries, pajamas, robe and a change of clothes. Melissa apparently lived beyond her salary as a nurse. The condo was expensive as were the furnishings, her wardrobe and jewelry. There was no evidence of drugs, prescriptions or alcohol except a small number of bottles of expensive champagne. Her pantry and refrigerator were well stocked with groceries indicating she cooked and ate most of her meals at home. The only thing he needed was her file before coming to L.A. and the source of her apparent wealth, in addition to the film and conversations from the gadgets he had installed. Perhaps Sloanberg could obtain her financial background on deposition.

Dr. Ronald Shepard was the next subject of Tim Charleton's

investigation. The first order of business was to obtain copies of the various contracts involving the doctor, the clinic and the HMO. They were public records so that was no problem. The clinic was owned by a corporation of which Shepard's share was forty-nine percent and Dr. Robert Jones' share was fifty-one percent. The HMO owned no stock, but simply contracted with the corporation to provide medical services to its members. Jones had retired with the signing of the contract. Shepard continued to practice and was CEO of the corporation. However, Alexander Garrison was Administrator of the clinic. Unofficially, he answered to the HMO. The doctors contracted with the corporation to provide medical and surgical services to patients of the clinic. The HMO was as far removed legally as it could possibly be from direct patient care. It had paid a large signing bonus to the clinic corporation, all of which went into the corporation owned by Jones and Shepard. Thereby the HMO was at arms length legally from any malpractice action. Each doctor was liable for his own actions and paid his own malpractice insurance. The clinic corporation was responsible for the actions of nurses and secretaries as its employees. Some very compentant, high priced legal talent had put this deal together.

Dr. Shepard had a large home in Beverly Hills. He was married and had two grown children. He lived a quiet life and continued to maintain an active surgical practice. He played golf regularly in the same foursome Wednesday afternoons and Saturday mornings at Wilshire Country Club. He was sixty-years old and in good health. His wife was ten years his junior and active in the country club and medical auxiliary. He had no extracurricular affairs and was active in the Presbyterian Church. He had never been a victim of a malpractice action. He and Jones had founded the clinic twenty-five years ago, which had become very successful and of excellent reputation. So much for another Mr. Clean.

CHAPTER 27

When Melissa returned home, little did she know that she would soon provide entertainment for an office full of middle-aged investigators. Michael was on his way over and she was too busy preparing for their liaison to notice any evidence of the invasion of her home which had taken place earlier in that day. She bathed, perfumed and dressed seductively from inside out. She prepared snacks, caviar and chilled two bottles of French Champagne. They had not been together in a week and she really wanted and needed him. Michael arrived promptly at seven and was overwhelmed by her beauty and ardor. The tension increased as they ate and drank until they no longer put off the inevitable. Afterwards, they held each other for a very long time, silently reliving their ecstasy. The whole scene had been captured in graphic detail and living color and was screened to the staff of the Legal Investigative Services. Tim said, "We certainly know what is going on in the private lives of the doctor and his nurse."

Sloanberg watched the film and listened to the dialogue in amazement.

Tim, "You really are an unscrupulous son-of-a-bitch."

"Is this the only copy of this film?"

"Yes."

"You'd better be telling me the truth. If I ever hear of it being passed around, I'll have your license. This goes in my safe and when I no longer need it as a possible bargaining chip, it will be destroyed."

Tim was somewhat surprised at Eric's reaction. He would have to warn his employees to keep their mouth shut.

There had been no conversation of the office, the suit or anything about their relationship except the intimacies of the evening. Now that he knew they were lovers, there was no further need for the camera so he planned to enter her condo again and remove it. The bug would be left in the hopes of catching a conversation relative to the lawsuit.

Sloanberg was a moral man. He was revolted by the film he had just seen, not so much its contents but the matter in which it had been obtained and probably been used by Charleton to entertain his associates. He hadn't asked because he didn't want to know. These were two young people who were in love and had a passionate relationship. He would never use this film or make their relationship public. The knowledge that it existed was all he needed to know.

With the knowledge he had gained about Dr. Shepard, it was time to depose him. He could not know what impact it would have on three young women.

The day of the depo arrived. The same cast was present with the addition of the witness and his attorney, Mark Smith.

Questioning began with Sloanberg inquiring about Shepard's education, medical background, and present clinical practice. He was a Mayo-trained surgeon with board certification in general surgery and limited his practice to abdominal surgery. He had practiced in the clinic for twenty-five years, starting by associating himself with Robert Jones, also a general surgeon. They eventually expanded the clinic to include other specialties. He was then asked about his relationship with the HMO, how it came about and details of the contract. He stated that the changes in the practice of medicine had made it essential that they become affiliated with a managed care group. The companies for whom the clinic provided medical care to their employees and their families demanded a cost effective contract. The HMO was the most reasonable way to go.

Sloanberg, "Was it also the most lucrative for you and your partner? Just how much were you and Dr. Jones paid to sign with them?"

Smith, "I object to that. It is irrelevant and immaterial to this deposition and is a matter of personal financial information which does not have to be revealed by my client."

"In the first place, the contract is a matter of public record and I'll place it in evidence if necessary. Secondly, it may go to motivation of this witness and his actions as they relate to this lawsuit."

"You have not filed on him?"

"All in due time. Your client is a major stockholder of the clinic and is technically the managing director of the clinic. That makes him responsible for the actions of the employees and agents of the clinic."

Sloanberg, "His contract does not support that hypothesis."

"I think it does and I'll introduce it to the court for a ruling. You do not have to answer that question now but we will proceed to other matters."

Sloanberg, "Dr. Shepard, did you receive a call from Alex Boomer about the effect of nitroglycerine on his chest pains several days before his fatal heart attack?"

"I don't remember."

"What would you say if I told you I have a witness who overheard that conversation and that your telephone log confirms that call?"

"I receive many calls each day and after I complete them, put most of them out of my mind. I do not remember such a call."

"Incidentally, a supeona is being served as we speak for your telephone log. I have nothing further for this witness at this time."

Shepard and his lawyer were visibly upset as they left the deposition. They proceeded to Smith's office.

Smith, "You didn't tell me that you had contact with Boomer before his death."

"I'd forgotten all about it until I was reminded by my secretary and Dr. Lawrence's clinic nurse."

"How did that come about?"

"Sue, my secretary, told me that the nurse was inquiring about a call from Boomer. Lawrence was asked about such a call at his depo and stated that he knew nothing about it. Apparently he asked his nurse if she had taken the call and she had denied it and inquired of the telephone operator. She had referred it to me because there was no other physician in the clinic at the time. Apparently, I did speak with him."

"Were you overheard?"

"Not to my knowledge."

"Are phone calls recorded or logged?"

"There is a telephone log which records the date, time and caller and disposition of all calls."

"And now that log is on its way to Sloanberg's office. Do you remember what he said and what you said?"

"No."

"Is it recorded in the patient's chart?"

"I doubt it."

"Do you realize this information, if true, will make you a defendant in the suit?"

Shepard returned to his office and made an appointment with William Blake, the CEO of the HMO and John Bailey, the HMO attorney. They met at Baileys office the next day and he informed them of the latest development.

"Smith says I'll become a defendant in the suit if there is indeed a witness to my conversation with the deceased."

"Is there such an individual," Bailey asked.

"I don't think there's a witness to the conversation, especially on my end. However, the telephone operator and Sue, my secretary, know that such a conversation did take place. Also Dr. Lawrence's nurse was told of it, but none of them could have heard what was said."

"Mrs. Boomer will testify as to the call and the contents as told her by the husband, however, that is here say. Besides she has much to gain, so her testimony will be prejudicial."

"Is it possible that someone on Boomer's end could have overhead it?"

"I have no way of knowing, but anything's possible."

"Perhaps his secretary and office personnel at ACME should be investigated in addition to Mrs. Boomer," Bailey said.

"I'll have my investigators go to work on it immediately. You're involvement will bring the HMO perilously close to legal jeopardy. That must be avoided at all costs. My job is to protect the stockholders and I'll do whatever is necessary to accomplish that."

Shepard, "I knew Blake would sacrifice the clinic in a millisecond if it became a liability. Perhaps I should warn Jones and consider moving the clinic funds to an offshore bank."

CHAPTER 28

Sherry had become alarmed about the management of ACME Electronics. The stock continued to decline in value and Epstein and the Board seemed unable to stop it. The company was floundering. She felt Elizabeth should be made aware of the crisis since her financial well-being was primarily related to the company stock. She called and they agreed to meet the next evening at an out-of-the-way restaurant.

When she left the office garage, she was vaguely aware of an unfamiliar vehicle behind her but soon lost sight of it and forgot about it. She went by home and changed clothes and proceeded to a suburban restaurant where Elizabeth was waiting for her at a corner table. Sherry ordered a drink and she plunged right into her concerns about the company.

Elizabeth, "I had no idea there were financial problems at the company. I never kept up with the business as Alex always told me not to worry about such things.

Besides, I have been so busy and emotionally distracted with everything that resulted from his death, I have not given a thought to the company. What should I do?"

Sherry, "I think you should employ a corporate lawyer to look after your interests. You are a major stockholder, after all. Perhaps the individual who audited the company, if there is no conflict with your malpractice attorney."

There was a minimum amount of small talk during the meal since they had little in common besides Alex and the company.

On leaving, Sherry noticed the same car in the restaurant parking lot. It seemed more than coincidental and she was somewhat concerned. However, she could not conceive why anyone would be following her. She saw no more of the car and soon forgot all about it.

Sherry was tired and emotionally drained by the meeting with Elizabeth. She was concerned about the status of the company and did not relish the idea of testifying. She did not notice that her home had been entered in her absence. The light was blinking on the answering machine and she checked and found there was a call from Eric Sloanberg. He wanted to see her at her convenience. She immediately called Elizabeth to make sure he was her lawyer and there was no objection to speaking with him.

"I don't know what he wants with me."

"He probably wants to discuss the tape and what you overhear of Alex's conversation with the clinic doctor. He was very interested when I told him about it."

John Bailey had his answer much sooner than he expected. Greg McKinna of Confidential Investigations Incorporated called him as soon as he listened to the tape of the conversation.

"Sherry Parker is the witness linking Shepard to the case. She was Alex Boomer's private secretary and apparently a friend of Boomer. There is also a tape of that conversation which is probably in the possession of Sloanberg by now."

"Is there anything in her life or past that we could use to insure her cooperation of silence?"

"I only checked her home and installed a bug so far. I'll have to do a more in-depth investigation of her past and present life."

Tim Charleton read the computer printout obtained from Maria's apartment with interest. She had meticulously documented her ploy at the clinic and the emergency department, and the results of her treatment at both places. She had outlined an encounter with Dr. Lawrence and his advice, as well as the conflicting advice given by Dr. Evans. She mentioned the apparent relationship between Lawrence and his nurse and the rapid turnover of patients, his comment about needless tests and consultations and the nurse's apparent concern about that comment. Dr. Evans, on the other hand, had urged her to either be admitted to the hospital or seek consultation with a cardiologist and indicated to fail to do so might jeopardize her life. What a difference in approach by the two doctors. She also documented her observations of Lawrence's three-hour visit to his nurse's apartment. Finally, she commented on her editor's rejection of her desire to write a story based on this information.

Sloanberg read the report with interest. It confirmed his suspicions about the clinic and the HMO. He certainly could use Maria as a witness to develop his theory concerning the motives for the events that lead to his client's husband's death. Added to Sherry Parker's testimony about Boomer's phone call from Dr. Shepard, he was closing in on adding the HMO as a defendant. He decided to interview Sherry rather than depose her and alert the opposition to knowledge concerning the case. His secretary, Lois, called ACME Electronics to ask to speak to Ms. Parker. She was informed that Ms. Parker was not at the office.

"Was she expected today?"

"Yes, she was usually in hours before this."

"Please have her return my call." She gave the private line which she alone answered. By 11:00 a.m, Lois decided to try Sherry's home number. The line was busy continuously for the next hour and she became suspicious. She reported this to Sloanberg. He suggested she contact Elizabeth Boomer to see if she had knowledge of Sherry's whereabouts. She did not but agreed to go by the home and check. On arrival, she noticed the alarm was off and the front door was ajar. She pushed it open. The normally meticulously neat entry and living room had been turned upside down. She called Sherry's name several times. There was no answer. She was afraid to investigate further and returned to her car and called 911 on her cell phone. The police were there in three minutes and entered the house with guns drawn. After a few minutes, one of the officers returned and told Elizabeth she should not go in and then he called for an ambulance.

"Why can't I go in?"

"There is a very bloody scene in there. Your friend has been viciously assaulted and is near death."

"I must try to help her." She ran in the house, found Sherry on her bed covered with blood completely naked and barely breathing. Elizabeth was shocked to near hysterics by the scene, but maintained self-control and tried to talk to Sherry. She was pale and unresponsive. She was bleeding from a large wound on the left side of her head, her left breast was almost amputated, there was an apparent stab wound in the right chest which was exuding bloody bubbles with each labored breath. Her hands were tied to each side of the bed board and her feet similarly to the foot of the bed by torn bed sheets. Miraculously she was still alive.

Paramedics arrived, freed her arms and legs, placed a Vaseline gauze pad over the chest wound, started an IV, intubated her and started positive pressure oxygen with an ambu bag. She was covered with a sheet, placed on a gurney and rushed to the ED accompanied by Elizabeth and a police unit.

They were met by the trauma team. She was quickly assessed, found to be in deep shock and suffering from a severe head injury. A chest tube was inserted into the right thorax relieving the hemopneumo thorax. The bleeding from the scalp and breast was controlled and the wounds dressed. She was then taken to x-ray for a CAT scan of her head and a chest x-ray. Routine trauma lab work was drawn. Type specific uncross matched blood was started in both arms while waiting for cross matching of six units. The respiration and blood pressure responded to treatment, but the patient remained unconscious. Her right pupil was dilated and she began posturing. CAT scan revealed a large subdural hematoma on the left with extension of bleeding into the cortex and the left ventricle. A neurosurgeon was called and the patient was taken to the OR. The hematoma was evacuated, but the extension into the ventricle and cortex precluded recovery.

In the rush to salvage the patient's life, a rape exam had not been done until one of the officers asked about it. He pointed out to the trauma surgeon that she had been tied spreadeagle to the bedposts and there had been slight bleeding from the vaginal area.

On return from the OR to the ICU, the emergency physician was summoned to ICU to complete this portion of the exam. It would be a necessary element of what was to be a murder investigation.

Dr. Evans' and Jackie Hart responded to the ICU reluctantly with the rape exam kit. Both felt this was an unnecessary medical intrusion on a dying patient. The exam ordeal was more brutalization of the patient. Samples were taken from the vaginal orifice, the cervix and the anal orifice. It was noted that both vagina and rectum were lacerated, most likely by a foreign object and there was a laceration of the top of the vaginal wall probably extending into the abdominal cavity. Blood had clotted in each of these areas. These observations were reported to the attending surgeon as well as the police. The surgeon started the patient on intravenous antibiotics to treat the potential peritonitis secondary to vaginal penetration into the abdominal cavity.

Elizabeth Boomer was an emotional basket case. To go through something like this so soon after her husband's unexpected death was almost more than she could bear. After all Sherry had been through, to be assaulted like this was beyond belief. She called Sloanberg to report what had happened. He was shocked. What was our society coming to? He had no reason to believe this tragedy could be related to the lawsuit, but it did cross his mind. Surely this was just a simple, everyday act of violence. Perhaps Elizabeth and the other people involved should be somewhat more observant and careful. He would call McAllen and Jim Bishop and at least notify them so they could warn their clients without drawing any conclusions for them. If she died or was mentally incompetent to testify, it would hurt his case against Shepard and possibly with the HMO, but he still had the tape.

CHAPTER 29

Nancy had not forgotten the last time Michael had been out late and come in drunk and disheveled with the same old excuse of being with his lawyer. When he called from the office and told her he was again meeting with his lawyer tonight, she became suspicious and decided to follow him and find out for herself. She rented a car, dressed inconspicuously and promptly at five o'clock, stationed herself near the clinic where she could watch the exit to the garage without being seen. She had not been there long when she saw his car. He headed west away from downtown toward West L.A. It was about a twenty minute drive to Melissa's condo. He parked in the garage and he let himself in with a keycard. He entered the condo with the same card and disappeared inside. She did not know how to proceed. About that time another car entered the garage, parked next to his and entered the condo. The occupant was a pretty young woman in a nurse's uniform.

Nancy was shocked. Her worst fears had been realized. She was shocked because her relationship with Michael had improved markedly recently. He had been more considerate, less critical and more loving. She was almost sorry she had found out, even though she recognized Melissa, she knew very little about her. Michael mentioned her only in relationship to the clinic and their social contact had been almost nil. She did not know whether to confront either one of them or just keep up the charade and hope the affair was a temporary passion which would soon pass. She wasn't even sure it was an affair. Perhaps it was just a meeting somehow related to the clinic and the trial. She assumed Melissa would be a witness for Michael but why would he lie about his whereabouts if that was the case? She would not mention her findings to either of them, at least for the time being. She went home shattered, struggling for control of her emotions.

CHAPTER 30

Tom Dougherty heard the report on the paper's police scanners and immediately notified Maria. She hurried to Sherry's home and arrived just as the ambulance was leaving. She decided to talk to the investigating officers and go to the hospital later. She was well-respected by the local police department because of favorable handling of controversial investigations. So she was given a detailed account of their early findings and conclusions. She was also allowed to peruse the crime scene with few restrictions. The bedroom was mute evidence to the brutal assault that had taken place. The bed was covered with blood and there was stains on the once beautiful wallpaper and carpet. The shredded sheets were still tied to the four posts of the bed, having been cut off Sherry's extremities to free her from the scene of her violation. The phone was knocked off the bedside table, as was a lamp and clock, both of which had been disconnected from their respective wall sockets by the violence of the struggle. The clock was stopped at 3:10, thus establishing the time of the attack. No weapon was found. The rest of the house had been searched and was in complete disarray. Every drawer was open and on the floor their contents strewn about the various rooms in a haphazard fashion. Even the kitchen had not escaped the devastation. Broken dishes were on the floor and the drawers and cabinets were virtually empty. The refrigerator doors were open and food was mixed with the broken dishes on the floor.

Maria questioned the lead investigator. "Who could be responsible for this kind of devastation? Surely not some deranged rapist."

Investigator, "So far that is the only theory we have until we have more information about the victim."

Maria, "Was she treated as violently as her home?"

Investigator, "She was beaten, stabbed, possibly raped and was forced to lie in that blood-soaked bed suffering the tortures of the damned for almost nine hours. I would be surprised if she survives and, unfortunately, only she might have the key that would enable us to catch this monster. So far we have not a clue and we can only assume this to be another random act of violence."

On route to the hospital, Maria assimilated what she had seen and been told. She could not believe this could be the work of someone without a more sinister motive. It appeared the house had been searched rather than vandalized and the victim tortured. This crime was more personal. It was either revenge or the attacker was seeking information by means of torture.

Maria entered the emergency department and was told there was a press briefing in progress in the conference room. Dr. Evans was at the podium and had just begun to relate the patient's injuries and her condition. The wounds were described in as much detail as was reasonable to the non-medical audience. He was asked about Sherry's chance for survival and was told less than ten percent. If so, would she make a complete recovery? "No, there would be severe brain damage." Maria asked if her family had been notified and if so, could they supply a possible motive? She was told, "As far as we know she has no family and we have little background on her other than her employment at ACME Electronics." Maria immediately made the connection between the company and the Alex Boomer case. She asked no further questions, hoping her colleagues had missed that. She would have to find out more about Sherry's background herself.

Dr. Evans recognized Maria but he was unable to make the connection with her ED visit until the end of the briefing. As she was leaving the conference room, someone gently touched her arm. She turned and saw Dr. Evans. She had hoped he would not recognize her.

Dr. Evans, "How are your heart palpitations?"

Maria, "I haven't had anymore. The Valium has worked very well."

Dr. Evans, "You did not take my advice then."

"No, I felt fine and my job has been very demanding recently."

Dr. Evans, "I hope I am wrong about your illness. Please reconsider."

"Yes, doctor," she replied in a tone all patients use when they have no intention of following their doctor's advice.

She hurriedly left the hospital before he had the opportunity to quiz her further.

On the way out she noticed Elizabeth Boomer sitting alone in the waiting room. She appeared to be crying. Maria recognized her from the many articles and pictures that appeared in the Daily Telegram. She took a seat next to her, hoping to find out what had brought her here. Information was soon in coming. Elizabeth was alone, upset and had to talk to someone, even a stranger. Maria seemed that sympathetic stranger. Soon she was pouring out the details of how and why she found Sherry, how they had become friends, what an irony it was for this tragedy to compound those of her previous life. The statements were quite general, avoiding details other than the fact Sherry had been Alex Boomer's secretary. With this much information, Maria would be able to fill in the details. She was genuinely sympathetic. She introduced herself to Elizabeth and neglected to tell her she was a reporter.

One week later, Sherry Parker died without having regained consciousness. The obituary was inconspicuous compared to the media frenzy concerning her murder. It was noted that she had no living relatives, her parents having died during her early teens. She had graduated from Purdue, been briefly married and moved to L.A. to take a position as executive secretary to the recently expired CEO of ACME Electronics. She had been a victim of a random assault in her home one week ago and had died from the injuries sustained in that attack. There was to be a grave side service in West Los Angeles at 2:00 p.m.

There was a rather sparse crowd mostly made up of fellow

employees from ACME, Elizabeth Boomer, a small group of media, two police investigators, two unspecified men apparently known to the investigators and Maria Gonzales. Elizabeth recognized her from the hospital and wondered why she was attending the funeral of someone she represented as a stranger. However, she was too caught up in the emotion of the tragic end of so tragic a life to give it more than a passing thought.

Maria avoided Elizabeth knowing that her presence here might be questioned. She was curious about the two strangers who were so obviously out of place. She would ask the police investigators later. She would also check into Sherry's life in Indiana, her parent's death, Purdue and the brief marriage. Somewhere the key to Sherry's murder might be found in her life prior to Alex Boomer. The detectives, Donald Jacobs and Mark Derey had attended the funeral more out of duty than grief for the deceased. Both had been with the LA Police Department for over fifteen years and had seen too many such victims, had been to too many funerals. The two strangers were not together and each represented different private detective agencies and were probably there for the same purpose as Jacobs and Derey, hoping the culprit had come to see the results of his handiwork.

After the services, the detectives approached Elizabeth Boomer and introduced themselves. "We're here hoping to find some lead to the death of your friend." They had responded to the 911 call and had recognized Elizabeth though she had been too distraught to remember them.

"If you're up to it, we would appreciate your help in identifying the mourners from ACME and any other familiar person present."

She was somewhat shocked but realized this would be part of their investigation. She regained control of her emotions, welcoming a respite from her grief.

"Perhaps the easiest way to help you is to point out those who are unknown to me. There are two men I have never seen before and a pretty, young brunette whom I met at the hospital after

Sherry had been taken to surgery. The rest are fellow employees of ACME and probably media."

"That certainly limits our prospects. We thank you very much, and you have our deepest sympathy."

By now the casket had been lowered into the ground and the mourners were disbanding. Elizabeth had wanted to talk to the young woman she had met at the hospital, but she had slipped away while Elizabeth was talking to the detectives.

CHAPTER 31

For a week now, Sherry's assault, medical progress and death had dominated both the print and electronic media. There had been no progress in the investigation, no clues to the identity of the murderer and no theories to the motivation other than another episode of random violence. The community was beginning to wonder if this was the first in a series of episodes to come. The media did little to discourage the fear of a serial killer.

Maria, however, could not dismiss the idea of some connection to the Alex Boomer death. Such a thought, though far-fetched, had some validity because of Sherry's relationship to the company and her boss. She decided to delve into Sherry Parker's early life in Indiana, college and life in LA. She convinced Tom Dougherty to send her to Sherry's hometown and university to obtain background for a human interest story on her before the media interest in this murder died down.

With the leads furnished by the obituary department of the paper, she started in the morgue of the Indianapolis Sentinel. She struck paydirt beyond her wildest expectations. The trial of Albert Parker had been headlines ten years ago. His conviction, imprisonment and the suicide of Florence Parker, the mother. After that Sherry disappeared from the media with the exception of the issuance of a marriage license to Sherry Parker and Charles Gault. This was followed in the public records section of the paper by a divorce decree. There the trail ended until she went to West Lafayette. She found nothing there except that Sherry had obtained a B.B.A. with honor. There the paper trail ended and there was no one at the school to furnish any other information. No one who might have known her when she was in school could be found.

She wondered if Albert Parker and Charles Gault were reachable. Parker would be easy to find unless he had been paroled. She went to the Indiana Office of Corrections and asked how to find the location of a prisoner, but struck a brick wall despite her press credentials. However, when she relayed the story of Sherry Parker's murder in LA and indicated that her father probably did not know that his only daughter was dead, the hard-bitten secretary then relented and went to her computer list of prisoners. Albert Parker was still alive and still in a correctional institution at Indianapolis.

"How can I arrange to visit him?" Maria

Secretary, "I can issue you a request for a pass to see him on family business, but the local prison officials and the prisoner himself have the final say."

Maria thanked her and prepared to make the pilgrimage. First she engaged the services of an investigative agency to find Charles Gault.

She called the prison and stated her business and advised the warden of the request for a pass form which she had received. She was granted a pass to meet with Parker the next day.

The prison was located in a dreary area several miles off the freeway. There was one two-lane, unmarked road leading to the main gate. The building was grey and stark surrounded by fifteen foot walls topped by another two feet of rolled barbed wire. There were manned turrets on top of the walls every two hundred yards. The entrance was two opposing gates made of steel bars electrically controlled from the guard house. She parked her car in the designated area and fell into the visitor's line. She was eventually admitted after being searched and was taken by bus to the cell block where Parker was housed. Since he was in a minimum security area, she was taken to a visitor's area along with fifty or sixty other individuals. Parker was brought in, taken to the table where Maria was waiting and seated across from her. He'd had no visitors in years, no contact with family since his wife had died. He was very curious why this young stranger had sought him out.

Maria was very depressed and apprehensive in this environment and came right to the point.

"I'm Maria Gonzales, a reporter for LA, doing a story about your daughter Sherry. I'm sorry to have to tell you that she is dead."

He was seized with the first emotions since the death of his wife ten years ago. He was convulsed in tears. Everybody in the room stopped to watch them. The guard approached and asked what the problem was. Maria told him of her news and he left stone-faced and without further comment. Maria supplied Parker with the details of Sherry's death, prompting another torrent of emotion. Despite Maria's prompting, Parker refused to discuss his abuse of his daughter, the trial or the events leading to the suicide of his wife other than to proclaim his innocence. Another dead end.

On her return to Indianapolis, Maria recontacted the investigative agency only to find that Charles Gault had been killed by police in drug raid. There the trail to Sherry's early life ended.

Maria returned to LA disappointed with her mission to Indiana. She thought about Elizabeth Boomer and wondered what she knew that had occasioned her discovery of the crime scene and her emotional response at the hospital and the funeral. Most wives did not have that close of a relationship with their husband's secretary. There was a missing link and she must find it. She had only uncovered part of Sherry's tragic life story, a part which, though interesting, probably had no relationship to the murder.

The headlines had detailed the brutality of the assault, the medical progress of Sherry and the speculation about a possible motive. The only clues found were blood-stained imprints of a man's shoe in the bedroom. DNA was taken from bloodstains on the bed and on the walls, but proved to be only compatible with Sherry. The killer did make one error. He did not use a condom during the rape, and therefore, left his DNA calling card. This would be of value only in rulings suspects in or out.

Maria's human interest story was put on hold temporarily.

Her latest findings were added to the computer summary of her HMO experiences and Sherry's murder.

CHAPTER 32

Sloanberg met with his staff to review his case and make decisions concerning presentation, plans and witnesses. Gary Gebhardt of his firm was chosen to be second chair and Denise Moody, paralegal to handle legal research. Marianne James, his secretary was to be responsible for scheduling witnesses, providing exhibits and motions when needed, taking notes and maintaining a general order of the presentation.

The death of Sherry Parker had been a blow to his case. She had been a witness to the phone call between Boomer and Dr. Shepard, which would have implicated the doctor, the clinic and the HMO. Now he had only the tape of the call, the clinic telephone operator and Melissa Hailey, the defendent's nurse and lover. The relationship between Melissa and the primary defendant could damage her credibility. Of course, Elizabeth Boomer could and would testify as to her husband's statement concerning the advice given him and also the statements given her about the call by Sherry.

Sloanberg called the meeting to order and stated the first order of business was to decide just who, besides Dr. Lawrence would be sued. He discussed the witnesses implicating Dr. Shepard and their credibility and admissibility. Mrs. Boomer's testimony about Sherry's story was pure hearsay as was that of Melissa. In light of Sherry's death, the judge might allow it. Both witnesses had their own baggage of prejudice.

Sloanberg, "Dr. Lawrence had an insurance level of one million dollars and my economist says that this case is worth many times that amount. The hospital, paramedics and ER doctors have no liability. Any contribution by them would be a pure gift. Besides, it would complicate the presentation of the case, might prejudice the jury against us. Besides we would be able to employ Dr. Evans, in addition to our cardiologist, as an expert. I believe we should add Shepard, the clinic and the HMO as defendants and delete the hospital, the paramedics and ED group. I also do not believe ACME Electronics has any exposure."

Gebhardt, "I agree with you. The major weakness is a question of admissibility of hearsay testimony. Denise should start right now researching any case laws supporting our position.

If found, motions and support should not be presented until the witnesses are called. So, if their testimony is denied, the jury will wonder what they were going to say."

Sloanberg, "Good point. I say let's gamble and go for it. Shepard and the clinic have deep pockets and the HMO pocket is infinity. Are we all in agreement?"

Everyone in the firm had learned long ago to trust Sloanberg's judgment implicitly, so there was no dissent.

Sloanberg, "Now, let's name our witnesses in order of presentation. Elizabeth Boomer should be first to tell her story and discuss her life with her husband, his death, her loss financially, and personally. I'll bring her back when we get to the tape and Sherry. Next we'll call our economist and then the new CEO of ACME and the auditor we employed to examine company books. Then we'll bring in our medical experts. We'll subpena Melissa, the clinic phone operator and Shepard's nurse and play the tape. We will put Dr. Shepard on as a hostile witness and close with Elizabeth. We may or may not use the paramedics, cardiac nurse and the doctor who tried to rescusitate. In addition to his opinions, Dr. Evans may be allowed to cover all that. He should since his opinions will be based on medical records. He was not a treating physician even though he is responsible for the medical care in the emergency department. Denise, see if there is any case law on that as a potential conflict. He will certainly be challenged because of our dismissing our suit against him and his group."

The lawsuit was amended to include Drs. Shepard and Jones,

the clinic corporation and the HMO. The hospital, city, paramedics, Drs. Evans and Williams and the ED group were all dismissed.

Sloanberg placed a call to Jim Bishop, Dr. Evans' attorney, to inform him of the dismissal and to enlist his aid in persuading Evans to agree to testify as an expert for the plaintiff. Bishop was elated and agreed.

Dr. Shepard was not surprised at being served with a complaint as his deposition had clearly identified him as a target. Fortunately, both he and Jones had transferred their funds to a bank in the Caymans, out of the reach of a potential judgment. He had only his home, personal possessions and his clinic salary and a million dollar malpractice insurance policy exposed. There was also a clinic malpractice policy on both Shepard and Jones. A copy of the complaint was also served on Martin Smith, Shepard's attorney.

CHAPTER 33

William Blake was feeling very smug this morning, having just completed another merger virtually doubling the assets of the HMO. His stockholders would be very happy. The company was now worth five billion.

His pleasure was short-lived. The process server gained access to his inner sanctum despite the protests of his secretary and presented him with his first bad news in a very long time. He had been hired as CEO of a fledgling HMO away from a small hospital chain. He was given carte blanche to expand the HMO by whatever means he chose. He began by listing both small and large companies to contract with the HMO. At the same time, he was developing relationships with other clinics and hospitals to provide medical services to the employees and their families of the companies he had enlisted. He cut employee benefit costs drastically, pleasing the corporate managers and he was soon deluged with proposals from other companies. Initially, he was hard-pressed to provide adequate medical care, but he began making sweetheart deals with providers. This lasted until he had a monopoly of both providers and consumers (patients). At that point, he started initiating medical policies and procedures which diluted the access and quality of medical care. Physicians, clinics and hospitals that refused to comply were frozen out, especially in industrialized areas. No compliance, no HMO affiliation, no patients. This formula worked like a charm. The companies cared only about the bottom line. The patients were like sheep and the physicians were powerless to do anything about it and the government could care less. The HMO was immunized from malpractice litigation by contractual arrangements with hospitals, clinics and physicians which placed all the liability on the professionals.

Blake was incredulous. He called John Bailey immediately. "How could this be? I thought your legal-eagle colleagues had placed so many contractual layers between us and the doctors that we had no malpractice liability."

"I thought so too but apparently Sloanberg is looking for a deep-pocket to test the waters."

"Get this dismissed. It could ruin us and destroy the whole HMO concept if we should lose."

Bailey read the text of the complaint listing the causes of action. In a separate communication was a list of witnesses and a subpena for William Blake.

Dennis McAllen also received a copy of the revised complaint and the list of witnesses composed by Sloanberg. He was pleased by the inclusion of the HMO and surprised by that of Dr. Shepard. It served his purposes. The plaintiff's attorney had unknowingly aided his defense plan by including the HMO in their action. Rather than having a group of entities which had little or no exposure, he now had co-defendants with significant culpability and deep pockets. He could join the plaintiff in blaming the tactics of the HMO for Dr. Lawrence's care. The complicity of Dr. Shepard was an even greater present. He called Dr. Lawrence to give him the good news.

Lawrence was far from elated. He still had to be subjected to the indignation of the lawsuit, his job was precarious, and his personal life was a mess. Recently Nancy was acting strangely. She was very cool, both personally and sexually. She questioned his every absence from home or the office, making it almost impossible to spend any time with Melissa. He could not afford to alienate either woman until his legal problems were over. A scandal would reflect badly on him with a jury and Melissa was a key witness to the impact of the HMO policies and procedures on the competency of medical practice at the clinic. His legal attack on the HMO would probably cost him his job.

CHAPTER 34

Jim Bishop explained the impact of Sloanberg's decision to Dr. Evans and urged him to accept the invitation to testify as a plaintiff's expert. He was relieved to be dismissed from the suit because of the impact on his medical reputation, but also the impact of not being listed by BMQA. On the other hand, he did not relish trashing a fellow doctor in court. About twenty percent of his medical/legal cases were for the plaintiff but his respect for the medical profession was such that he only felt comfortable testifying against extremely incompetent doctors. In this case, he believed Lawrence to be ethical and compentant, this maloccurrence having resulted from the HMO policies. The fact that the HMO was a co-defendant eased his conscience about accepting the assignment.

CHAPTER 35

Buffy Rogers was always uncomfortable when returning home especially after dark. This particular evening she felt particularly wary though there seemed no tangible reason. The alarm was on as she had left it, the door was locked and the lights were still on in the hall and on the porch. On entering, she carefully locked the front door and went straight to her bedroom. There she was confronted with the source of her intuition. The struggle was brief, but violent. She was no match for the powerful stranger and soon lay mortally wounded as she was subjected to the ultimate violation. The intruder had left unnoticed and the neighbors remained unaware of another episode of senseless violence in their midst. She was twenty-two years old, a graduate of an inner city high school and a local business college. Her ascent out of the ghetto had been painful and slow. She lived in an upscale apartment near the old neighborhood but had remained streetwise. She was proud of her job and education and looked forward to achieving the American Dream. All that ended on this summer night. The next morning when she failed to arrive at the clinic and her phone was continuously busy, the manager called the police to check on her. The apartment was locked, the alarm was on and the porch and hall lights were on. Her car was in the driveway and locked. The patrolman peered in the window of the living room and was shocked to see everything in complete disarray. He and his partner broke in and found a young black female, naked, covered with blood, with extremities tied to the four posts of the bed. The house had been tossed and clothes, pictures, dishes, clock, telephone, everything was scattered on the floor. Furniture was overturned and broken. Buffy's body was cold, the blood was clotted and there was no sign of life. Her throat had been cut so deeply that the trachea muscles and all vessels of her neck been severed. There was a large hematoma on the left side of her head. There was no obvious wounds of the chest or abdomen. There were no other obvious wounds.

The sergeant arrived, called the medical examiner and the detectives and then notified the manager of the clinic. He in turn called a meeting of the clinic personnel and notified them. Buffy had worked there only six months and had not developed any close friends, but there was shock and sorrow among the personnel. A tragedy that usually happens to a stranger and only merits a passing acknowledgment in the media had now come very close to home. However, since her background was unknown and she lived near a violent neighborhood, no one was able to identify with the tragedy. Perhaps there was a new serial killer at work in LA.

The police, remembering the recent murder of Sherry Parker, approached it that way. Blood samples were taken, the scene was photographed from every angle and the apartment was searched through all the rubble for a weapon, a finger print and blood spatters or footprints. None was found. The body was taken to the morgue for a post. The neighbors were canvassed and no one had seen or heard anything. Buffy had kept to herself and developed only nodding acquaintances with her neighbors. There had been no arguments with any of them. She had been quiet, kept to herself and entertained no one.

Maria heard about this on the police scanner and immediately remembered Sherry. She got to the scene before the body was removed and was sickened by the sight of Buffy and the devastation of the apartment. It was all too reminiscent of the previous murder, if not a "copy cat" killing, it was done by the same person or persons. The police gave her all the information they had and she asked the medical examiner to call her when he scheduled the autopsy. Her repore with the various police agencies was good because she was never uncomplimentary of law enforcement in her articles and she was always willing to translate for officers who were not bilingual. When she got home she added the details of this murder as a footnote to her summary of the HMO suit, only because Buffy had worked at the clinic.

CHAPTER 36

The media blitz of what was characterized as the second of a potential series of serial killings had a noticeable effect on the patient population of emergency rooms throughout the city. On the one hand, there was a decrease in the number of minor illnesses because people were staying home in droves. On the other, there was a significant increase in the number of rape and molestation cases. Many women who had ignored date rape, assault, and rape by friends, neighbors and relatives were coming in droves. They were reporting every such event for fear it might be the "bedpost rapist". Instead of one or two rape exams per day, there were ten or twelve. As a result, many rapist were taken off the street. However, the one they really wanted to arrest continued to leave them without a clue.

In the midst of this plethora of assaults and alleged assaults, the mayhem of the streets continued. At 10:00 a.m. the paramedics called in a shooting associated with a failed bank robbery. An off-duty police officer approached the local bank to deposit his check. He noticed a car with its motor running, double-parked near the front door. On closer observation, he noted all activity inside the bank had come to a halt. He felt he had happened on a robbery in progress and decided to intervene. He only had a thirty-eight caliber revolver with six cartridges in it, his off-duty weapon. He drew his gun, walked up to the car and told the driver to put his hands on the steering wheel and not try to warn his colleagues. About that time, the other two ran out of the bank holding automatic weapons. Thinking retreat was a better part of valor, he ran back to his car and called for backup. The perps were not aware of what was going down until they were in the car and the driver was screeching out of the parking lot.

"Officer needs help." Calls bring dramatic results and soon, in addition to him, there were six police cars, a highway patrol car and two sheriffs following the robbers car through the middle of town at speeds in excess of sixty miles per hour. Soon there was also a motorcycle cop leading the parade of LA's finest. Suddenly one of the perps smashed out the back window and extended an AR-15 and started shooting at his perusers. The first one down was the motorcycle cop. He was on his side traveling down the street at the same speed he had been going on his bike, which by now was in the gutter. Miraculously, the parade missed him. The driver of the fleeing car lost control and plowed into a telephone pole and several kiosks near a shopping center. The officers opened fire on the car when the occupants failed to exit as ordered. The rifleman was hit in the head ending his criminal career. The driver was hit in the neck and the third individual surrendered.

The trauma team was alerted to the imminent arrival of four critically injured individuals, one of which was an officer. They assembled quickly and the emergency department physician stood at the door to triage the injured. The first to arrive was the motor-cycle cop who was in surprisingly good condition considering he had been hit in the chest with a round from an AR-15. It turned out he was wearing his vest for the first time today and the impact had only knocked him off his bike. The damage he sustained was a broken left ankle and severe cement burns on his arm, hip and left leg. It turned out that he did have a severely contused lung. The next to arrive was the rifleman who was D.O.A. from a clean shot through the head. The driver was critically injured from a bullet which transacted his trachea and left carotid. He was immediately sent to surgery as it was not possible to repair either the artery or the trachea in the emergency department. Luckily none of the other officers were injured. The Chief and virtually the whole precinct descended on the E.D. to see first hand what had happened.

Maria had also caught this incident on her scanner and proceeded directly to the hospital. She was met at the door by Dr. Evans who had just triaged the last of the wounded. He recognized her and inquired as to her health. She insisted there had been no recurrence of her palpation or chest pain and she was still taking the Valium. He eyed her skeptically, but did not pursue the subject. She also recognized two detectives among the hordes of police milling around the emergency department, Glenn Holmes and Vincent Ladd. She asked them for details of the shooting and they readily complied. She also inquired if there had been anything new on the Buffy Rogers murder. They stated that nothing more had been discovered except that she had been raped and sodomized with a blunt object just as Sherry had. The one significant fact was the DNA match of the semen in both women. That fact was still not for publication and hoped that it might be significant. They also did not want the rapist to read about it and start using condoms in his future crimes. This blunt prediction caused her to have a cold chill. Obviously the police were convinced there was a serial killer at work in LA and he would continue to strike until he was caught or killed. They were no closer to solving these crimes than when Sherry's body was first discovered.

She interviewed Dr. Evans and two of the officers involved in the bank robbery and chase. The condition of the wounded were upgraded, the only change being the death of the person shot in the neck during surgery. The story of the discovery of the robbery and the ensuing chase was graphically described by Officer Murkle who first noted the suspicious circumstances in the bank and took part in the chase.

Maria returned to the newspaper offices and wrote the story of the failed bank robbery. Accompanying her account of the chase was a photograph of the dead felon on the street, hands cuffed behind him with an officer standing over him with his gun leveled at the felons head. Police take it seriously when someone shoots at them or even points a gun at them. She also updated the story of the death of Buffy Rogers carefully avoiding any reference to the sperm samples. She noted that it was being treated as a serial killing and no new information was available except the results of the autopsy. She knew this information would heighten tension in LA but her job was to desciminate the news as it happened regardless.

CHAPTER 37

Officers Holmes and Ladd had not yet interviewed the two private investigators they had seen at Sherry's funeral. Ralph Nichols was a lone operative. He was known to take cases that the more reputable investigative firms shunned. His reputation was shady but he had never been arrested. He numbered among his clients drug kingpins, mafia dons, and other unsavory characters. He did jobs for them their underlings were unqualified to do. It was usually spying on unfaithful wives or girlfriends, skimmers, identifying potential witnesses and locating them. Some of the subjects of his investigations ended up dead, but not at his hands. No murder or assault had ever been traced to him directly. Andrew Kurtz, on the other hand, had legitimate clients but his activities were questionable. His specialty was obtaining secret formulas from competitive chemical industry and pharmaceutical firms to peddle or to obtain for a particular client. He also investigated key officers or employees of companies either to lure them away to a competitor or to destroy them, thus weakening their employers. He numbered among his clients well-known corporations as well as small local industries. Holmes and Ladd decided it was time to find what possible interest either or both of these individual may have in Shevvy Parker. They first went to the office of Ralph Nichols, needless to say he was not overjoyed to see the two officers. He had been interviewed many times before when something happened to someone close to one of his clients. He always professed his innocence and claimed client privilege and could never be implicated in whatever incident was the subject of police scrutiny. This was no exception. Holmes came right to the point.

"Why were you at the funeral of one Shevvy Parker?"

"The notoriety of the case interested me."

"Were you employed to investigate any aspect of her death?"

"You know that I cannot and will not answer that question."

"You realize her murder is a subject of an on-going police investigation and withholding information is a felony."

"I am neither withholding nor do I have any information about her death."

Nichols was a large man, powerful from the years he had spent in prison body building. In his early twenties he had served five years for assault in the performance of his duties as an enforcer for the local loan sharks. He had developed contacts with crime figures for whom he now worked. Prison had been a very unpleasant experience and he was unwilling to chance a repeat so he carved out a career in which he worked for his former bosses just above the law. It was extremely doubtful that he was involved in these murders but why was he at the funeral?

Holmes and Ladd were no more successful in their investigation of Kurtz. He was a small, nattily dressed man of forty and with a pronounced German accent. He had immigrated to the United States approximately ten years ago after being involved in an industrial spying incident in Germany. He was not convicted, therefore the INS was unaware of his indictment and processed his citizenship application summarily. His white-collar crimes in the United States had never been provable though the bunko units knew him well.

Questioning was no more productive than it had been with Nichols. He maintained America was a free country and funerals were public affairs and he, therefore, had as much right as anyone to be there. He did not know Miss Parker, her relatives or her coworkers. He simply read about the incident in the paper and was curious. He terminated the interview abruptly without further comment.

Holmes, "Perhaps we should have the detectives assign someone to these characters and see just who they are working for at the moment."

CHAPTER 38

Dennis McAllen had followed the accounts of both Sherry and Buffy with interest and consternation. He had counted on using both as defense witnesses for Dr. Lawrence since he found Dr. Shepard had counseled the deceased by phone. Now he had only Betty Sue Givens, Shepard's nurse, and Melissa Hailey to tie him to the phone call. He did not know that a tape of that conversation existed. By including both Shepard and the HMO as defendants, Sloanberg had made McAllen's job much easier.

Dr. Lawrence arrived for his appointment to plan strategy or at least listen to his lawyers plan. McAllen was all business and his usual brusk self. He advised his client of the change in Sloanberg's strategy and explained the advantages to his defense.

"I'll put you on the stand first to discuss your medical care of the deceased including the prior relationship with him and his company, the physical exam, its purpose and the findings. You will also testify to the reasons for the return visit, your treatment and its rationale. Finally, you will deny receiving a call concerning the nitroglycerin. You do not know if such a call was made, was received, and if so, by whom? You will not testify as to the events surrounding the deaths since you were not there."

"When I bring you back, it will be to explain your usual routine of caring for a patient with the history Boomer gave and how it was modified by the principle's laid down by the HMO. My cardiologist expert will testify concerning the chances of survival and the risks involved with invasive diagnostic procedures and treatment of such a case, as well as those of bypass surgery. Hopefully, he will destroy the myth the media portrays that bypass surgery is little more dangerous than an appendectomy."

"I plan to subpena Shepard's nurse and Melissa Hailey to testify about the call-back, and Melissa will also testify about the HMO regulations and their effect on the practice of medicine at the clinic and on you in particular."

"Obviously I will use some of their witnesses. Barry Sherwood, who you have met, will join the team as my assistant. Any questions?"

Lawrence, "How much have my chances improved?"

"Your liability is unchanged. If the jury buys the HMO theory, your percentage of damages may be significantly reduced. "

Michael could hardly wait to get out of that office and be with Melissa to tell her what he interpreted as good news. It was five thirty p.m. by the time he reached her condo. He was wary that he was being followed and took a secuitous route to his destination, delaying his arrival by thirty minutes. He searched the area visually before going in but saw nothing out of the ordinary.

Melissa was on edge because of his lateness, but was ecstatic when he finally arrived. She insisted on making love before conversation, food or drink. Her appetite was ravenous, besides she felt safe and content in his arms.

Afterward he told her of his apprehension at being followed as well as the conversation with his attorney. Melissa was also apprehensive since her home invasion especially with a serial killer on the loose. She had purchased a Glock nine millimeter and learned how to shoot as a majority of young women in Los Angeles had done. She kept it by her bedside. She had also changed the locks and upgraded her alarm system. For the first time in several years, she was nervous about living alone, however, she knew that she could not pressure Michael to leave Nancy at the present time.

CHAPTER 39

McAllen and Sherwood decided to let Sloanberg depose William Blake, CEO of the HMO and Alex Garrison, manager of the clinic. They knew the HMO attorney would make a motion to squash the suit against the HMO on the grounds that it did not control, hire or guarantee the physicians quality of care. The court would decide this motion before subpoenas could be issued for these depos. In the meantime, McAllen would depose Betty Sue Givens and a subpena was issued.

Betty Sue was twenty-two years old, married to a resident physician for one year, and a recent graduate of a nursing school where she had met her husband. She had found employment as the clinic nurse for Dr. Shepard shortly after graduation and marriage. In order for them to financially be able to marry, it was necessary for her to work until her husband finished his residency and started his practice. Their life was chaotic and with conflicting schedules. He worked long hours, nights and weekends and moonlighted at ER's on his off-hours. She, on the other hand, worked nine to five, five days a week at the clinic and spent many lonely evenings and weekends.

It was on such a night that she became the third victim of the "bedpost rapist". Dr. Carl Windser returned home at 7:30 a.m. from a twelve hour shift at the ER to find the apartment door ajar and Sue naked, spread eagle, tethered to the four posts of the bed and covered with blood. She was dead from multiple stab wounds to the chest and the abdomen and a blow to the head. Despite his training and experience, having seen many such victims in the ER, he was devastated with shock and grief. He called 911 before passing out.

The police and paramedics responded promptly and found Windser in a complete state of shock. He was inconsolable. He kept repeating, "I didn't have to work last night. I was just doing someone a favor. If I'd only been home, this would not have happened."

The paramedics knew him from one of the ER's he worked and tried to console him to no avail. The Windser marriage had been extremely happy in spite of their limited time together or perhaps partly because of it. They felt like they were stealing what little time they had.

The paramedics were of no use here and left as soon as possible. The scene was too much for even individuals who saw so much tragedy daily. It was especially traumatic because of their acquaintance with Dr. Windser. It was personal.

Police detectives Holmes and Ladd from Homicide responded. The scene was almost a carbon copy of the other two home invasion murders. The condition of the victim, the blood and the rubble in the apartment and the lack of a weapon or other obvious clues. The only difference was the existence and presence of a grieving husband. Could he be responsible? He would have to be questioned, even though it did not seem reasonable. His grief and lack of blood-spattered clothing were against any involvement.

Holmes, "Where were you when this happened?"

Windser, "I worked at the County Hospital ER all night, and I arrived home just before I called 911, only to find this terrible scene. Again he was wracked with sobs and unable to continue.

"We should wait until later to finish this. I think he is not our man. "

"Do you have friends or relatives we can call to be with you?"

"I have a sister who lives in LA."

"We will call her for you."

The ME arrived. He surveyed the scene and started his crew to work taking pictures, blood samples and looking for a weapon, footprints, fingerprints, or just anything that might identify the killer.

Ladd called the hospital Emergency Room and inquired about Dr. Windser's schedule last night, whether he was there all night, what his mood was like, etcetera. His alibi for the night was completely air-tight.

The ME established the time of death at between twelve and three a.m., eliminating the husband as a suspect.

The nurse who supplied this information at the Emergency Room inquired what their interest was. She was told only that Windser's wife was found dead. She was very upset and volunteered to come stay with him until his family could arrive. The detectives were happy to be able to have someone to comfort the husband and then told her about the incident. They could question him about enemies, prowlers, etcetera later when he had regained control of his emotions.

Maria heard the report on her police scanner and hurried to the scene only to find an almost exact duplication of the two previous homicides. The detectives allowed her complete access to the apartment and to the facts they had so far. She was introduced to the husband, but made no attempt to question him on the advice of the detectives.

Eventually the body was removed by the ME. Dr. Windser was taken to the home of his sister who had arrived in the meantime and the crime scene was cordoned off for further investigation by the forensics team.

Maria returned to her office and transferred her notes to the computer. She re-read everything she had compiled about the murders looking for anything that might tie them together. At first they seemed to be the random violence of a serial killer just as the police and media believed. However, on closer scrutiny, she noted that the last two victims had worked at the clinic. Could that be significant?

Holmes and Ladd again attended the funeral of a murder victim hoping to find someone out of place. On this occasion Dr. Windser identified everyone there as a family member of one of the two of them, a friend or someone associated with one or the other of them at their respective jobs. The only strangers were members of the media and the police department. They made an appointment to question Dr. Windser the next day.

Maria again spoke with the detectives and inquired about the results of the autopsy. She died of "hemorrhage from the stab wounds of her chest." She was also raped and sodomized with a blunt object. The DNA of the seminal fluid matched that of the other two victims. The only additional finding was an early pregnancy. The head wound in this case was not lethal and she was probably conscious for at least part of the attack.

"Did her husband shed any light on the murder?"

"We haven't questioned him extensively yet, but we are to meet with him tomorrow."

Maria thought about mentioning the job relationship of the last two victims but decided against it for the time being.

Dr. Windser had regained his composure by the time he met with the detectives.

"Did either of you have any enemies you know of?"

"No."

"Were there any problems in your marriage?"

"Absolutely not. We loved each other completely and never had a major argument."

"Have you noticed anyone following either you, or who appears out of place in the neighborhood, coming to your door as a repairman, salesman, etc."

"No, but I was away from home at work for long and irregular hours."

"Did your wife mention anything of this nature or anything at work which might be significant?"

"No."

"Did you have any disputes at the hospital or ER with patients who might be capable of such a thing?"

"I saw my usual quota of drunks, pimps, murderers, rapists and the other dregs of society in the ER, but there was nothing unusual about my relationships with any of these people."

"Were there any family problems on either side—old boyfriends, girlfriends, or other potential enemies from the past?"

"No. Is there anything else? This questioning is very upsetting to me. Was there anything unusual about the autopsy?"

"Only the pregnancy."

With that, Windser completely lost control. He obviously was unaware of her pregnancy until now. The officers had not meant to be unkind, but assumed he would have known, especially being a physician. They had a patrolman take him to his sister's home as he was too upset to drive.

CHAPTER 40

Sloanberg read the paper concerning the murder of Sue. He didn't immediately make the connection with his witness who he knew only as Betty Sue Givens, not Sue Windser. McAllen called him to ask what was happening to his witnesses.

"What do you mean?"

"Don't you read the papers."

"Yes, of course I do."

"The latest victim of the 'bedpost rapist' was Shepard's nurse, your witness to his conversation with Boomer."

"Holy shit! Someone is sabotaging my case."

"Mine too."

"Now what will you do?"

"I'll have to regroup."

He was not about to disclose his tape of that conversation until the time of trial.

However, it could be a problem introducing the tape without any witnesses to identify it and the circumstances under which it was taken. There was Melissa, of course, but her testimony would be hearsay and might not be admissible. What a terrible coincidence to lose the three people who could directly tie Shepard and thence the clinic and the HMO to his case. He must see that Melissa was warned to be more cautious but how could he do that without tipping his hand.

Michael and Melissa needed no warning. Two employees of the clinic had been murdered and the female employees were all scared to death. Melissa had already taken precautions but she felt herself unsafe living alone. Alarms and security buildings had not protected the other three victims. She emplored Michael to move in with her but both realized that was impossible now. She did convince him to buy a gun to protect himself and her when they were together. He purchased a snub-nosed 38 which was easily concealed on his person but loaded it with black talon ammo. If he had to shoot someone, he wanted it to be lethal.

CHAPTER 41

Nancy, like the remainder of the female population of LA, was also terrified to be alone. More than ever, she resented Michael's absences from home and demanded they be curtailed. Of course, she had a more compelling reason to try to keep him home, jealousy. She knew he was having an affair with his nurse and would do anything possible to end it. Her demands only increased the tension between them, but served to decrease his opportunities to be with Melissa. However, Nancy gave up following Michael and Melissa in deference to her fear of being out in LA by herself.

Her reaction was typical of what was happening all over Los Angeles. The media coverage was constant and graphic. Restaurants, bars, theaters were all virtually empty. Traffic was dramatically reduced. The police presence was all-encompassing. LA was like a city under siege. All of this was somewhat inappropriate since the crimes had taken place in the privacy of the victims homes.

It had now been a month since the last murder, yet the media blitz continued as if it were yesterday and the prevailing fear had not diminished at all. The police were no closer to a solution now than when they investigated the first crime. They had interrogated every known sex offender, drug addict and felon in the area. They had exhausted interrogation of known informants. Nothing. They had reexamined the evidence from each crime scene, delved more deeply into the personal lives of the victims and their families and searched for any possible relationship between the victims themselves. None of this brought them any closer to the killer.

Holmes and Ladd continued their investigation of Kurtz and Nichols. It had been unusual for them to show up together anywhere especially at the funeral of someone neither professed to know. They did not travel in the same circles, work for the same clients or take the same types of cases and had never been known to work together before. The first objective would be to try to learn what type of case each was presently working. That would require the expenditure of great deal of shoe leather, but that was the only lead they had. They drew straws and Ladd lost. He drew Nichols a much more dangerous and distasteful assignments since he would be invading the world of the local syndicate. Having worked on vice in his early years with the force, Ladd was familiar with the clubs, nudey bars, pimps, whores and both upper and lower echelons of the syndicate. Following Nichols lead him through these old haunts. He apparently was tracing the activities of a skimmer known as Jake. When Nichols had enough evidence on Jake and presented it to his employer, there probably would be an assassination. Ladd was faced with a moral dilemma, whether to intervene and blow his assignment and endanger his own safety or let nature take its course. For the greater good, he decided on the latter.

 He expected one of the locals to take care of the chore but was surprised to find that Nichols was a full-service employee. He found, arranged for and imported a hit-man from Detroit to execute Jake. This was accomplished efficiently and brutally as an object lesson to anyone who might decide to get greedy. Ladd actually witnessed the murder but was powerless to prevent it or arrest the hitman and still maintain his anonymity. This was a new dimension of private investigator Nichols and Ladd would use this information to put him out of business when his present assignment was finished. He could not even imagine what bearing this information might have on the serial murder case.

 Surveillance of Kurtz was much more difficult. Holmes found himself following his quarry to country clubs, office buildings, company outings, executive symposiums, sporting events, charity affairs, etcetera. Kurtz traveled in the most prestigious circles, but it was obscure just who he was working for or what project he was pursuing. He was always in the company of executive types and attractive women. This assignment seemed to be leading nowhere as it was virtually impossible to find out what project he was working on and for whom. However, he finally struck paydirt. Completely out of character, shortly after the hired killing Ladd had observed, Kurtz met with Nichols and another man in a small diner in Pomona. The third man seemed to be known to Kurtz, but not Nichols. He was well-dressed, middle-aged and could have been a client of Kurtz. The three talked, ate and went their separate ways. Holmes tried to tail the third man, but lost him when he entered a cab. Of his weeks of surveillance, the only significant event was the meeting between Kurtz and Nichols. This was really the odd couple but it did lend credence to their attendance at Sherry's funeral.

CHAPTER 42

Shortly before Sherry died, she had alerted Elizabeth Boomer to the financial problems besetting ACME Electric because of her husbands death. On the advice of Sloanberg, she had consulted Kenneth Brock, the auditor who had evaluated the company's financial status. He confirmed Sherry's analysis. Elizabeth, the auditor and Gary Gebhardt, assistant to Sloanberg, made an appointment to meet with the executive committee of ACME to ascertain the present state of company finances. The results of that meeting were depressing. The stock had fallen precipitously, borrowing power was non-existent, employee morale was low and the company was behind on its debt service. Bankruptcy was imminent. As a result, Elizabeth would soon face financial ruin. Since this was a related problem, Gebhardt resolved to discuss a solution with Sloanberg. Elizabeth inherited forty percent of the company stock and it might be prudent for her to force the company into Chapter 11 bankruptcy and replace the CEO and the rest of the Board with individuals who could restore the company's profitability.

Sloanberg approved this plan. He also decided to limit the discovery phase of the malpractice case and move the trial along as rapidly as possible. Accordingly he called Dennis McAllen.

Sloanberg, "Rather than finishing the depo with Dr. Lawrence, would you be willing to have an informal meeting with you, me and the Doctor? I want to know what he is going to testify to since my major advisory is now the HMO. I would also like to have the same arrangement with Melissa Hailey. Both would be protected by your presence, and if at any time you felt either of their rights were being abridged, we would immediately stop the proceedings. Nothing said would be on the record and we all would be honor-bound to treat these interviews confidentially."

McAllen, "You are really reaching. I'll have to think about that and talk to my client. In the meantime, I want to depose your experts."

Sloanberg, "I'll arrange it. Please give me an answer as soon as possible on the other matter."

CHAPTER 43

The cardiologist, a Doctor Joseph Hulsey, was a small man, fifty-one years of age with impeccable credentials and significant experience in courtrooms. Despite McAllen's badgering, his testimony was very simple and damaging to Dr. Lawrence.

"With proper consultation and tests, including angiography, Boomer's disease would have been readily diagnosable and treatable. He probably could have been cured by angioplasty which has a mortality risk of approximately two percent, about the same as a gallbladder operation. If he had required bypass surgery, his mortality risk would have been significantly less than ten percent. The doctor was negligent by not referring the patient to a cardiologist. He is doubly negligent by not referring following the exercise-induced chest pain. Nitro was acceptable treatment for angina thirty years ago, but not today with all the surgical procedures which are available."

No questions were asked about the HMO procedures as motivation for Dr. Lawrence's failure to be more aggressive. Such testimony would be extremely damaging to the HMO and hopefully, helpful to Dr. Lawrence. However, it was felt that it would be preferable to save this for the trial itself.

McAllen made an appointment with Michael Lawrence and Melissa Hailey to discuss Sloanberg's proposal. They were extremely curious as to the need for this meeting and somewhat apprehensive. They left the clinic together at noon, had lunch together and arrived at McAllen's office promptly at two p.m. They were ushered into the conference room and McAllen began immediately in his usual abrupt manner.

"Mr. Sloanberg has proposed an informal meeting with each

of you to discuss your testimony rather than to depose you. His primary focus is now the clinic and the HMO rather than you, Doctor. You are not being dismissed from the suit by any means, but by involving the other entities, he feels he can obtain a much larger settlement, thus leaving you off the hook for any amount in excess of your insurance. There is no guarantee. The decision will be up to the judge and jury. This fits in with my original "the devil made me do it" defense for you. It is being handed to us by the actions of Dr. Shepard and the strategy of Mr. Sloanberg. The only downside, is that Sloanberg will have a preview of your testimony and thus be better able to prepare for your cross-examination at trial. You two are the only defense witnesses I plan to use. The rest of our case will be cross-examination of their witnesses. Do you have questions or objections?"

There was a stunned silence. Melissa was the first to break it.

"What is my part in this?"

McAllen, "Your testimony, I presume, will be that the principles and policies imposed by the HMO has lowered the quality of care provided by all the doctors at the clinic and was responsible for the type of care received by Alex Boomer. I understand that Alex Garrison sought your services to spy on Dr. Lawrence and help keep his practice within the HMO guidelines. Is that correct?"

"Yes, I can honestly testify to all that. In addition, Sue told me about referring a call from Boomer to Dr. Shepard. In addition, Shepard called me in and threatened to fire me because of my prying about the call."

McAllen, "I was not aware of your knowledge concerning Boomer's call to Shepard. That will be very helpful. What about you, Doctor?"

"I was under the gun to follow the HMO guidelines in treating and diagnosing patients. I was threatened with dismissal by Garrison if I varied from the company line. The nitro test was a reasonable rationale for Mr. Boomer considering the circumstances and is within the standard of practice for his type of presentation.

Had I received the call that Shepard did, I would have sent him to a cardiologist and he would have been diagnosed and treated properly and be alive today. When the suit was filed, Garrison was concerned only about keeping the clinic and the HMO out of it, not about Boomer's death."

McAllen, "You both have used the term threatened. Does that just mean being fired or possibly something more sinister? "

Dr. Lawrence, "Fired and blackballed concerning employment elsewhere."

Melissa, "Fired and a veiled threat of exposure of my personal life."

McAllen, "Ms. Hailey, I assume by that you mean exposure of your affair with the doctor."

Melissa, "Yes, I wasn't sure you knew."

McAllen, "Of course I knew, and on that subject, you two must be as discrete as possible until this trial is over otherwise the jury might develop a feeling of moral outrage against both of you. In addition Melissa, your testimony might be discounted as prejudiced to help your lover."

After assurances from McAllen, it was decided to accept Sloanberg's proposal.

CHAPTER 44

The admonition concerning discretion was only in the mind of the lovers. Many knew or strongly suspected their relationship was far more intimate than doctor and nurse, especially Nancy. This particular day, she happened to drive by the clinic just as Michael and Melissa drove out of the garage. She followed them to the restaurant and watched as they entered arm in arm. She was enraged. She had previously made up her mind to ignore the affair and hope it would die of its own momentum, but she could no longer ignore it. She would confront Michael tonight.

CHAPTER 45

The discussion started as a very cold and calculated recitation of the facts as Nancy knew them. Michael tried to deny the relationship but Nancy would have none of that.

Nancy, "Please don't insult my intelligence. I know that you have been having an affair. All the nights that you have spent with your lawyer you have been with her. You must make a decision. Either this ends now or our marriage ends now."

Michael, "I could not end it now even if I wanted to. In the midst of the trial, I cannot afford the publicity of a scandal and a divorce. Besides Melissa is a vital witness in my defense. Please don't do anything until the trial is over."

Nancy, "I cannot continue to live with you knowing that you are sleeping with that tramp."

Michael, "Is there no way that we can put off any action until the trial is over? My professional and financial future is at stake."

Nancy, "I don't give a damn about your future. You have deceived me and lied to me for months and I will not tolerate it any longer. I want you to move out tonight."

She was very cool and deliberate. No tears, no tantrums, just a determination that he had never seen in her before. There was no reasoning or logic that would change things.

Though he was quite shaken by the events of the evening, he calmly went to their bedroom and gathered the essentials of clothes and toiletries together, put them in a suitcase and left the house without another word. Once in his car, he called Melissa, briefly told her what had happened and asked if he could spend the night. She was ecstatic but hardly prepared for the Michael who appeared at her door shortly. She had dressed seductively, opened a bottle of wine, prepared snacks just as she had always done when they were to be together.

He was visibly upset, sullen and short tempered. He had no interest in food, drink or her. He had told her only briefly what had happened but refused to discuss it further and would make no commitment as to their future.

She was hurt and confused coming down emotionally from the illusion that now she would have him all to herself, to wondering if she would lose him entirely. It seemed that the love affair, too hot to cool down, had indeed suffered a deep freeze. She could only hope it was temporary.

CHAPTER 46

When Dr. Evans arrived at McAllen's office he was surprised to see Jim Bishop in the waiting room. Since Evans had been dismissed from the suit, Bishop was no longer involved in the case but was allowed to sit in on the depo by arrangement with McAllen and Sloanberg. The same cast of characters of the previous deposition with the exception of those dismissed and the addition of Shepard's lawyer were gathered in the conference room. Dennis McAllen made a preliminary statement concerning the change of status of Dr. Evans from the defendant to the expert and inquired if there were questions before swearing the doctor.

Mr. Bailey, "Why is Dr. Evans represented by counsel if he is no longer a defendant?"

Bishop, "I do not represent him for this procedure. I am just interested in the case since I was previously involved."

Bailey, "I will object to your presence if you advise him or in any way act as his counsel."

Bishop, "Perhaps you have forgotten that an expert has a right to counsel if he chooses."

Bailey, "My objection stands and I will take it to the judge, if necessary."

McAllen, "Let's cut the trivia and proceed. Swear the witness."

McAllen questioned Evans about his education, medical background in emergency medicine and expert witness experience. He proceeded to ask him about his review of the records concerning Alex Boomer.

McAllen, "What records did you review?"

Evans, "Clinic records, ED records and pathology records."

McAllen, "What are your conclusions?"

Evans, "That the patient died of coronary occlusion of the left anterior descending coronary artery."

McAllen, "When in your opinion did this occur?"

Evans, "When the patient collapsed at the office."

McAllen, "Was there anything that could have been done when he collapsed by fellow employees, paramedics, or the emergency personnel to resuscitate him?"

Evans, "No. Everything was done that could have done to resuscitate him. He was given CPR by the office personnel, treated properly by the paramedics and the ER personnel. He was essentially dead of a fatal heart attack when he hit the floor."

McAllen, "Do you believe that he was treated properly by Dr. Lawrence prior to the attack?"

Evans, "No."

McAllen, "Why?"

Evans, "His complaints at both office visits were strongly suggested of accelerated angina."

McAllen, "What is that?"

Evans, "Accelerated angina is the prelude to a heart attack."

McAllen, "How was he not treated properly?"

Evans, "The symptoms were suggestive enough to have alerted his doctor to the possibility of an impending heart attack. Further tests should have been done or the patient referred to a cardiologist for more definite tests."

McAllen, "The patient was given a prescription for nitroglycerin. Is that not a treatment for angina or a test for angina?"

Evans, "Nitro is treatment for angina and could be used to test for angina, but that is out of date. Now we have lab tests, exercise tests and angiography to make that diagnosis."

McAllen, "How would have such tests made a difference in Boomer's case?"

Evans, "The proper diagnosis could have been made for certain and appropriate treatment instituted which would have prevented his heart attack."

McAllen, "What treatment?"

Evans, "Balloon angioplasty, laser treatment or coronary bypass surgery. Any of these procedures would have been curative."

McAllen, "How about risk?"

Evans, "In an individual of Boomer's age and health, the risk would have been minimal."

McAllen, "Do you believe that Dr. Lawrence violated the standard practice by not prescribing these tests?"

Evans, "Yes."

McAllen, "Do you believe that violation directly lead to Mr. Boomer's death?"

Evans, "Yes."

McAllen, "If I told you that Dr. Lawrence was under some pressure from the clinic and HMO for which he works to avoid the expensive tests and procedures, would that alter your opinion?"

Bailey, "I object to that question. The inclusion of the HMO and clinic in this suit is under appeal and a ruling has not yet been handed down."

McAllen, "What is your experience with HMO's and their gatekeepers?"

Bailey, "I object on the same grounds."

McAllen, "That is a general question going to the experience of the doctor about HMO's in general. Doctor, you can answer."

Evans, "My experience has been very negative. Gatekeepers do not call back promptly, even in emergencies. They object to necessary x-rays, CAT scans, MRIs and other essential tests and procedures and refuse hospital admission of patients who are acutely ill. Managed care is a system that places the economic need of the company above the medical needs of the patient. In my specialty of emergency medicine, it negates many of the gains made of the last twenty years in the care of acutely ill and injured patients."

Bailey, "That's a nice speech for the local medical society, but there are no statistics to back any of those comments."

McAllen, "Mr. Bailey, this is not a debating society. Dr. Evans is an expert witness, and as such, was asked an opinion question and responded. That is what an expert is suppose to do."

McAllen, "There is evidence that Dr. Lawrence did not receive the call from Mr. Boomer about the effect of nitro on his pain, but that Dr. Shepard answered that call. He assured the deceased that relief from nitro was expected and that he need do nothing further except to take that nitro when he has chest pain. Dr. Lawrence was not notified of that call and it was not logged in Boomer's chart. Is that a violation of the standard of care?"

Smith (Shepard's attorney), "This witness is an ER doctor and is not qualified to answer questions concerning continuing care and clinic procedures."

McAllen, "In this state, a licensed M.D. can answer questions as an expert concerning any other M.D. In addition to emergency medicine, Dr. Evans is certified in surgery the same as your client."

Evans, "Yes, it's a violation in two ways. First, the advice is wrong. Nitro, as pointed out earlier, is not a primary treatment for angina. Second, Dr. Shepard was under a moral and ethical obligation to notify Dr. Lawrence of anything pertaining to diagnosis and treatment of his patient. He, at least, should have made a note in the chart and called it to the attention of the patient's doctor."

McAllen, "I have nothing further. Does anyone else?"

There being no further questions, the deposition was ended.

Bishop and Evans stopped for a drink before returning to their respective offices. Bishop, "McAllen was pretty easy on you. It was as if you were his expert. It appears that he and Sloanberg were in cahoots to go after the HMO and Shepard."

Evans, "That's fine with me. Lawrence is primarily responsible but if he's operating under the constraints of the clinic and HMO, he's only partially responsible."

Bishop, "This trial will be very interesting."

Michael and Melissa had spent a night of fitful sleep without any of the intimacy that had been such an integral part of their relationship. She was noticeably upset and on the edge of tears. He was cool and uncommunicative. This partially related to his concern over the impact of the separation and pending divorce on his trial and career. In addition, his realization that his marriage was over and a period of his life was over, was a sobering thought. The finality of the change puts a damper on the passion of the love affair which had been a motivating factor. Hopefully these emotions were temporary and would soon pass.

In the meantime, he must find a place to live and try to make the best of the situation and apply damage control to his reputation.

CHAPTER 47

Things were awkward at the office with Melissa. She had been deeply hurt and could not understand his feelings. She was an emotional wreck and was barely able to function.

His first patient was a large middle-aged man who was dressed expensively but with a complete lack of taste. When Melissa brought him back to the treatment room she asked what his problem was and he responded that he just wanted to talk to the doctor and refused to give her any information. When she tried to take his temperature, pulse, and blood pressure, he also refused to submit to that. Nor would he undress.

He rudely told her that he came to see the doctor and not some nosey sexpot of a nurse. With that she left the room and informed Michael of the encounter. Michael entered the room, introduced himself and asked the patient what he could do for him. The name on the chart was Sam Jones, but the patient did not offer to introduce himself or accept the handshake offered by the doctor.

Jones, "I'm not sick. I'm here to talk to you about the trial."

Doctor, "Are you an investigator, an insurance agent, a lawyer or what?"

Jones, "I'm none of those things. I'm here to give you some advice."

Doctor, "I'm getting all the advice I need from my lawyer. I see no reason to waste my time any further."

Jones, "I came here to deliver a message and I'm not leaving until I finish. Do not ring that buzzer."

With that he opened his coat revealing a shoulder holster with a large automatic.

Jones, "Are you ready to listen?"

Michael was thoroughly frightened and submissive now. "Yes."

Jones, "When you testify in your trial, just talk about your care and treatment of Boomer. Do not try to implicate anyone else. Do you understand?"

Doctor, "Yes."

Jones, "If you do not follow my advice, someone near and dear to you will pay the price. Do not discuss this conversation with anyone. Do you understand?"

Doctor, "What is your interest in this matter?"

Jones, "That is none of your business. Just do as you're told if you and your family and friends are to remain healthy."

He turned and left the room without another word. Michael was shaken. He was on the verge of passing out. Melissa entered the room and found him sitting in the patient chair, pale, wet with perspiration and shaking uncontrollably.

Melissa, "What is the matter?"

Doctor, "I can't tell you."

Melissa, "Did that man do or say something to you? You look horrible. I'll get one of the other doctors to check you."

Doctor, "No, no, I'll be okay in a minute. Just leave me alone."

Melissa, "I can't leave you like this. I want to help you. Is it about last night?"

Doctor, "No, no. That has nothing to do with it. Please don't keep quizzing me. I'll be all right in a few minutes and I'll tell you later."

Melissa left the room hurt and confused because he wouldn't confide in her. She was convinced that this somehow was related to the man he had just seen. Because of his rudeness and refusal to give her any information, she had taken particular notice of him. He was six foot four inches, weighed about 250 pounds, white, dressed in an expensive tan checked suit with a striped shirt and loud patterned tie. His face was scarred as from acne, his nose was askew as if it had been broken and his eyes were blue and cold. His hair was iron grey and thick. All told, he was an extremely unattractive, hard looking character whose photo would be appropriate on the bulletin board of the post office. Michael finally recovered his poise and somehow got through the rest of the afternoon's patients. He had to discuss this encounter with someone and Melissa was not only the only person available, but she was also a potential subject of the threats. As soon as they arrived at her condo, he told her the whole story of Sam Jones. She was horrified to think that someone could walk into the clinic, flash a gun and make such threats.

Melissa, "You must tell the police."

Michael, "What can they do? We don't know who this person is or how to find him. Even if he were arrested, it's my word against his and he would simply be released to carry out his threats. He's obviously hired by someone interested in the malpractice case but we don't know what that is either."

Melissa, "At least call your lawyer and get his advice."

Michael, "If his purpose was to scare me, he succeeded. I haven't dealt with people like that since my residency. His threats seemed to include you by the way he used the word friend. We both need to be cautious. Perhaps I should live here until this is all over after all."

Melissa was overjoyed at the last statement. She had been crushed when he indicated his plan to find a place of his own. Maybe this strange character had helped keep Michael near her.

McAllen seemed more concerned by threats to Michael than anything else that had happened to him. He actually showed a degree of compassion which seemed totally out of character.

McAllen, "We will have to assign bodyguards to both of you and expedite the trial to decrease the time you will have to live with this threat. I'm convinced it's real. I can't imagine who might do such a thing. Certainly not the plaintiff or her company. That leaves Dr. Shepard, the clinic or the HMO. I find it difficult to believe that any legitimate or professional organization would employ such tactics. I will assign a private investigative firm to protect both of you and try to find out the primary source of the threats. In the meantime, be observant and watch your backs."

Michael, "What could he mean by his demands concerning my testimony?"

McAllen, "It would seem he would want you to take all the blame and simply defend your actions as being within the standard of practice."

Michael, "To change the subject, Nancy found out about Melissa and threw me out of the house and refused to avoid the divorce proceedings until the trial is over."

McAllen, "Which comes as no surprise. There is none so blind as lovers who are trying to conceal an affair. We simply have to deal with it as best we can. Try not to rub it in the public's face. Don't start dating publicly and try to avoid open confrontations with your wife."

Michael and Melissa both felt somewhat relieved to have discussed both subjects with McAllen. He was sort of a father-confessor to them and the only friend they had at the moment.

CHAPTER 48

As soon as they left his office, McAllen called Jack Burge of Private Investigations, Incorporated and made a luncheon appointment to discuss the latest turn of events. Burge was a retired LAPD detective whose reputation was above reproach. They met in a downtown men's club and McAllen told him the story of the case and the threats and gave him Melissa's description of Sam Jones.

McAllen, "I want you to do two things. Protect my client and his lover and try to find out the origin and the reason for the threats."

Burge, "That's a heavy assignment and could be expensive."

McAllen, "Put it on my tab. Hopefully, the malpractice insurance company will pay for it."

Burge, "Can I go to the P.D. for help?"

McAllen, "If you can do it without disclosing the client's or the reasons."

Burge, "The description of the perp does not sound familiar. Perhaps they can help to identify him. Give me the names, addresses and places of employment of your clients."

Burge went directly to Parker Center and met with Steve Dunbeck, the sergeant in charge of the CID. He described Sam Jones, told him of his attempt to intimidate the witness and inquired if the P.D. knew anyone of that description. The answer was a qualified negative, but a promise to follow up with officers in his division. He returned to his office and met with Emily Matthis and Robin Price and gave them their assignments to protect Michael and Melissa. Both were very competent at their job, black belts in karate and expert marks persons. It would be very easy for both to fit into jobs at the clinic and live in the condo occupied by Michael and Melissa. He called McAllen to make those arrangements and it was accomplished easily and confidentially.

McAllen arranged for Michael and Melissa to meet separately with Sloanberg to discuss their proposed testimony. He also informed him of the threats to Michael and suggested they try to expedite the trial. Sloanberg agreed. The meeting was scheduled to be held at McAllen's office to avoid knowledge of it leaking to the other defendants. Because of the threats, Michael was reluctant to be as open as he had been with McAllen. He only wanted to discuss his exam and treatment and the prescription for nitro. Under intense questioning by Sloanberg, he did not mention HMO guidelines or Garrison's threats to fire him in reaction to the suit. Melissa was equally vague about the quality of care issues and her knowledge concerning Dr. Shepard and the call from Boomer.

Sloanberg called for a break to confer with McAllen privately. "What is going on? Neither of these people are telling me what you indicated. I can't help your client if he and his lady continue to stonewall me. I'll be forced to depose them and put them under oath. This was a bad idea."

McAllen, "I'm as surprised as you are. They must have been more frightened than I thought. I arranged security for them and expected that would relieve their fears. Let me talk to them before we give up."

McAllen, "Why aren't you two telling Sloanberg what you told me? If you don't there is no deal and he will bury you, Doctor."

Michael, "At least we'll be alive. The threats of that thug scare me a hell of a lot more than anything the courts can do to me."

McAllen, "I've arranged security for you both and we'll get this trial over as soon as possible. We're also trying to find out who Sam Jones is and who he's working for. Just tell Sloanberg what you told me. It will go no further than this room until you testify in court. By then we should know who threatened you and why, and be able to put him behind bars. If not, you can back out before you take the stand."

They reluctantly agreed. When they returned to the conference room, both told Sloanberg everything they had discussed with McAllen. They also told him the details of the threats. Sloanberg explained his plan to lay the majority of the blame on Shepard and the HMO. He also indicated that he would investigate the source of the threats.

CHAPTER 49

Sergeant Dunbeck circulated a description of Sam Jones to all LAPD divisions without explaining why and asked for ID only. There was no response until it came across Inspector Ladd's desk. The description vaguely fitted that of the killer he had witnessed doing the syndicate murder. Ladd notified Dunbeck that there had been a hired gun from Detroit recently who possibly could be his man. There was no other response and the trail ended there. Dunbeck was frustrated by his failure to ID Jones, however, he assumed if an out of town enforcer had been imported, someone was serious about their threats. He called Burge and reported his findings hoping to learn the reason for the inquiry. Burge thanked him but added no details and asked for the identity of the officer who had made a possible ID. Dunbeck complied wondering if some time in the future this might involve him. Burge sought out Inspector Ladd and explained that the person Ladd had identified as an out of town hitman could be someone who threatened his clients. Ladd replied if those individuals were one and the same, the threats were serious. He would not say more. Burge reported his findings concerning Sam Jones to McAllen, along with the warning from Inspector Ladd. The bodyguards were placed both at the clinic and in the condo. One of them was nearby wherever Michael and/or Melissa might be. Each was supplied with electronic warning devises to be carried with them at all times. Jones description was given to a sketch artist who prepared photograph like drawings of him. All of this did little to calm Michael and Melissa's fears. They worked different shifts almost daily, took alternative routes to and from the clinic and spent their free time cloistered in the condo. The precautions approached those of a protected mob informant and put a severe strain on their romance.

McAllen and Sloanberg met with the judge who was to preside and petitioned to expedite the trial date. He explained that the defendant and a potential witness for the defense had been threatened. Judge Sherry Levine was outraged that someone was attempting to interfere with the justice system. She demanded details of the threats and was given the facts as the attorneys knew them. They also pointed out the financial problems of ACME Electronics and the mood and the virtual siege state of LA because of the "Bedpost Rapist." The judge looked at her calender and agreed to expedite the trial. She set a date ten days hence for hearing of motions to be followed immediately by jury selection.

Judge Levine presided at the motion hearing with all attorneys present. Sloanberg for the plaintiff, McAllen representing Dr. Lawrence, Smith representing Dr. Shepard and the clinic corporation, and Bailey representing the HMO. Smith and Bailey were upset by the accelerated trial setting as well as the fact that their clients were defendants. Smith presented a motion to dismiss Dr. Shepard based on the fact that he had not rendered any care to Mr. Boomer. McAllen opposed the motion and the judge asked Sloanberg and McAllen their basis for including Dr. Shepard.

Sloanberg, "We have a witness who will testify that she has personal knowledge that Dr. Shepard was the person who received the call from Boomer and advised him to continue nitroglycerin and reassured him that was all the treatment necessary." McAllen, "That same witness will link the clinic to the case because of Dr. Shepard's negligence and his position as director and owner."

Smith was annoyed and demanded to know the identity of the witness.

Judge Levine, "For reasons that will become clear in the trial, the identity of that witness will not be made known until he or she is called to testify. Motion denied. Shepard and clinic stays in."

Somewhat taken aback by the Judge's ruling, Bailey presented the following motion.

Because the HMO contracts with the clinics and the doctors to provide patient care, and depends on the contractee to hire competent physicians and ancillary employees and to maintain quality control, therefore the HMO has no responsibility for the negligence of said physicians and employees.

Judge, "Mr. Sloanberg, what say you?"

Sloanberg, "We will present witnesses who will testify that despite the elaborate contractual screen designed to protect the HMO from liability, we have proof that there was an exchange of stock between the HMO and the clinic, which made each a stockholder of the other, thereby nullifying its immunity."

Judge, "Motion denied pending the presentation of such evidence. Any other motions?"

McAllen, "That Doctor Lawrence's liability be limited to his malpractice coverage if he is found guilty of malpractice."

Judge, "On what basis?"

"That the method of medical practice was strictly controlled by rules and regulations imposed by the HMO leading to the alleged negligence of Dr. Lawrence."

Judge, "Motion denied pending evidence to be presented at trial. Any other motions?"

Bailey, "I move for a continuance based on the previous motions and the implications to my client and the need for additional time for preparation of our defense."

Smith, "I join in that motion."

Judge, "Motion denied. The trial will proceed with jury selection starting Monday."

The hearing was adjourned. Smith and Bailey were distressed at the developments and on return to their offices scheduled same day appointments with their respective clients.

Dr. Shepard was extremely upset and angry when he was told of the failure of the motion to dismiss him. "I thought the only witnesses who could link me to that phone call were dead."

Smith, "I thought so too. Can you think of anyone else who

had any knowledge of your conversation with Mr. Boomer?"

"No one except Lawrence's nurse. Sue apparently told her and I met with her and chewed her out for meddling in my business."

"Tell me the details. I was not aware that anyone else knew about that call."

"Apparently Lawrence found out at his deposition that Boomer had called the clinic and spoken with someone else. He had his nurse check with the personnel and Sue told her that I had taken the call. I told Melissa to mind her own business if she wanted to continue to work for the clinic. Afterwards I didn't hear anything else about it. She must be their witness. Rumor has it she is also Lawrence's mistress."

"Is there anything else you haven't told me?"

"Nothing except the stock transaction between the clinic and the HMO must be a public record. We can claim Melissa's testimony is hearsay and try to discredit her on the basis of her personal relationship with the Doctor. The stock ownership is more damaging to the HMO than the clinic, but you and the clinic are in the suit to stay."

An equally distressing scene was taking place in Bailey's office. On being told of the developments, William Blake was livid with rage. "I thought you and your corporate colleagues had covered the stock swap so deeply it could never surface."

Bailey, "I did too since it was an off-shore transaction. However, it is in the public record of the Cayman Islands."

Blake, "Who is the witness concerning the HMO control of medical practice?"

"Dr. Lawrence for one and most likely his nurse also."

Blake, "Can you not control their testimony?"

"Possibly and it has been suggested to Dr. Lawrence that he not try to implicate anyone else. Based on what I heard this morning he may not be taking that advice."

Blake, "Do you realize a suit of this magnitude has a potential for a multi-million dollar judgment that could not only bring down the HMO but make all others fair game? Do whatever is necessary to convince them of the error of their ways."

"I realize all too well."

CHAPTER 50

Judge Levine was a fifty-five years old, widowed from a physician, attractive for her age, childless and completely dedicated to her job. Politically she was a moderate republican and no-nonsense jurist. She and her husband had met while they were in college and married while both were in professional school. Despite their diverse professions and careers, their life together had been extremely happy. Dr. Levin had been a very successful surgeon who died suddenly of a ruptured aortic aneurysm when he was fifty leaving his wife a large nest egg. She resigned her position with a prestigious law firm and hibernated for a year. Shortly after that time, she was offered a judgeship which she accepted. She was able to assuage her grief and immerse herself in her work. She became a hard working conscientious judge, well respected by both the plaintiff and defense bar.

The court was called to order promptly at nine a.m. with all parties present. The jury pool of fifty individuals was brought in. The judge explained the process of selection and what was expected of the panel members as well as those chosen.

The court was in the affluent west side of LA and it was expected that the jury members would be as open minded as possible and intelligent enough to grasp the somewhat complex issues of this case. There are no racial or ethnic issues involved. All the parties of the suit are in the upper echelon financially so there should be no prejudice on that basis.

In questioning, the lawyers will try to discover any prejudice for or against physicians, insurance company or HMO's. There had been significant publicity concerning this case, much of which was slanted one way or the other. An attempt would be made to find those members of the panel who had not followed the case in the media or at least had not been swayed by it. Questioning would attempt to discover anyone who had a bad experience with either physicians or insurance companies or managed care medical systems. Many lawyers maintain that a case is won or lost in the jury selection process.

Twelve jurors were selected out of the first twenty seven interrogated. Eight were white, three black and one Hispanic. Five were female and seven were male. One white man was a sixty-seven year old retired executive of an aircraft manufacturing company. Three of the women were unemployed housewives in a thirty-five to forty-five year old age bracket. One woman was a divorced thirty-year old secretary. The other a twenty-seven year old single television producer. One of the black men was a fifty-year old postal worker, another was a thirty-two year old bartender and a third was a twenty-five year old carpenter. The Hispanic was a thirty five year old new car salesman. One of the other men was a thirty year old computer salesman. The final juror was a forty five year old owner of a hardware store.

Both legal teams seemed satisfied with their selections. Sloanberg had successfully challenged a paramedic, an insurance executive and medical technician. McAllen had successfully challenged a golf pro of Boomer's country club, a female housewife who had been involved in malpractice litigation and an ER nurse. Smith and Bailey each challenged two individuals who openly complained about managed care during their questioning.

Jury selection required only two days and opening statements were to begin Wednesday with the plaintiff's attorney going first. He would be followed by McAllen, Dr. Lawrence's attorney and then Smith and Bailey for Dr. Shepard and the HMO respectively. Sloanberg had prepared his statement to contain not only his allegations of negligence against Dr. Lawrence, but also those of Dr. Shepard, the clinic and the HMO. The other attorneys would wait to see what Sloanberg said before they planned their rebuttal.

CHAPTER 51

It had been two months since Michael had left home and moved in with Melissa. He had little communication with Nancy during this period what with preparing his defense, trying to maintain a reasonably normal medical practice and trying to avoid exposure to the threats of Sam Jones. He'd called her to warn her about the threats and her possible exposure to danger and to discuss the monetary problems associated with their separation.

He was surprised to have a call from her when he returned to the office from court and more surprised that she wanted to see him. Not knowing what to expect, he told Melissa he would be late, without explaining the reason and immediately drove to what used to be his home.

Nancy greeted him warmly. Despite everything else that had happened in his life, he had missed Nancy. The trauma of the separation had left him with a mixture of emotions. He realized that he still loved her and had reservations about their pending divorce. She was prettier than he remembered and was dressed and made up very attractively. She was even more appealing because things had been somewhat tense with Melissa. They made small talk about her school, his practice, the lawsuit and business matters that were of mutual interest. These topics were interspersed with embarrassing silences and sips of wine. Finally Nancy came to the point of the meeting. Somewhat flustered, she said, "Michael, do you remember the last time we made love?"

"Of course I do."

"Well, you scored better than either of us ever expected. I'm pregnant."

There was a stunned silence. He had never considered the

possibility. Neither of them had ever talked about having children. That was something for the future. A future that would never happen for them. The Rubicon had been crossed. They could never repair their marriage, even for a child. He finally said, somewhat brutally, "What do you expect me to do about it?"

"Nothing. I just thought you ought to know."

He had tried to talk her into waiting until his malpractice case was settled, but he knew now that was not going to happen. He would be spending all his time with lawyers or in courthouses. After the news, they had little more to say to each other and parted quite formally.

Thought he had not told Melissa why he was going to be late, the receptionist had let it slip about Nancy's call and she put two and two together. She had been apprehensive and depressed about their relationship for some time. Michael had seemed distracted and distant. He had been fractious with her and their lovemaking infrequent and perfunctory. She felt she was loosing him already and now when Nancy calls he goes running to her.

When he arrived home, he seemed even more distant than normal.

"What did she want?"

"How did you know where I was?"

"The receptionist told me she left a message and I just assumed you were at her beck and call."

"That's not the way it is. I don't run over there every time she calls. I've spoken to her before and this is the first time I've seen her."

"What did she want that was so important this time, then?"

"She wanted to tell me she was pregnant and is filing for divorce immediately."

"Is it yours?"

"Of course it's mine. She wouldn't get involved with someone else until the divorce is final. She's not the type to do that."

"Oh, no. She certainly wouldn't do something like that even

though I'm a shameless slut."

"I don't think that at all."

"You certainly implied it."

Both of them were angered by this exchange and they finally dissolved into a strained silence.

Melissa slept very little that night. She had never considered the possibility of a pregnancy complicating the already strained relationship. She had refused to allow herself to accept the fact that Michael and Nancy slept together and made love during the time he was still living at home. This latest development stunned her and forced her to the realization of facts that she had not allowed to her level of consciousness. She was devastated. How would Michael react? Would he be so guilt-ridden that he would return? Would he have second thoughts about his feelings for Nancy? Or would it slowly destroy their relationship? She realized there was nothing she could do and that was the most difficult part for her. For the first time she realized what it was like to be a mistress.

Michael also slept very little. He was stunned by this development. Added to the trial with its possible financial disaster, the potential of a shattered career and the fear of a deadly assault, he was almost crazy. In addition, all of this has driven a wedge between him and Melissa. How could he deal with all his problems.

CHAPTER 52

It was a crisp, clear November day when the participants congregated at the Santa Monica courthouse for the beginning of the civil trial of the decade. There was something for everybody—a defendant doctor who was young, handsome and in the midst of a divorce and living with his beautiful nurse-mistress, two prominent malpractice lawyers, a socially prominent victim of alleged malpractice and a clinic and HMO, both of which provided medical care to a large segment of Southwest Los Angeles. The trial had been expedited for reasons not clear to the public and the media. However, it had been set to coincide with the holidays, something which plaintiff's attorneys love due to the perceived generosity of juries at that time of year.

The courtroom was packed. Not only the local media congregated, but the networks were also generously represented. This trial promised to be explosive because of the reputations of the two primary attorneys, Sloanberg and McAllen, the pre-trial publicity and the precedent setting inclusion of an HMO. Because of her early investigational article, which was still on hold, Maria Gonzales was a prime local print journalist assigned to cover the trial.

Promptly at 9:00 a.m. on a Monday morning, Judge Levine called the proceedings to order. The jury was brought in and Mr. Sloanberg was called on to begin his opening statement.

"Your honor, ladies and gentlemen of the jury, a young man has met an untimely death due to the negligence of the doctor and medical group he had trusted to maintain his health. The facts, medical records and witnesses to be presented to you will prove beyond the shadow of a doubt that this man did not have to die, that his wife did not have to become a widow and his children did not have to become orphans. Witnesses will tell you that Alex Boomer had a physical exam by the defendant doctor less than a week before his death, was told to quit smoking, lose weight and exercise, but his general health was good. Following the advice of the defendant doctor, while exercising on a treadmill, he developed chest pains. He returned to that same doctor, who prescribed nitroglycerine and told him to dissolve the tabs under his tongue and call him if the pain recurred. It did. He called the clinic and spoke to another doctor who told him to just take the nitro when and if pain recurred and shortly thereafter Alex Boomer collapsed and died in the boardroom of his company.

A prominent ER doctor will testify that paramedic and ER treatment, though heroic, could not revive him. A renown cardiologist will testify that with the first episode of exercise-induced chest pain, the patient should have been referred for a cardiac workup, which to a reasonable medical certainty would have discovered a coronary blockage easily accessible to surgical correction.

Alex Boomer did not have to die. We cannot bring him back, but we can recompense his wife and children monetarily for their loss and we can punish the doctors and medical group responsible for his death. Thank you."

Judge, "Do any of the defense attorneys wish to make opening statements at this time, Mr. McAllen?"

"No, your Honor, I will reserve my comments until Mr. Sloanberg has put on his case."

"Mr. Smith?"

"No, your Honor, I will wait until a more appropriate time."

"Mr. Bailey?"

"No, your Honor, I will wait pending the disposition of my motion to dismiss the HMO."

Judge, "Mr. Sloanberg, call your first witness."

Sloanberg, "I will call Mrs. Boomer."

Elizabeth Boomer was duly sworn. She was dressed with subtle good taste and appeared calm but her countenance bore the strain of her loss.

The first questions concerned her name, address, relationship to the deceased, how long she had been married to Alex, their relationship, his job, travel, stresses and his position at the time of his death. All the general questions that had been asked and answered at her deposition.

"Mrs. Boomer, was your husband's health good?"

"As far as I knew he had a physical about a week prior to his death and was told his health was good, but that he needed to exercise, lose some weight and quit smoking."

"Did he follow those suggestions?"

"He started exercising and dieting but he had not yet quit smoking."

"What happened when he exercised?"

"He bought a treadmill and was using it when he first developed chest and left arm pain. He stopped and the pain went away."

"What did he do next?"

"He called Dr. Lawrence who had performed the physical and reported the incident."

"What did Dr. Lawrence do?"

"He told Alex to come to the office immediately. He was examined and given a prescription for nitroglycerine with instructions to use the medicine if he had another such episode and report the results to him."

"Did he?"

"Yes, he had another episode, took the nitro and the pain stopped."

"Did he follow those instructions?"

"Yes."

"What happened?"

"He called the office and spoke to a different doctor who told him to continue the exercise and use the nitro for pain if it recurred."

Smith, "Objection. In her deposition, Mrs. Boomer stated that she presumed that her husband talked to Dr. Lawrence again, not some other doctor."

Sloanberg, "Since that deposition, we have new evidence that will not only confirm her last statement, but also identify the other doctor as Dr. Shepard."

Judge, "What evidence is that?"

Sloanberg, "A tape recording of the actual conversation."

Judge, "Recess for fifteen minutes. Councils into my chambers. I want to hear this tape before I rule on the objection."

In the judge's chambers, the taped conversation between Boomer and Doctor Shepard was played and Sloanberg explained how and where it was obtained. Smith objected on the grounds that he had not been informed of the existence of the tape and that the only witness to the retrieval of that tape and the identification of it was Sherry Parker and she was now dead.

Sloanberg, "Mrs. Boomer, can certainly identify her husband's voice and Dr. Shepard identifies himself on the tape. In addition, Sherry discussed the tape and how it was found several days before she was killed."

Judge, "Objection's overruled and the tape can be entered as an exhibit and played for the jury."

The judge and lawyers returned and Mrs. Boomer's testimony was to resume.

Sloanberg, "Before continuing with this witness, I wish to enter this tape recording from Mr. Boomer's office phone as Exhibit A and play it for the court."

Judge, "You may proceed."

The tape in which Dr. Shepard identified himself and responded to Boomer's questions about his chest pain and the nitroglycerine was played.

Sloanberg, "Mrs. Boomer, can you identify your husband's voice on that tape?"

Elizabeth was crying softly on hearing her husband's voice. "Yes." The answer was so soft as to be almost a whisper.

Judge, "I understand how painful this must be for you but you must speak up. Please repeat your answer and then we'll take a morning recess."

She composed herself and again answered, "Yes." During the recess Sloanberg assured her that she was doing fine and tried to comfort her as best he could. When the trial resumed, Elizabeth was still on the stand.

Sloanberg, "Just before the recess, you testified that another doctor, the other defendant physician reassured your husband that he needed nothing more than the nitro for his chest pain, no EKG, no stress test, no referral to a cardiologist, no further visits to the clinic."

Elizabeth, "That is right."

"Did you discuss this with Mr. Boomer?"

"Yes."

"Did either of you have any qualms about that advice?"

"I did. Alex didn't voice any."

"Three days later you were called to the ED of Southwest Hospital. Tell us what happened."

"I was told that Alex had fainted in his office and had been brought to the ER. The paramedics had been called to the office and were unable to resuscitate him. The doctors at the ER were also unable to do anything for him." She was again visibly upset.

"You talked to the director of the ER. What did he tell you?"

"He assured me that everything possible was done for Alex, both at the office, in transit and in the ER, but he didn't respond to any of the treatment. He suggested an autopsy to learn what caused his death."

"And was that done?"

"Yes."

"What was the diagnosis?"

"A heart attack."

"Do you believe that could have been prevented?"

All three lawyers leaped to their feet and objected.

Sloanberg, "I will withdraw the question. I am finished at this time but reserve the right to call her to the stand again."

Judge, "Mr. McAllen."

McAllen, "You have my deepest sympathy for the death of

your husband, but I must ask you a few questions to clear the circumstances surrounding his death. You have testified that your husband was a hard-driving executive who traveled extensively, ate irregularly, was overweight, slept poorly and irregularly and smoked excessively. Were those last options not consistent with the cause of his heart attack?"

Sloanberg, "The witness is not a doctor and cannot give medical opinions."

Judge, "Sustained."

McAllen, "In the lay press, is that lifestyle not associated with heart attacks?"

"Yes."

"Is it not reasonable that the lifestyle was responsible for his death rather than the negligence of Dr. Lawrence?"

Sloanberg, "I renew my objection to this line of questioning on the same grounds of my previous objection."

Judge, "Sustained."

McAllen, "I have no more questions."

Judge, "Mr. Smith."

Mr. Smith, "Thank you, your Honor. I too am sympathetic with your loss and I'll only keep you a few minutes. Would you please explain how you came to know about the tape that was played a few minutes ago."

"Shortly before her death, Sherry Parker came to see me and gave me the tape."

"Did she tell you where she got it?"

"Yes."

"And what were the circumstances surrounding that?"

"Alex's office had been sealed after his death. An audit of the company was ordered shortly thereafter. Sherry was helping the auditors find the documents they needed and she went into his office. She noted the telephone answering machine was blinking and she checked it for messages. Apparently Alex had not erased the conversation with Dr. Shepard, and she brought me the tape. She had heard the conversation when it occurred."

"So you only have the word of a dead woman for the authenticity of the tape?"

Sloanberg, "Objection. The tape speaks for itself."

Judge, "Objection sustained."

Smith, "To your knowledge was your husband ever treated by Dr. Shepard or any other clinic doctor except Dr. Lawrence?"

"No."

"Do you consider that telephone conversation treatment?"

"He gave the wrong advice which prevented my husband from getting proper treatment which would have saved his life."

"I move to strike that answer as unresponsive. Nothing further."

Judge, "The court will be adjourned for lunch break and testimony will resume at 2:00 p.m. The jurors are reminded not to discuss the case during the recess."

After the recess, Mr. Sloanberg called Dr. Evans as his first expert witness. After questions concerning his training and experience, he was asked about the case at hand.

Sloanberg, "Dr. Evans, you have reviewed the documents supplied concerning Alex Boomer's exam and office visit by Dr. Lawrence, have you not?"

"Yes."

"What other documents have you reviewed?"

"The paramedic report, the ER chart and the autopsy report."

"Did you reach any conclusions concerning Dr. Lawrence's care of the patient?"

"Yes."

"And what conclusions did you reach?"

"That Dr. Lawrence failed to comply with the standard of care in his treatment of this patient."

"Why is that?"

"Mr. Boomer complained of chest pain on exercise and Dr. Lawrence prescribed nitroglycerine rather than referring the patient to a cardiologist for the tests."

"Do you believe that failure resulted in Mr. Boomer's death?"

"Yes."

"How is that?"

"Had Mr. Boomer been seen by a cardiologist and appropriate tests done, an accurate diagnosis of his heart disease could have been made and proper treatment been instigated."

"What tests?"

"An angiogram."

"And what would that have shown?"

"The autopsy revealed a ninety-percent occlusion near the origin of the LAD with a clot which completely occluded the artery resulting in the patient's death."

"What is the 'LAD'?"

"The left-hand anterior ascending coronary artery which nourishes a large area of the left ventricle of the heart. It is called 'the widow maker' in medical circles because it is the most frequent coronary artery involved in sudden death."

"If an angiogram had been done, how would that have prevented the patient's death?"

"Discovery of the ninety-percent occlusion would have led to treatment which would open the artery and prevent the formation of a clot."

"What kind of treatment?"

"Balloon angioplasty and/or by-pass surgery, both of which are routine in such cases and carry only a minimal risk."

"I have nothing further at this time."

Judge, "Mr. McAllen."

"Thank you, your Honor. Dr. Evans, is nitroglycerine not a standard treatment for angina pectoris?"

"Yes."

"Why then do you believe that Dr. Lawrence committed malpractice when he prescribed nitroglycerine?"

"Thirty years ago nitroglycerine was virtually the only treatment for angina, but with the advent of balloon angioplasty and by-pass surgery, nitroglycerine is only a temporizing measure to control chest pain."

"What about nitroglycerine as a test for angina? Incidentally, what is angina pectoris?"

"Angina pectoris is pain in the center of the chest usually radiating into the left arm or the neck or the jaw that is due to decreased circulation of the heart with a loss of its oxygen supply. Nitroglycerine can be used as a test for angina by relaxing the coronary vessels, it can temporarily improve circulation of the heart and relieve anginal chest pain. However, it is only temporary and does nothing to permanently correct the problem."

"If the protocol in the clinic and the HMO prevented Dr. Lawrence from referring patients to cardiologists or the use of expensive tests and treatments, do they share the responsibility for this patient's death?"

Smith and Bailey, "Objection. Assumed facts not in evidence."

McAllen, "Dr. Evans is an expert witness and as such can answer a hypothetical question."

Judge, "Objection overruled."

Evans, "In my opinion, they do."

McAllen, "Doctor, if Dr. Lawrence was using nitroglycerine as a test and never received a phone call concerning the results of the nitroglycerine on the chest pain, does that change your opinion concerning his responsibility in the matter?"

"It would modify that opinion if I accepted nitroglycerine a legitimate test for coronary disease which I do not."

McAllen, "I have nothing further."

Judge, "Mr. Smith?"

Smith, "Doctor, have you seen any protocols of the clinic or HMO which would have prevented Dr. Lawrence from doing his job?"

"No."

"How then can you comment on that?"

McAllen, "Objection. He was asked to answer a hypothetical question.

Evidence concerning the protocols will be introduced during the defense portion of the trial."

Judge, "Objection sustained."

Smith, "I have nothing further."

Judge, "Mr. Bailey?"

Bailey, "Doctor, in your deposition you made some negative comments about HMOs. Is that an opinion based on the fact that the gatekeeper concept makes your job in the emergency room more difficult and decreases your income?"

Evans, "My opinion is based on the fact that American medicine as we have known it is being systematically destroyed by managed care and patients are suffering because of it. I believe Mr. Boomer's untimely death is a prime example of the results of the greed and incompetence of that system."

Bailey, "This witness should be disqualified and all of his testimony stricken from the record because of his obvious prejudice."

Sloanberg and McAllen both leaped to their feet with objections.

"Mr. Bailey's trying to prejudice the jury against Dr. Evans."

Judge, "Sustained. Mr. Bailey, you opened the door by your question. Dr. Evans is eminently qualified to express opinions on this subject as well as the malpractice issue."

Bailey, "I have no further questions."

Judge, "Court will be recessed until tomorrow a.m."

CHAPTER 53

Maria Gonzales had sat through the trial all day and returned to the paper immediately after court was recessed. She went directly to Tim Dougherty's office.

"This trial is headed exactly where I predicted. The clinic and the HMO are being dragged in kicking and screaming. I think it is time to publish my article which was submitted to you last summer."

Dority, "It is too prejudicial. The HMO will have their attorneys in my office fifteen minutes after the paper hits the street."

Maria, "Both the clinic and the HMO are defendants. Can't we publicize them like we have Dr. Lawrence?"

"Not yet. Just write your summary of what went on today."

She stalked out his office and to her desk to write her daily article which would be only a rehash of the testimony with a slightly slanted opinion.

Sloanberg and his staff arrived at the courthouse at 7:30 a.m. They were met by an entourage of media, which all but barred their entrance into the building. There was a cacaphony of shouted questions from the assembled members of the press, and a thicket of microphones thrust forward towards the attorney.

"Do you really believe Boomer's death was preventable?"

"What about Dr. Lawrence's pending divorce? How will that play with the jury?"

"Who is the mystery witness?"

Sloanberg ignored these and many other questions shouted at him until the doors closed behind him and his colleagues.

They entered the elevator and proceeded to the cafeteria where they were to meet with their first two witnesses of the day—the pathologist who did the autopsy and a cardiac surgeon. Both were experienced witnesses and their preparation required only a few minutes from each.

When court was called to order promptly at 9:00 a.m., the pathologist was sworn. He testified as to the post mortem findings of the deceased. He was led through the autopsy report confirming the findings and conclusions. The cause of death was stated to be a coronary occlusion of the LAD by a fresh clot superimposed on a partially obstructed artery cutting off all the blood supply to a major portion of the left ventricle. This in turn caused the fatal arrhythmia. Otherwise the autopsy was normal. All the other organ systems were entirely within normal limits. The autopsy report was then entered into evidence as exhibit B. The defense attorney had no questions.

The next witness was William Sumner, a cardiac surgeon. He was first questioned as to the effects on the heart of a lesion such as described by the pathogist. He agreed that a blood clot, superimposed on the partially obstructed LAD would cause sudden death and resuscitation would be all but impossible. He also stated that the symptoms exhibited by the deceased should have aroused the suspicion of doctors caring for the patient.

"Doctor, what should have been done?"

"The patient should have had an angiogram which would have clearly demonstrated the obstruction of the LAD. Once that was accomplished, establishing the diagnosis of angina due to that obstruction, balloon angioplasty or bypass surgery should have been performed to open the artery before the fatal clot formed."

"Would any of these procedures, the angiography, the angioplasty or the bypass surgery have been risky?"

"Yes, all three carry a risk roughly equal to an appendectomy or gall bladder operation."

"Would nitroglycerine or other medicine designed to open the coronary arteries have been just as effective as surgery?"

"No, those medicines only relieve pain temporarily. They do

not cure the problem or prevent clot formation leading to death."

Sloanberg, "I have a schematic drawing of the circulation of the heart which has been enlarged for the jury. Would you, please, show us where the obstruction was and what area of the heart would be involved?"

Dr. Sumner complied by using the drawing in the autopsy report and duplicating the lesion on the enlarged schematic. He then added the clot showing the result of complete obstruction and the large area of the left ventricle which was deprived of blood and oxygen.

Dr. Sumner, "The loss of oxygen to that area would interfere with the electrical conduction mechanism producing a cardiac arrhythmia or arrest which was incompatible with life."

Sloanberg, "Show us on that drawing what a bypass would look like and what it would accomplish."

He drew the bypass around the obstruction and indicated the blood flow through the bypass would nourish the area of the heart previously supplied by the LAD.

"Could that not have been accomplished after the patient had his heart attack?"

"Not in this case because the patient was already dead."

Sloanberg, "I have nothing further."

McAllen, "Nitro and other drugs dilate coronary arteries and relieve anginal pain, do they not?"

"Yes."

"Could such drugs not have prevented this attack?"

"They didn't in this case."

"Could nitro be used as a test for coronary heart disease?"

"Yes, but it's non-specific."

"How about this case?"

"It relieved pain temporarily but did nothing to prevent the fatal attack as shown by the drawing."

"What should have been done when the patient's exercise-induced pain was relieved by nitro?"

"The patient should have been seen immediately by a cardiologist for an angiogram, which would have shown the obstruction. He should then have had an angioplasty and if that didn't work, taken to the O.R. for a bypass."

"I have nothing further."

Mr. Smith, "Doctor, aren't patients still treated for angina with nitro and other drugs?"

"Yes, but it doesn't work with patients like the deceased."

"The answer is nonresponsive. Yes or no, doctor?"

"I cannot answer a simple yes or no to that question."

Smith, "Your honor, please instruct the witness to answer my question."

Judge, "He should be allowed to explain his answer since he is an expert witness."

Smith, "I have nothing further of this witness."

Judge, "Mr. Bailey?"

Bailey, "I have nothing."

Judge, "It's time for the noon recess."

CHAPTER 54

The afternoon session was not exactly scintilating. The first witness was an economist whose assignment was to estimate for the jury the monetary loss to the Boomer family of Alex's untimely death.

The gist of the testimony was as follows. Mr. Boomer's salary was one million a year at the time of his death and with estimated growth of the company, his salary would rapidly increase to two and one half million per year. His age at death was forty-five, giving him an expected earning capacity of between twenty and thirty million during the rest of his productive years. That was in addition to stock options, with a value of ten million at the time of his death. With the anticipated growth of the company, and its potential value as an IPO, his stock options might conservatively be valued at twenty-five million. Had he survived, his net earning and worth would have been at least fifty million. All these projections were based on his value to the company as its CEO.

The only defense attorney to cross-examine the economist was Mr. Bailey.

"Mr. Brock, you audited ACME Electronics shortly after Mr. Boomer's death, did you not?"

"Yes."

"What was the condition of the company's finances at that time?"

"It was unstable, to say the least."

"Based on your audit, what was the stock worth at that time?"

"Conservatively, it was worth five dollars a share."

"How many shares outstanding?"

"One hundred thousand."

"So the total value was five hundred thousand."

Brock, "That does not include other assets such as building, tools, money owed it and unfilled orders."

Bailey, "What is the total value of those assets?"

"Approximately $250,000."

"How about the IPO?"

"It's on hold at the present time."

"So the twenty-five million you estimated is really only $750,000."

"The reason for that is the loss of Boomer. The present and future of the company was totally dependent on his ingenuity and leadership."

"Is it not true that ACME is presently in Chapter 11 bankruptcy?"

"Yes, again due to the loss of Boomer."

"Yes or no?"

"Yes, but..."

Bailey, "I move to strike the rest of the answer since it is based on speculation."

Judge, "Motion denied. Mr. Brock is an expert and as such is allowed to explain his answer."

Bailey, "I have nothing further."

Sloanberg, "Mr. Brock, what is the status of Mrs. Boomer's finances at the present time?"

"She is living off her husband's insurance and her savings."

"What is the status of the bankruptcy proceedings?"

"The company is in the process of reorganization with the objective of employing a new CEO who can return the company to its profitability and protect the assets of the stockholders."

CHAPTER 55

Court was adjourned after Brock's testimony. Maria quickly returned to her office and met with Tim Dougherty.

"Two things of significance happened today. First there was a question put to Sloanberg about his mystery witness. This happened prior to the beginning of today's session and no answer was given. The more I thought about it, the more I wondered if there was a relationship to the accelerated scheduling of the start of this trial."

"How so?"

"Could it be that there is a security problem with the witness, whomever he or she may be?"

"Come on, this a civil trial, not a syndicate trial."

"I understand that but the amount of money damages being bandied around is $50 million and that is serious change to any defendant or insurer involved.

"The other thing disclosed today was the fact that ACME Electronic is bankrupt and is being blamed on the death of the defendant. In addition, Mrs. Boomer is broke. Can I include speculation about these facts in my article today?"

"You can with the exception of linking the mystery witness to the scheduling of the trial."

The article which appeared reported a summary of the testimony of the three witnesses, but also included closing questions, "who is the mystery witness?", "who has the most to loose if there is a very large plaintiff's award?"

CHAPTER 56

Needless-to-say, Sloanberg was very upset about the article. He was afraid speculation about a mystery witness might increase the danger to Michael and especially Melissa. He had hoped to have Melissa on and off the stand as a surprise to everyone as much for her safety as for the value of her testimony.

Neither was he happy about the revelation concerning the bankruptcy proceedings against ACME Electronics. Even though it was public record, he didn't want the facts to become general public knowledge. However, there was nothing he could do but maintain a "no comment" posture.

CHAPTER 57

On arrival at the courthouse the next day, Sloanberg and Elizabeth Boomer were met with a barrage of questions about the mystery witness and the bankruptcy proceedings against ACME Electronics. Sloanberg and Boomer were surrounded by his staff and the local police to provide a wedge though the entourage of media. Both simply replied "no comment" to their queries.

When safely inside, Sloanberg again cautioned Elizabeth and his staff about refraining from comments about these subjects and any other aspects of the case. They proceeded to the cafeteria where they met with a nattily attired black man in his early forties. They introduced themselves to Mr. Percy Smythe, who had been brought to the U.S. from the Cayman Islands to introduce and testify concerning certain records of stock transactions between the HMO and the clinic trust.

Sloanberg briefed him concerning American court proceedings but was assured by Smythe that he was very familiar with the civil court proceedings in America having been called upon to testify many times in similar circumstances. He was quite circumspect and seemed capable in his job and for his current assignment.

Court was called to order and Judge Levine inquired if Mr. Sloanberg was ready with his next witness. He indicated that he was and called Mr. Percy Smythe, who was duly sworn.

Sloanberg, "Mr. Smythe, what is your position in the Cayman Islands?"

Smythe, "I am the recorder of records for the federal government of the Cayman Islands."

"You have brought copies of certain records with you which

pertain to this trial."

Bailey, "Objection, lacks foundation."

Judge, "Rephrase, Mr. Sloanberg."

"Thank you, your Honor. Mr. Smythe, the records I referred to deal with a stock transaction between a clinic trust of Drs. Smith and Jones and an HMO do they not?"

"Yes they do."

"Can you briefly explain the nature of that transaction?"

"As part of a sale of the clinic to the HMO, the clinic trust received 500 shares of HMO stock with a par value of $250,000 American and other valuable considerations. In turn, the HMO received 51% of the shares of the clinic stock giving it a controlling interest."

"Are there other provisions?"

"The above transaction was solely recorded in the Cayman Islands and any profit to either entity from the above interest was to accrue to respective accounts in the Bank of Cayman. Only the trust officers of the HMO and CEO could draw from the respective accounts."

"Under the laws of your country, does this arrangement establish partial ownership and control of each party concerning the opposite entity?"

"Yes, sir."

"To make this clear, the HMO has a controlling interest of the clinic and the clinic is a significant stockholder of the HMO."

"Yes, sir."

"From your understanding of the corporate laws of your country as well as those of the United States, is there any reason why this relationship would not apply to these companies in the United States?"

Bailey, "Objection. The witness is not a lawyer, is not familiar with United States Corporate law."

Judge, "Sustained. This is a legal point which I will have to rule on later."

Sloanberg, "Thank you. I have nothing further of this witness.

I would like to have these documents marked as Exhibits."

Bailey, "Cross-examination, your Honor?"

"Mr. Smythe, how did you come into possession of these records?"

"They are public records in my country."

"How did Mr. Sloanberg obtain the records?"

"He sent a legal representative to the Hall of Records and inquired if such a transaction existed. A search was made and the records found."

Bailey, "Is it not a breach of Cayman Islands government policy to make such records public?"

Smythe, "Not at all. You're possibly confusing bank records with legal documents."

"How much were you paid to find, transport and testify concerning these records?"

"My expenses, and $100 and hour for the time spent."

"You indicated a familiarity with the American Court System. Have you made a practice of providing similar services to legal firms in other countries?"

"Part of my job is to provide such information when sought by a legal representative of a court or other reputable government agency."

Bailey, "I have nothing further."

CHAPTER 58

After the noon recess, Mr. Sloanberg called Dr. Joseph Hulsey, a renown cardiologist to the stand. The initial questions concerned his qualifications. He was a Mayo trained cardiologist, chief of cardiology at the Cleveland clinic, author of a text book on cardiology and a foremost authority on angiography and angioplasty and other related invasive procedures. After establishing his credibility, Dr. Hulsey was asked the following hypothetical question.

Sloanberg, "Doctor, a forty-eight year old, slightly obese, slightly hypertensive, hardworking executive comes to your office for a routine physical. He smokes a pack of cigarettes daily. He has no complaints. His past medical history is negative. He is not diabetic, has no family history of carcinoma, diabetes, high blood pressure or heart disease. The exam is entirely normal except for a blood pressure of 148/92 and twenty pounds overweight. His lab, chest x-ray and EKG are normal. You advise him to start exercising, lose twenty pounds and stop smoking and to follow-up with regular visits.

"He follows your suggestions and about a week later reports that, while on a treadmill, he developed pain in his mid-chest with radiation to his left arm which subsided shortly after resting. At this point, what would you do?"

Doctor, "I would have him back in the office and do an exercise cardiogram."

"What would expect to find?"

"With that history, I would expect to find an abnormal EKG."

"If you found an abnormal EKG, what would you then do?"

"I would admit him to the hospital and schedule an angiogram."

"In this patient, by autopsy, we know what an angiogram would have shown, do we not?"

"Yes, an narrowing of the LAD."

"In such a case, what would you have done?"

"I would have performed angioplasty."

"And if that did not clear the obstruction, what would you have done?"

"I would have referred the patient to a cardiac surgeon for bypass surgery."

"Why is that?"

"A lesion such as described in the pathology report is a time bomb for sudden death, just as happened in this unfortunate case."

"Doctor, would you ever just prescribe nitroglycerine as a test for coronary disease or primary treatment for angina in such a patient?"

"Never!"

"Why is that?"

"Nitroglycerine only provides temporary relief of pain in such a situation. It does nothing to cure the disease."

"Did you ever use nitroglycerine as a test for coronary disease?"

"No."

"Why is that?"

"The relief of pain due to nitroglycerine is non-specific for coronary disease. It might relieve pain from a gall-bladder attack, for example."

"In your opinion, nitroglycerine had no place in the treatment or diagnosis of this patient, is that correct?"

"Yes, sir."

"I have nothing further, Judge."

Judge, "Mr. McAllen?"

McAllen, "Dr. Hulsey, you indicated that nitro does relieve heart pain, did you not?"

"Yes."

"You indicated also that there are more reliable tests for coronary disease but you do not rule out its use for relief of pain and thus the suggestion of pain due to coronary disease, is that not correct?"

"Yes, but..."

"Just answer the question, yes or no."

"Yes."

"That being the case, you could not say that the prescription of nitroglycerine for relief of pain and as a suggestion of the cause of the patient's chest pain is below the standard of practice, could you Doctor?"

"No, but..."

"You've answered the question. Thank you, Doctor. I have nothing further."

Judge, "Anything further, Mr. Sloanberg?"

Sloanberg, "No, your Honor. The plaintiff rests, but reserves the right to call additional witnesses later on in rebuttal."

Judge, "That being the case, the court will stand in recess until Monday morning, at which time Mr. McAllen will begin the defense."

CHAPTER 59

Sloanberg and McAllen met briefly in the men's room after checking to assure themselves that no one else was present.

McAllen asked, "When do you want them at your office?"

"Let's make it early so it will be less likelihood of their being observed. Say, 7:30 a.m. Saturday?"

Saturday a.m. promptly at 6:30, Michael left the condo and took a convoluted route to Sloanberg's office. He was admitted to the suite by Denise Moody and ushered into a small conference room. Sloanberg introduced Dr. Lawrence to Lois Puckett, a trained witness consultant and Mary Anne James, his personal secretary. He had previously been introduced to Ms. Moody. Shortly thereafter, Melissa arrived dressed in jeans, a sweatshirt and tennis shoes. She too had been very careful to avoid being followed. She was introduced to Denise and Mary Anne.

Coffee was served and Sloanberg briefed the group on the purpose of the meeting and the reason for secrecy.

Michael and Melissa were all too aware of the precautions and they had been living like this for weeks now.

Sloanberg, "Within the next week or ten days, both of you will be called to the stand. Somebody does not want you to testify or at least testify to the facts which somebody does not want exposed. Melissa has already been dubbed as a mystery witness by the press though she was not identified by name. Her true identity is either known or suspected by whoever does not want her to testify. Michael's situation is slightly different. The whole free world knows he will take the stand, but the concern is to what he will say, therefore the cloak and dagger aspect of this meeting. If our adversaries knew you were meeting with me, the scope of your testimony would be quite apparent to them.

"With that background, we come to the purpose of this meeting. First of all, I want your assurances that your testimony will be as we discussed at our previous meeting. Do I have that?"

Michael, "Yes, I have no choice."

Melissa, "Yes, despite the threats and fear."

Sloanberg, "That agreed to, the second purpose is to prepare you for the onslaught of cross-examination by either Smith or Bailey or both. These gentlemen are extremely competent and completely unscrupulous. There is an enormous sum of money dependent on their performance, therefore I have brought in Lois Puckett to prepare you to deal with them. And I'll now turn the meeting over to her."

Lois Puckett is a forty-year old, conservatively dressed, divorcee, attractive for her age with an all-business approach to her profession and to people in general. She had been working in the legal field for ten years starting as a legal secretary, educating herself as paralegal, then a BA in psychology and finally a law degree. She had no desire to practice law and eventually became an invaluable consultant to high profile attorneys helping them to pick juries and preparing witnesses.

Puckett, "Dr. Lawrence and Ms. Hailey, both of the opposing attorneys are very capable and will attack you personally and professionally. You can expect an attempt to destroy your credibility with the jury and media because of your relationship. Your professional competence, Doctor, will be attacked not only for your care of the deceased, but also your work in the clinic. Your loyalty to your employer and to your wife will become an issue. Ms. Hailey, you will be characterized as a scarlet woman. Your professional conduct at the clinic and loyalty to your employer will be trashed.

"It will be extremely difficult to avoid striking back in anger or, in your case, Ms. Hailey, breaking down in tears. But you both must avoid these reactions at all costs. The omnipotence of the medical profession does not tolerate this kind of treatment very well. You must be calm, honest, matter-of-fact and answer questions as simply and briefly as possible. On the other hand, do not get caught in a yes or no situation. If the attorney demands a yes or no answer which requires explanation, appeal to the judge stating that a yes or no without explanation might convey an erroneous impression.

"Don't answer too quickly. Be sure you understand the question and that the attorney has finished asking it before you answer it. Don't allow them to hurry you or fluster you. Look at the attorney who's asking the questions. Don't look at the jury, but don't avoid them. Try to take them into your audience as you would if you were speaking with someone in your den where there are additional interested people.

"Don't try to verbally fence with the attorney. He does this for a living, you don't. Remember, you know more about medicine than the attorney does. He will try to convince you otherwise, but don't let him. You also know as much or more about the facts of this case as he does. If not, you shouldn't be a witness.

"If asked to comment on a document or a deposition, read it carefully taking all the time necessary and being sure you understand both the document and the meaning of the question.

"The demeanor of both attorneys is designed to confuse you, upset you emotionally and make you look like you are lying. Keep this in mind. These people are your adversaries, actually, your enemies. They will do or say anything to accomplish their objectives to destroy your credibility.

"What I have described is a general overview of cross-examination. The individual characteristics of these attorneys is not particularly important except to say that they are extremely good at what they do. Any questions?"

Both Michael and Melissa sat in stunned silence. The enormity and unpleasantness of the process had been brought home to them graphically, and they were fully aware of the potential consequences."

CHAPTER 60

On the fourteenth green of the Wilshire Country Club and Golf Course, the screeching of his cell phone interrupted John Bailey's concentration on the back swing of a birdie putt causing the ball to go wide right and long. He was both irritated and embarrassed as the other members of his foursome glared at him.

He was very impatient with the caller but almost immediately responded to the message with anger and a sense of urgency.

Bailey, "I'm going to have to leave you gentlemen and take care of business."

Jack, "Nothing should be more important than a golf game. You should leave that gadget at home when you play with us."

Bailey, "I'm sorry but this is urgent."

He called the golf shop and asked for someone to send a cart to the fifteenth tee for him. On arrival at the locker room, he called Blake and asked him to come to his office within the hour. He refused to give a reason over the phone. Blake arrived shortly before Bailey and was waiting in the lobby of the building when Bailey arrived.

Blake, "What is so damned urgent to drag me to your office at lunchtime on Saturday?"

Bailey, "I have just been informed that both Dr. Lawrence and Ms. Hailey spent this morning in the offices of Sloanberg. This was a clandestine meeting attended by Sloanberg, his secretary, paralegal and Lois Puckett, his jury and witness consultant. That could mean only one thing. They're going to testify against the clinic and the HMO as we had feared. We must make contingency plans. I am unable to reach either Martin Smith or Ronald Shepard, but I will keep trying."

Blake, "We must do whatever is necessary to prevent that from happening, especially the Hailey woman. Can we destroy their credibility on the stand?"

"Possibly the doctor since he is a defendant and any attempt to blame the HMO would seem self-serving. The woman is less vulnerable. Even though she is in an extra-marital relationship with the doctor."

Blake, "Shall we go to plan B?"

Bailey, "Not until we consult with Smith and Shepard. Lawrence will testify first next week when the defense starts presenting its case. We may get an indication of the tactics from that. I can minimize any damage he might cause if there is no corroborating witness."

Blake, "So we'll do nothing until we talk with our colleagues and see what Dr. Lawrence has to say."

CHAPTER 61

Michael and Melissa returned home by separate and circuitous routes. She stopped at the deli for their lunch. They were unaware that their clandestine meeting had been observed and reported and that their every move was under constant surveillance. It was just as well that they did not know. They had been frightened enough by the threats of physical harm, but the added prospect of being crucified by unscrupulous lawyers and the media made life almost unbearable. Added to that was the increasing tension between them because of their extraneous problems.

When Michael walked in, Melissa threw her arms around him and began crying uncontrollably. He held her close and tried to comfort her. This soon escalated into the most passionate love making they had ever experienced. The fear engendered by all of their problems intensified their desire more than anything since the initial passion of their mutual discovery. Afterwards they lay in each others embrace for a long time without speaking. They realized it was them against the world.

CHAPTER 62

When court was called to order Monday morning, McAllen's opening statement was the first order of business.

McAllen, "Your honor and ladies and gentlemen of the jury. Dr. Michael Lawrence is a well-trained, conscientious member of the local medical community. He is not responsible for the death of Alex Boomer. He did a routine physical, found his patient to be overweight, a heavy smoker, and with a very stressful job which prevented him from sleeping, eating and exercising in a healthy manner. The exam was otherwise normal including x-rays, lab and EKG. The patient had no complaints. So far, even the plaintiff's attorney could find no fault with his care to this point.

"After the physical, the patient was advised to lose weight, quit smoking and exercise. No negligence there. But while exercising, Mr. Boomer developed chest and arm pain. Did that complaint require the immediate dangerous and expensive tests suggested by the plaintiff's experts? Dr. Lawrence thought not. After all, the most likely source of such pain was due to exercising muscles of the chest and arms which had been underutilized for years. Did he consider the possibility of the pain being due to his heart? Yes, he did and he prescribed nitroglycerine as a test. Is that negligence? No. Nitroglycerine has been a drug used to relieve heart pain since the dawn of modern medicine. He prescribed nitroglycerine not as a treatment but as a test to rule out heart disease. Simply, if nitro stopped the pain, heart disease must be considered and other tests needed to be performed. Unfortunately, Dr. Lawrence never had the opportunity to follow-up. He was never informed of the results of that nitroglycerine test, therefore, had no opportunity to order more specific tests. Dr. Lawrence and other witnesses will explain how this happened and why you should find him not guilty of negligence. Thank you."

CHAPTER 63

Dr. Lawrence was called to the stand and duly sworn. He appeared younger than his thirty-six years, but mature and professional. He physique was athletic and his facial expression was pleasant but serious. He exhibited little of the tension thrust upon him by the lawsuit, the pending divorce, the physical threat and the restriction of freedom occasioned by all these things. He wore a dark blue pin-stripe suit and white shirt with a button-down collar and a subdued red tie. He appeared both handsome and professional.

McAllen questioned him about his education, training and medical experience, all of which was impressive. He outlined his background with ease and candor.

McAllen, "Dr. Lawrence, did your negligence result in the death of Alex Boomer?"

Michael, "No, sir."

"Explain."

Michael, "I did a complete physical on him, found nothing abnormal in his medical history or exam. I advised him concerning lifestyle changes and otherwise gave him a clean bill of health."

McAllen, "When he called and told you about the exercise-induced chest pain and arm pain, what did you think and what did you do?"

Michael, "I had him back in the office, re-examined him and did another EKG and gave him a prescription for nitroglycerine."

McAllen, "Why did you prescribe nitro?"

Michael, "I was convinced his pain was due to unaccustomed activity and muscle pain of his chest and arm muscles. Heart pain was in my differential diagnosis and that is the reason why I prescribed nitro, not only to protect his heart but as a test. If it relieved the pain, I would have considered heart disease more seriously and ordered more specific tests."

McAllen, "Why'd you not do that?"

Michael, "I never received a call back from him."

McAllen, "His wife testified that he did indeed called back and was told to just take the nitro when he had pain and exercise less vigorously. Did you give him that advice?"

Michael, "No, I never received a call from him."

McAllen, "Who did he talk to?"

"I have been advised that he called the clinic when I was not there and the call was transferred to Dr. Shepard."

McAllen, "Did Dr. Shepard notify you of the call or make an entry in Boomer's chart?"

"No."

McAllen, "Have you discussed it with him?"

"No."

McAllen, "Why?"

Michael, "He refused to discuss that or any aspect of the case with me. I have been told that this suit is my problem and to not implicate the clinic, any other doctors or the HMO."

McAllen, "Are you saying that you were threatened or coerced?"

"Yes, I was told I would be fired and black-balled in the medical community."

"By whom?"

Michael, "Both Dr. Shepard, the Medical Director and Alex Garrison, the CEO of the clinic."

Smith, "Objection. Here say."

McAllen, "The doctor has a right to testify to conversations to which he was a party."

Judge, "Overruled."

McAllen, "Doctor, we've heard a lot from so-called experts that you should have ordered more specific, invasive and dangerous tests immediately when you were first told of the chest pain. How do you respond to that?"

Sloanberg, "Objection to the term "so-called" experts. These doctors have duly qualified as experts and their respective fields."

Judge, "Sustained."

McAllen, "Sorry, your Honor. Doctor, shall I repeat the question?"

Michael, "No. In my judgment, heart disease was an unlikely cause of the patient's pain, therefore I felt my more conservative approach was appropriate. In addition to being somewhat hazardous to the patient, these procedures are quite expensive. In this era of managed care, we are discouraged from ordering expensive tests, surgery, hospitalization and ER visits. The doctors at the clinic have repeatedly been cautioned against practicing medicine as it was practiced prior to the advent of managed care."

McAllen, "Cautioned by whom?"

Michael, "Dr. Shepard, Mr. Garrison. There are written directives to that effect from the HMO which are incorporated into the policies and procedures of the clinic."

Bailey, "Objection. Not in the evidence."

McAllen, "The doctor is testifying to the P & P under which he practiced at the clinic."

Bailey, "He has no evidence of the source of those P&P."

Judge, "Sustained as to the HMO."

"Doctor, have you read those P&P's?"

"Yes, and the medical staff has had seminars on P&P's, some of which have been conducted by utilization employees of the HMO."

McAllen, "Do you have any notes or handouts from any of those meetings?"

"Yes."

"Provide them to the court."

McAllen, "Do you believe that Dr. Shepard was acting on those Policies and Procedures in his advice to Mr. Boomer?"

Smith, "Objection. This doctor cannot testify to the motivation of another doctor."

Judge, "Sustained."

McAllen, "I have nothing further at this time."
Judge, "It's time for the morning recess."

CHAPTER 64

During the recess Michael and McAllen found a private corner of the hallway to confer.

McAllen, "You did very well. I think we got everything in that we wanted for the time being."

Michael, "Sam Jones and his threats were all we left out."

McAllen, "That will come later. Hopefully, just before Melissa testifies."

Michael, "She's scared to death."

McAllen, "Rightfully so. She's potentially more damaging than you."

Michael, "Who's my first dragon to slay?"

McAllen, "Sloanberg and he'll be easy with you. Go to the bathroom, take a deep breath and compose yourself."

Judge, "Come to order. Doctor, you are still under oath. Mr. Sloanberg, you may proceed."

Sloanberg, "Doctor, your C.V. is quite impressive. You've had significant training in the diagnosis and treatment of coronary disease, have you not?"

Michael, "Yes, sir."

Sloanberg, "You do not dispute any of the testimony of the plaintiff's expert about diagnosis and treatment of heart disease, do you?"

"No, sir."

"Then why did you not order any of the tests available to you on Mr. Boomer?"

Michael, "As I explained, while coronary disease was in my differential, I did not consider that diagnosis to be the most likely cause of the patient's pain and therefore did not feel warranted in exposing him to the added risk unnecessarily. In addition, I was under significant pressure to avoid specific and unnecessary tests."

Sloanberg, "Your judgment was wrong, wasn't it?"

Michael, "Yes."

"And Alex Boomer paid the price for that error, didn't he?"

"Yes, but ..."

Sloanberg, "You've answered the question, I have nothing further."

Judge, "It's a little early but in the interest of continuity, we'll take the lunch break now."

McAllen and Michael found a restaurant not too far from the courthouse where their privacy was assured.

Michael, "I thought he was on our side, sort of."

McAllen, "You're still the primary defendant and he has to make a case against you in order to go after the other defendants. You will remember he did not attack your testimony concerning the pressure to avoid expensive testing and procedures. He also used the word "judgment" in describing your treatment. The judge will instruct the jury that an error in judgment is not necessarily malpractice."

Michael, "I guess I should be somewhat comforted by those tidbits."

McAllen, "Indeed you should. If you were the sole defendant, Sloanberg would have ripped you to shreds. What you have to be concerned about is the cross by the next two or whichever one is designated to attack you."

Michael, "Would it be both, do you think?"

McAllen, "I think Smith will carry the burden since his client is the most vulnerable at this point. You will be asked about your relationship to Shepard and Garrison, the Principles and Procedures of the clinic, the threats to your career and what you knew and when and how you know about Shepard's phone conversation with Boomer. Can you deal with all that?"

Michael, "Just the facts, man, just the facts."

McAllen, "It's time to eat and get back to the salt mines."

The trial was called to order at 2:00 p.m. and Martin Smith began cross-exam of Dr. Lawrence.

Smith, "Doctor, you and your attorney have made several allegations against my client in order to excuse your own bungling. I want to examine those one at a time. First of all, it has been alleged that your medical care was influenced by Policies and Procedures of the clinic, dictated by the HMO. Is that correct?"

Michael, "Yes, sir."

"Have you ever read such a document?"

"Yes, sir."

"Can you produce such a document?"

"No, sir, but ..."

"You have answered the question. You have also indicated that both my client and the administrator threatened to terminate your services and black-ball your medical reputation if you did not adhere to these phantom Principles and Procedures. Is that true?"

"Yes, sir."

"Do you have anything in writing or any witnesses to the threats?"

"No, sir."

"Finally, you allege that you personally never received the phone call from Mr. Boomer reporting his response to nitroglycerine. Is that true?"

"Yes, sir."

"You further allege that Dr. Shepard took that call and never informed you or made a notation in the chart. Is that correct?"

"Yes, sir."

"Do you have any proof of that?"

"Yes, sir."

"And what is that?"

"The telephone tape that was introduced by my attorney and will be verified by my nurse."

"You mean, Melissa Hailey, your mistress?"

McAllen, "Objection. Inflammatory and not in evidence."

Judge, "Sustained. Mr. Smith, it is not permissible to trash the defendant and a potential witness in this courtroom."

Smith, "I beg your pardon, your Honor. I withdraw the question. I have nothing further."

McAllen, "Your honor, redirect this witness."

"Doctor, to your knowledge, does there exist a written document concerning the principles and procedures that you described?"

Michael, "No, sir."

McAllen, "How then do you know about it?"

"These P&P's were communicated to the personnel orally, discussed in clinic seminars by utilization reviewers and mentioned to me on occasions when I violated any of them."

"Was it on such an occasions when you personally violated these guidelines in the care of a patient that you were called in by Dr. Shepard and Mr. Garrison and threatened?"

"Yes."

McAllen, "By the way, were you ever criticized by either of these gentlemen about your care of Mr. Boomer?"

"No."

McAllen, "Were there records kept of any of the meetings at which guidelines were discussed either with you personally or in general meetings with the personnel?"

Michael, "Not to my knowledge."

McAllen, "Did Dr. Shepard ever contact you about Mr. Boomer's call?"

Michael, "No, sir."

"Have you seen his chart since his death?"

Michael, "Yes, sir."

McAllen, "Was there any kind of notation about the phone conversation between Dr. Shepard and the deceased?"

Michael, "No, sir."

McAllen, "You heard the tape of that conversation. Did you not?"

Michael, "Yes, sir."

McAllen, "Can you identify the voices on that tape?"

Michael, "Yes, sir."

McAllen, "Who were they?"

Michael, "Dr. Shepard and Alex Boomer."

McAllen, "I have nothing further of this witness. I now would like to call Mr. Alex Garrison and treat him as a hostile witness."

Judge, "So ordered."

McAllen, "Mr. Garrison, you are the administrator of the clinic which is a defendant in this lawsuit?"

Garrison, "Yes, sir."

McAllen, "Does the clinic have written guidelines concerning care of patients specifically when hospitalization, surgery, x-rays, MRI's, consultations and other specific modes of patient care can be ordered by the clinic physician?"

Garrison, "No."

McAllen, "Is there a general attitude about these things on the part of management which is communicated to medical personnel by word of mouth, either individually or in meetings?"

Garrison, "Yes, but the doctors are expected to practice medicine according to their training and community standards as well as economic principles."

McAllen, "But the more expensive medical procedures are restricted, are they not?"

Garrison, "In the interest of economics there is a restriction of such procedures to absolute necessity."

McAllen, "Most of the procedures mentioned and many others must be approved by Utilization Committee regardless of the desire of the physician and the welfare of the patient, is that not correct?"

Garrison, "Yes that is what is meant by "managed care".

McAllen, "Doctor Lawrence mentioned that he was disciplined and threatened by you and Dr. Shepard for violations of this unwritten code. Is that true?"

Garrison, "I believe that is true."

McAllen, "Did you keep records of those meetings?"

Garrison, "No."

McAllen, "Does the Utilization Committee keep records?"
Garrison, "Yes."
"What do those records consist of?"
Garrison, "The patient's name, the procedure, requesting physician, diagnosis and disposition."
McAllen, "There's no record of the discussion of the reasons for request, of the procedures and the reasons for approval or rejection or the ensuing discussion, pro and con. Is that correct?"
"Yes."
McAllen, "The only consideration is cost. Is that right?"
Garrison, "No, sir. "
McAllen, "The way you people practice medicine is sort of like the camel which resulted when the committee was asked to design a horse. Is that not correct?"
Smith, "Objection."
Judge, "Sustained. Your question is inappropriate."
McAllen, "Withdrawn. I have nothing further of this witness."
Judge, "Is your next witness available?"
McAllen, "Yes, your Honor. I call Mr. William Blake, also as a hostile witness."
Judge, "So ordered."
Blake was sworn.
McAllen, "Mr. Blake, you are the CEO of the HMO which is a defendant in this action. Is that correct?"
Blake, "Unfortunately so for the present."
McAllen, "Does that answer refer to your position or to your perception of the involvement of the HMO in the lawsuit?"
Blake, "The action against the HMO which is illegal and is on appeal."
McAllen, "Thank you for clarifying that for us. When the HMO took over the clinic, did it make certain requirements regarding the method of practice to be performed by the doctors?"
Blake, "Only that they consider the best interest of their patients and practice within community standards."
McAllen, "Were they not already doing those things?"

Blake, "We would not have contracted with them if that had not been the case."

McAllen, "Are you stating for the record that the HMO did not require certain changes in practice patterns?"

Blake, "No, there were certain minor changes designed to comply with the standards and objectives of the HMO."

McAllen, "Can you enumerate those changes for us?"

Blake, "There was to be a Utilization Committee to consider and approve certain medical procedures and decisions."

McAllen, "Was there a specific list of such procedures that require approval by the committee?"

Blake, "Yes."

McAllen, "Please list those procedures."

Blake, "It's hard to be specific."

McAllen, "Try."

Blake, "Hospitalization, some elective surgeries, some consultations, and some lab and x-ray procedures."

McAllen, "Anything else?"

Blake, "That pretty well covers it."

McAllen, "What was the purpose of such interference with the practice of medicine by the doctors?"

Blake, "Sometimes doctors get carried away and order things that are unnecessary."

McAllen, "Does that mean you can't trust your doctors?"

Blake, "No, of course not. Sometime in their training they are taught to order unnecessary procedures for academic reasons and they develop habits of over utilization."

McAllen, "Is it not true that the HMO interferes with medical judgment solely for economic reasons?"

Blake, "No, I resent that inference."

McAllen, "Dr. Lawrence stated and Mr. Garrison verified that he had been disciplined and threatened for violating that economic code on several occasions. Would he have been disciplined if he had sent Mr. Boomer to a cardiologist when he reported chest pain on exercise?"

Blake, "That would have been a decision of the Utilization Committee."

McAllen, "In other words, the committee would have been able to decide whether Mr. Boomer lived or died, but Dr. Shepard spared the committee that choice."

Bailey and Smith joined in objection.

Judge, "Sustained. Mr. McAllen, you will have your opportunity to summarize your case later."

McAllen, "I have nothing further of this witness, and the defense rests."

Judge, "On that note, the court will be in recess until Monday morning. The jury is admonished not to discuss this case with each other or any witnesses, attorneys or principles."

CHAPTER 65

Maria Rodriguez returned to her office at the paper and wrote her story of today's events. She included the fact that Melissa Hailey had been identified as a witness and the possibly the "mystery" witness. After recounting the day's events to Tim Dougherty, she again sought his permission to write her editorial of her initial story for the Sunday edition.

Maria, "The facts concerning limiting care by the clinic and the HMO were brought out in court today and Melissa was identified as the 'mystery' witness and also Dr. Lawrence's paramour. With these facts plus the fact that the three young women murdered were all related to the case in some way, I don't believe a carefully written story would be libelous."

Tim, "The operative words are 'carefully written'. I know how your imagination can run wild. Write it and let me approve it, but do not even speculate about the three murders being related."

Maria, "Can I use my own experience at the clinic?"

"Yes."

With glee, Maria set about composing what she hoped would be a Pulitzer Prize winning piece of journalism.

CHAPTER 66

Blake, Bailey, Smith and Shepard met in an out-of-the-way bar in West L.A. None were pleased with the day's events. Blake was particularly upset with his attorney.

"Why did you let McAllen attack me as you did?"

"Based on the known facts, he was within his rights. There was no way to stop it."

"How much damage did he do?"

"That's hard to estimate."

"What are our chances of our appeal to be dismissed from the trial?"

"Slim to none considering the facts about the stock swap. The HMO is now considered an employer rather than a contractor. I have a corporate lawyer who is an expert in this field, but I have little hope of winning the appeal. This expert will try to convince the jury that the HMO really had no control over medical practice of the clinic physicians. So far, we have only Lawrence's testimony about HMO control of medical practice and yours, of course."

Bailey, "Are there any physicians in the clinic likely to testify against us?"

Blake, "No. They're all afraid of their job security."

Bailey, "Then, the only real damaging potential witness is the Hailey woman. She was there before the HMO came in and can testify to changes in medical care, utilization meetings, specific cases and the tape of Dr. Shepard and Boomer."

Blake, "She must not testify then."

Smith and Shepard nodded ascent.

CHAPTER 67

If this group thought things were bad now, they only had to wait until Sunday morning. Maria's expose started in the upper left-hand corner of the Telegram, consumed another full-page inside Section A complete with pictures of the clinic, Dr. Lawrence, Dr. Shepard, Mr. Blake and all four attorneys.

In the article she recounted the history of the clinic, its sale to the HMO and summary of the Boomer case and testimony so far. She included a summary of her own experiences detailing the difference in treatment and advice between the clinic and the emergency department. She identified Melissa Hailey as the so-called "mystery witness" and mentioned the fact that of the three women murdered by the bedpost rapist, one was Alex Boomer's secretary and two were employees of the clinic. No inference was made as to any possible relationship to the trial, however.

CHAPTER 68

Monday morning Judge Levine called the lawyers into her office before the case resumed.

"I assume you've all read the article in yesterday's Telegram."

Bailey, "Yes, and I move for a mistrial."

Judge, "Anyone else?"

Smith, "I join in that motion."

Sloanberg, "I oppose the motion."

McAllen, "I also oppose the motion."

Judge, "I'm going to meet with the jury and question them as to the impact and then I'll rule."

Jurors one by one all agreed that the article with the exception of Maria's personal experiences was no more than a summary of the testimony they had heard and would not influence their deliberations. They felt her personal experience was just sensational journalism. Based upon these interviews, the judge rejected the motion for a mistrial.

CHAPTER 69

During the recess, while the judge was questioning jurors, Maria received a call on her cell phone from Inspector Ladd.

"I read your article and it touched a nerve. Could we meet sometime today to discuss some parts of it?"

"Sure, when the trial adjourns this afternoon."

"They haven't started with testimony yet. The judge is meeting with the lawyers. I'll call you."

The judge appeared at 11:45 a.m. and indicated the testimony would resume at 1:30 p.m.

CHAPTER 70

The afternoon session was called to order promptly and Judge Levine asked Mr. Smith if he was ready to proceed with his opening statement for the defense of Dr. Shepard.

Smith, "I plan to make no statement at this time. I would like to call Dr. Shepard to the stand."

Judge, "Proceed. Dr. Shepard, you are still under oath."

"Dr. Shepard, please state your qualifications."

Shepard, "I graduated from Harvard Medical School in 1960 and completed a surgical internship and residency at Mass General Hospital. I then opened my offices in West L.A. in association with Dr. Jones in what eventually became the clinic. I am a board certified surgeon and limit my practice to general surgery."

Smith, "You do have a general medical background, do you not?"

"Of course."

"You are familiar with treatment of heart disease?"

"Yes."

"Did you speak to Alex Boomer on the phone approximately six months ago."

"I don't remember."

"There has been testimony that in the absence of Dr. Lawrence you took a call in which he complained of chest pain on exercise relieved by nitroglycerine."

Shepard, "I do not remember that incident as I do not remember telephone calls from other doctors' incidents unless they're calling on an emergency basis."

"If you did receive such a call, would you have considered it an emergency?"

"No, a heart patient with exercise-induced chest pain relieved by nitroglycerine would not seem to be an emergency. Nitroglycerine is a standard drug for angina."

"Would you have notified his doctor or made a notation in the chart?"

"I probably would have notified his doctor, but not made a notation in the chart."

"Would you have felt it necessary to see such a patient immediately?"

"No."

"Would you have ordered a cardiology consult or any special tests?"

"No."

"Why?"

"It's not my place to order tests on another doctor's patients. I would have told him to contact his doctor and make an appointment."

"Is that what you did?"

"I do not remember anything about the incident."

Smith, "Nothing further."

Judge, "Mr. McAllen?"

McAllen, "Your training and experience as a surgeon would not qualify you to take care of a cardiac patient, would it?"

Shepard, "I am a doctor. I went to medical school and I've had occasion to treat cardiacs in my training and practice."

"But you're not conversant with the modern, sophisticated tests for coronary disease and the indications for their use."

Shepard, "I read medical journals and go to post-graduate symposiums where these things are discussed."

"But that is not a part of your everyday practice, is it?"

"No, but..."

"You've answered the question. I'd like to refresh your memory about your conversation with Mr. Boomer. I'd like to play the tape of that conversation."

Smith, "Objection. There's no foundation that the tape actually represents such a conversation."

McAllen, "Surely Dr. Shepard will recognize his own voice."

Judge, "Objection overruled. Play the tape."

"The tape was that of a phone conversation in which Boomer identified himself as a patient of Dr. Lawrence and was calling to report that he had chest pain on exercise which was relieved by nitroglycerine. Dr. Shepard assured him that was good and keep taking nitro as he needed."

McAllen, "Doctor, is that your voice on the tape?"

Shepard, "Yes."

McAllen, "Does that refresh your memory?"

Shepard, "No."

McAllen, "But you did talk to him and gave him advice over the phone with no knowledge of his history, did you not?"

Shepard, "The tapes speaks for itself."

McAllen, "You gave medical advice over the phone to a patient you knew nothing about, who had a disease for which you were not qualified to treat, did you not?"

"Yes, but I am a doctor."

"Yes, you are a doctor but you're no omnipotent. I have nothing further."

Judge, "Mr. Smith, do you have another witness ready?"

"Yes, your Honor. I would like to call Dr. James Finley."

He was duly sworn.

Smith, "Dr. Finley, you are an internist at the clinic, is that correct?"

"Yes."

"Please give us your professional background."

Finley rattled off a litany of college, medical school, hospital training in internal medicine and cardiology and fifteen years of experience in private practice.

Smith, "Having reviewed the chart and depos pertaining to this case, do you believe that Dr. Shepard was negligent in his care of Boomer?"

"No."

"Why is that?"

"He simply gave general advice to the patient of another doctor. The advice was within the community standard of practice in dealing with another doctor's patient over the phone."

"Do you think he should have seen the patient immediately or referred him to a cardiologist?"

"No. There was no apparent emergency and the advice given was correct considering the circumstances."

"Thank you, Doctor."

McAllen, "That advice proved to be wrong, didn't it?"

"Yes, but Dr. Shepard had no way of knowing that at the time."

"Would a few questions concerning his recent medical history have helped clarify the situation?"

"They might of helped."

"Knowing only what you got from that taped conversation, would you have handled the situation differently?"

"No."

"Are you aware of the guidelines of the clinic concerning tests, hospitalizations, consults, etcetera?"

"I'm aware of a utilization committee."

"Is the function of that utilization committee to disapprove expensive medical procedures in order to save money for the clinic and the HMO?"

"The function is the prevent over utilization of medical services."

"Does that process interfere with the way you practice medicine?"

"It's sometimes inconvenient."

"It proved to be very inconvenient for Mr. Boomer, didn't it? I'm finished with this witness."

Court was recessed for the day.

CHAPTER 71

When Maria returned to her office, Inspector Ladd was waiting for her.

Maria, "What can I do for you?"

Ladd, "I read and re-read your article in yesterday's Telegram and it started me thinking. For instance, I had never connected those deaths with the malpractice trial.

Do you have any information you couldn't write about?"

"Not really. It just seemed strange that three supposedly serial killings would have a connection to that clinic and the decedent's wife."

"What do you mean by 'connection' to the Boomer woman?"

"Remember when Sherry was taken to the hospital? It was Mrs. Boomer who found the injured woman in her home. She was also in the waiting room of the hospital and was very upset. Doesn't that seem a little strange?"

"Yes, but Sherry was Boomer's secretary. And the other two were Clinic employees."

"Maybe it means nothing but it seems like the odds would be against it."

"Well, this is just another imponderable, like the two private eyes we've been investigating being at one of the funerals. Keep me informed."

"You too."

CHAPTER 72

With a miserable performance by Dr. Shepard and Dr. Finley, it was up to Mr. Bailey to try to salvage the HMO. He had planned to use Blake, Shepard and Garrison, but McAllen had fired preemptive strikes against all three and he didn't think he could rehabilitate any of them. He would have to depend on his corporate lawyer to convince the judge and jury that the HMO is not responsible legally for the practice of physicians whom it did not control. He might have to dump on the clinic, discreetly, of course.

CHAPTER 73

The next morning Bailey asked to put on his first witness. He called Jackson Warfield, Esq., a corporate attorney.

Bailey, "Mr. Warfield, please state for us your educational and professional qualifications."

Warfield enumerated his educational background which included Harvard undergraduate school, Harvard Law School and a variety of post-graduate courses in corporate and health law. His practice for ten years had been with a large San Francisco firm which specialized in Health Law. Most recently with the advent of managed care, HMO's, PPO's and capitation schemes, he had been the principle attorney of the firm in this segment of health care law. He had been the primary counsel for cases that had led to landmark decisions in the field.

Bailey, "Mr. Warfield, in your professional experience, you have handled many cases in which malpractice was alleged against a managed care provider, have you not?"

Warfield, "Yes, sir."

"You have won all of these cases, have you not?"

"Yes, I have."

"Many of these cases have been appealed. Is that true?"

"Yes."

"So far your clients have prevailed in appellate court?"

"Yes."

"On what basis?"

"On the basis that they were simply contractors and were not responsible for the acts of employees of the contracting facility."

"All of those defendant providers have had contracts with treating facilities which specified that relationship, have they not?"

"Yes."

"Have you examined the contractual relationship between the defendant HMO and the clinic in this case?"

"Yes."

"Does that contract comply with the standards approved by the appellate courts?"

"Yes."

Bailey, "I have nothing further."

Judge, "A cross-exam?"

Sloanberg, "Yes, your Honor. Mr. Warfield, you say you have examined the contract between these two defendants?"

"Yes, sir."

"Have you also been provided with the documents from the Cayman Islands which are exhibits in this case?"

"No, sir."

"How can you testify knowledgeably if you have not seen all the documents?"

"Unless they change the whole concept I have outlined, they're irrelevant."

"Would you please read these documents and tell me if they are irrelevant or if they influence your testimony in any way."

Bailey, "Your Honor, can we have a recess so Mr. Warfield can study these documents both for accuracy and content without the added pressure of continuing to sit in the witness chair?"

Sloanberg, "Your Honor, such a learned legal consultant should be able to read and recognize these contracts for what they are and render an opinion as to their bearing on the impact of his testimony."

Judge, "I think it's reasonable to allow Mr. Warfield to examine these exhibits without the pressure of doing it from the witness stand. Recess of ten minutes granted."

Bailey and Warfield retired to a small room near the court and read the material provided by the court. After the recess they returned and cross-examination resumed.

Sloanberg, "Were you able to study the material in privacy

and evaluate it?"

"Yes, sir. Thank you."

"Do you have an opinion as to whether this material influences your previous testimony?"

"Yes, sir. And it does not."

"And why is that?"

"These legal papers simply indicate a stock-swap between the Clinic and the HMO which does not influence the contractual relationship between those two entities."

Sloanberg, "The fact that the HMO owns forty-nine percent of the Clinic stock does not change your testimony?"

Warfield, "No sir."

Sloanberg, "Why?"

"First of all, this exchange was done in a foreign country and the courts here would not recognize its legality. Secondly, the stock was used in lieu of money and there are no provisions for HMO control of the operation of the Clinic."

Sloanberg, "That is the most creative legal theory I have heard in a long time. In your mind does not stock ownership carry with it control?"

Warfield, "Not always."

Sloanberg, "Why then do we all get voting proxies from companies and mutual funds in which we own even an infinitesmal number of shares?"

Warfield, "I can't answer that."

"I have nothing further."

Judge, "Mr. Bailey, do you have other witnesses?"

Bailey, "No, your Honor."

Judge, "Mr. Sloanberg, do you wish to summarize now?"

"No, your Honor. I have several rebuttal witnesses before summarizing, but I was taken by surprise by the timing and I would ask for a recess until tomorrow."

Judge, "Recess granted, but be prepared in the morning."

CHAPTER 74

It was near the lunch hour when Michael returned to the Clinic. Robin Price, his bodyguard, followed at a reasonable distance. So far there had been no attacks or further threats.

When he got to his office, he found all his appointments had been canceled for the day and he ordered lunch be brought in for him and Melissa. He brought her up to date on the progress of the trial and told her that she needed to be ready to testify by tomorrow afternoon. He had a meeting with his divorce lawyer at 5 p.m. today and following that he was to be prepped by McAllen for his testimony tomorrow afternoon.

CHAPTER 75

Robin excused herself and left Emily Mathis to watch over their clients. She indicated she would return in time to accompany Michael to his 5:00 appointment and cautioned them to stay together until she returned. By 4:30 Robin had not returned and Michael decided to leave without her. He gave Melissa the address and phone number of Willard Barnes, his divorce lawyer and told her he would call before he left to meet with McAllen. He also instructed her to inform Robin of his itinerary. They embraced passionately. Their relationship had regained the love and intimacy which had been temporarily lost and was like new all over again.

CHAPTER 76

When Michael left the office it was almost dark. In November, daylight disappears between 4:30 and 5:00. He felt somewhat uncomfortable without his trusty bodyguard. For several weeks she had been a constant shadow of his every move. In the parking garage he looked around carefully before approaching his car. Seeing no one, he hurriedly unlocked his car, checked the backseat for intruders, got in and relocked the doors. He drove out alert to every car leaving the garage. Seeing nothing suspicious, he made the short drive to the office building on Wilshire, drove into the garage and again observed the area for anyone who might have followed him. Seeing nothing, he hurried to the elevator and took it to the thirteenth floor suite of Willard Barnes.

He was ushered into the offices promptly and offered coffee by a pretty secretary who assured him Mr. Barnes would be with him momentarily. Barnes had been recommended to him by McAllen as the best divorce attorney in L.A. His client list was like a Who's Who of Hollywood. In fact, many familiar faces graced the walls of his office somewhat like the trendy watering holes of L.A. Michael was unimpressed by this garish display of client appreciation. All he wanted was an attorney who could get him out of his domestic disaster as quickly and cheaply as possible.

Barnes made his entrance shortly. He was a small, balding man in his late fifties, without any of the sex appeal one might expect from someone who dealt routinely with the most famous and beautiful women in the world. He was pleasant but intense and matter of fact.

"Dennis has briefly told us about your problems, both legal and domestic. Why don't you fill in the details? Please be completely frank and honest with me. I represent you, and I am in no way judgmental."

Michael, "It's a long and complex story which I'm sure is quite similar to those you hear daily." Michael told him about Melissa, how the affair began, ended and began again. How his wife caught him, her pregnancy and the relationship of all this to his malpractice case. Barnes listened patiently, if not sympathetically.'

"Your wife wants half of everything, child support and a hefty alimony plus her legal fees. Of course, she expects full custody of your son."

"I'm willing to do all that. The only problem is that I may not have an income after the trial. I certainly don't want to run up legal expenses fighting over a bare bone."

"We'll have to talk to your accountant to assess your present and potential financial situation. The problem is that she is demanding a settlement based on your present income without taking into consideration the results of your legal and employment situation. She is very vindictive, and her attorney is famous for exploiting his clients emotions."

The secretary at that point knocked and entered the room. "Pardon me for intruding, but there is an emergency call for Dr. Lawrence." She ushered him to a private office to take the call.

CHAPTER 77

"Michael, I think someone followed me home and neither Robin or Emily is here. I'm frightened and I think someone is trying to get in. Please come home now."

"I'll be there in ten minutes. Get out your gun and call 911. Don't go near a door or a window."

"Please hurry."

Michael left the office, only explaining that there was an emergency at home. As he walked through the waiting room, he expected to see Robin but she wasn't there. On entering the parking garage, he looked for her car but did not see it. He ran to his car, unlocked it, got in and felt in the glove compartment for his gun. He stuck it in his belt and hurried out of the garage. After his testimony, someone must have figured that they were ignoring the warnings and Melissa was going to be the next witness. Remembering Sam Jones, he was frightened. He only hoped that police or bodyguards were there before he got home. But he steeled himself in case that didn't happen. He drove with abandon but the late afternoon traffic was horrendous.

CHAPTER 78

Melissa beeped the bodyguards but there was no response. She retreated to her bedroom, bolted the door, opened the bedside table drawer looking for her pistol. It wasn't there. She had checked this morning and it was in it's place at that time. What could have happened to it? She called 911 and told them the nature of her emergency. They tried to keep her on the phone, but she hung up when she heard the glass break. She heard heavy footsteps in the hall.

She had locked the door. Suddenly she saw the knob turn but the door did not open because of the dead bolt she had had installed. A man's voice swearing. "I know you are in there and this door is not going to keep me out, bitch." She thought she recognized the voice but was too terrified to place it at this moment. It was a man's voice, deep and threatening. She had heard it before, but where? He started banging on the door, but it was sturdy and did not give. He kicked at the knob area but it still held fast.

The pounding stopped momentarily. Melissa was terrified. The phone rang but she was afraid to answer it. She did not want him to know she had called for help.

The pounding on the door started again and intensified. The sound was different. He was using an instrument of some sort. The wood began to splinter. She knew she only had a few more minutes before the door would no longer offer her any protection.

Her only weapon was time, time to give the police or Michael a chance to save her. When the door gave way, what could she do to stall him and delay the inevitable? She must remain calm and in control of her senses. Suddenly she recognized the voice. It was that of the man who had come to the clinic and threatened Michael.

That horrible beast of a man who frightened Michael half out of his mind. The thug who the police said was a brutal hit man.

The door splintered and she was confronted with a big, powerful, ugly man dressed in blue jeans, a pullover sweater and a black stocking cap. He was holding a club larger than the batons carried by the cops. He had used it to splinter the door. There was a large knife in his belt.

She remembered reading about Buffy and Billy Sue. How frightened they must have been. Would she meet the same fate? Was this the same man?

His face was drenched with sweat and beet red with rage.

He swore and said, "I warned your boyfriend and told him to pass it along to you, but you both ignored it."

"What did you warn him about?"

"Didn't he tell you?"

"No."

"Neither of you were to testify against my employer."

Maybe she could stall him.

"Who is your employer?"

"Some lawyer. I'm not going to play 'Twenty Questions" with you. I come to silence you permanently and have some fun first."

"Like those other women? What did they do to you?"

"What makes you think I did them?"

"Did you?"

She was petrified but she knew she would live only as long as she could keep him talking.

"Yeah, it was me."

"Why?"

"I was hired to do them just like I was hired to do you, but I think I'm going to enjoy you more. I knew I had to have you when I saw you at the clinic. The others were not in the same class—one was queer, another was black and the third was pregnant. When they were begging, the first one told me sex with a man was repulsive to her and the last one begged me not to hurt her baby.

"Enough small talk, take off your clothes."

He removed his sweater and jeans. His arousal was obvious.

She almost wished he would go ahead and kill her. The torture and rape would be a terrible ordeal to end her life with. But she still had hope. If she could only maintain her composure and stall him until help arrived, even if she had to endure his brutalizing her.

He was getting impatient now.

"Take off your clothes, or I'll rip them off."

She knew that the end was near. She could only stall him by removing her clothes slowly and seductively. Maybe she could prolong the agony a few more minutes.

She still had her uniform on. It was nylon and clung to every curve. She slowly unbuttoned it and stepped out of it leaving her covered by a white form-fitting slip with lace at the top and bottom.

"Take the rest off. I'm getting impatient." He was obviously very excited. It was almost as if he thought this was a seduction.

She pulled the slip over her head revealing her transparent bra, bikini panties and pantyhose.

"Take the rest off now."

She had run out of time.

He took off his shorts, picked her up, threw her on the bed and mounted her. She screamed and struggled but to no avail. He was too powerful.

At that moment, Michael appeared in the door with a gun drawn.

"Stop and get off her or I'll blow you away."

Jones raised his knife. "Drop the gun or I'll kill her now." Michael fired. Jones brought the knife down reflexively as he was knocked off the bed by the impact of the bullet. He was moaning like a wounded animal. Melissa screamed with pain. Her chest was instantly covered with blood but she was still conscious. The police and paramedics burst in and told Michael to drop the gun, which he did. The cop handcuffed him. Michael said, "You idiot, I just shot that s.o.b. who stabbed my girl."

Melissa saw what was happening and confirmed Michael's story. Jones was on the floor doubled over in pain and swearing at nobody in particular. The cop asked Melissa what had happened. She explained that Jones was going to rape and kill her as he had the other three women, that he was the "bedpost rapist."

She was barely conscious. The paramedics started an I.V. and oxygen. They called for a back-up unit for the gunshot victim. They called Southwest E.R. and explained what they had. Melissa had a stab wound in the left-upper chest and a blood pressure of one hundred over forty. The other unit arrived momentarily, started an I.V. and oxygen on Jones after assessing his injuries. He had been shot in the left side just below his ribs and there was no exit wound. He was in shock with a blood pressure of fifty over zero and a thready rapid pulse. Both patients were taken stat to the Emergency Department for care by the trauma team. Two policemen rode in the ambulance with Jones who was handcuffed to the gurneys. Michael rode with Melissa.

CHAPTER 79

On arrival at the E.D., both units were met by Dr. Evans and the trauma surgeon, Dr. Patricia Blakenship. Evans followed Melissa into the trauma room, quickly assessed her, and ordered trauma lab, stat chest x-ray, and six units of uncrossed O negative blood. He told his nurse to contact the chest surgeon stat. Dr. Lawrence had followed her into the trauma room and was watching helplessly. Evans noticed him and recognized him from the trial.

"Is Ms. Hailey your nurse?"

"Yes, how is she?"

"She has a chest full of blood and is in shock. I'm getting blood for her and am going to insert a chest tube right now. A chest surgeon is on his way to take her to surgery."

Melissa was conscious and heard the conversation. "Am I going to die?"

"No, but you are going to have surgery to repair whatever damage has been done inside your chest."

"Michael, I love you. Stay with me."

"I love you. I'll be with you all the way."

Dr. John Jackson arrived. He examined Melissa and explained what he was going to do. The chest tube had drained two liters of blood which was saved for possible auto transfusion. She was taken to the operating room then.

CHAPTER 80

Evans now joined Blakenship in the other trauma room. After two units of type specific uncross matched blood, Jones was now conscious. Blakenship was examining the abdominal x-rays when Evans walked in. Bullet fragments were scattered in a horizontal pattern across the upper abdominal cavity from the entrance on the left side to an area near the right side, probably in the liver. She said this bullet is some type of fragmenting missile, which has probably traversed his left kidney, spleen, colon, stomach and the left lobe of his liver. His abdomen is distended and tender. He is in severe pain and deep shock.

"Is he salvageable surgically?"

"I doubt it. I'm not sure we can even get him to the O.R. alive."

CHAPTER 81

The officers at the scene had notified homicide on their way to the hospital and Inspectors Holmes and Ladd had responded. They overheard this conversation and asked the doctors if they felt it was reasonable to try to get a death-bed statement from the patient.

Evans, "What's the point? He was shot by Dr. Lawrence protecting his lover."

Ladd, "He made statements to the girl implicating himself in the bedpost murders, indicating that he was hired to commit those crimes and also to kill Ms. Hailey. We want to know who hired him."

Evans and Blakenship looked at each other, conferred briefly and then asked the detectives what they could do.

"Just tell him he's dying and we'll do the rest."

Evans, "That's pretty cold."

Ladd, "If you knew what this s.o.b. did to those women and to a small-time hoodlum, you wouldn't think twice."

Ladd had recognized Jones.

Evans, "All right, I'll do it." He approached the gurney and looked down at the patient who was conscious. His skin was pale and moist. His blood pressure was sixty over zero, with two units of blood running in each arm, wide open. Surgery would not save this man. "Mr. Jones, these detectives want to ask you some questions. I must inform you that you're going to die. We cannot save you."

Jones, "I'll talk to them."

Ladd, "You have been informed that you are going to die. Are you willing to make a deathbed statement about killing those women and who hired you to do it?"

Jones, "Hell, yes. I was hired to kill those three women by two private investigators named Ralph Nichols and Andrew Kurtz to keep them from testifying in some trial. Nichols contacted me and he and I met with Kurtz and some lawyer who did not introduce himself. They paid me $50,000 for each and I was to rape them, tear up their homes and make it look like some sort of serial sex fiend. I was to get $100,000 for the nurse."

Ladd, "You make this statement of your free will in front of these witnesses with a certain knowledge that you're going to die?"

"Yes, I have nothing else to lose."

The two arresting officers, Holmes and Ladd, the two doctors and two nurses witnessed the statement.

Evans to Blakenship, "I thought I had seen everything, but this is new. Are you going to take him to surgery?"

"I don't think he can survive the trip. Just keep up the fluids and give him narcotics if necessary."

Ladd to arresting officers, "Stay here and finish your paperwork and be sure our perp does not get up and walk out. Stay until the coroner has done his thing."

Ladd to Holmes, "We need to go find two very shady private eyes and tie this case up in a blue ribbon."

CHAPTER 82

In the O.R., Dr. Jackson on opening Melissa's chest, found it filled with blood again. The branch of the pulmonary artery and vein to the left upper lobe of the lung had been severed as well as a large irregular laceration of the lung tissue itself. Because of the condition of the patient, it was decided to simply resect the left upper lobe rather than to make an attempt to repair the vessels and the lung tissue. This was done quickly, the bleeding controlled, the blood volume replaced by transfusion and the patient was returned to SICU in stable condition. Dr. Jackson explained his findings and the surgical procedure to Michael and assured him that Melissa should recover completely with no residual.

CHAPTER 83

Maria Rodriguez had heard the call on her police scanner and she hurried to the hospital unaware of the people involved and the relationship to her expose. On arrival she saw Ladd and Holmes in the E.D. police room.

Ladd, "You certainly can add to your Times story tonight. The cast of characters from the trial are here. Your possible mystery witness is in the O.R. undergoing surgery for a stab wound. The hit man who stabbed her is dying in the Emergency Department from a gunshot wound inflicted by Dr. Lawrence. And Dr. Evans has been taking care of all of them. In addition, the hit man is a professional from Detroit, who was hired by someone to kill those three women last summer. He just made a deathbed confession. He was also hired to kill Melissa Hailey, but Dr. Lawrence walked in on the assault in progress and shot him. Apparently both the Doctor and Ms. Hailey have been living under a threat of death for some months. We don't have the whole story yet. The doctor is a basket case with all that has happened to him, and we have gotten all we're going to get from the perp. He died a few minutes ago. We're going to arrest the private investigators who hired him. Then, perhaps, we can get the rest of the story. Please keep all this confidential until we have made the arrests. The rest of the media is unaware of all that I've told you."

Maria, "Can I go with you?"

Ladd, "No it's too dangerous and it might take some time to find them. I'll call you when we have them in custody and you'll get an exclusive on the story."

CHAPTER 84

After he had looked in on Melissa, Michael decided he should call McAllen. It was now after midnight and a very sleepy and grumpy voice answered.

Michael, "Melissa is in the hospital. She was assaulted and stabbed earlier tonight and I shot the assailant and he is dead."

With that, McAllen was wide awake and asking all the details. Michael filled him in as best he could.

McAllen, "Are you in custody for the shooting?"

"No, the cops walked in just after I fired and handcuffed me. Melissa was still conscious and told them I had saved her life. They removed the cuffs and have said nothing further to me. They are too interested in what Jones told them to bother with me."

McAllen, "Tell me the rest of it. What did he say?"

"I can't now. I'm too upset. I just saw my lover being assaulted and killed a man."

"I'll be right down as soon as I can get there. Don't leave."

CHAPTER 85

Before leaving for the hospital, McAllen called Sloanberg to appraise him of the dramatic events. He was instantly alert and astounded.

McAllen, "I thought your trial schedule might be affected."

Sloanberg, "Of course it will be. Melissa was to be my next witness. I'll have to petition for a recess until all this is sorted out."

"What about the impact of the other murders?"

"If one of the defendant organizations is responsible for hiring Jones, that will just about cook their goose. I'll be right down to find out the rest of the story."

CHAPTER 86

Inspector Holmes and Ladd called Steven Dunback at his home and gave him a very skimpy review of the facts including Jones death and his contracts by Nichols and Kurtz. They needed the help of his men to find and arrest the two private investigators. Ladd was to take three officers to arrest Nichols, and Holmes was to be accompanied by three members of the force to arrest Kurtz. Dunback wanted to be a part of this operation and agreed to go with Holmes.

Nichols lived in a small apartment in Inglewood near LAX. They needed five officers to deploy themselves in such a manner that escape would be impossible. Since Nichols was unaware that he was wanted, Ladd expected no resistance and no attempt for the suspect to flee. Despite the fact that it was now 2 a.m., Ladd knocked on the front door and identified himself. Nichols came to the door and asked what he wanted. He was read his rights, cuffed and taken to the station without incident.

Kurtz had a home in Santa Monica. His arrest was planned and executed in a similar manner, again without incident. He was booked in the same station but without the knowledge of Nichols. They were held in separate areas of the jail and so far were unaware of the reason for their arrest other than for questioning. Being streetwise, each demanded an attorney before questioning.

CHAPTER 87

Ladd and Holmes returned to the hospital hoping to question Melissa and Dr. Lawrence. Melissa was still in ICU and under sedation, but Michael was still at the hospital and agreed to talk to the officers.

Ladd, "Melissa indicated that both of you had been threatened by Sam Jones, is that true?"

Michael, "Yes. He came to the clinic several weeks ago and threatened me not to testify in the malpractice trial. He also, indirectly, threatened Melissa. We told my attorney and he provided two bodyguards. We have lived in fear since then and have been very isolated."

"By-the-way, where are the bodyguards?"

"They were supposed to have been with us before this all happened."

"Who are they?"

"Robin Price and Emily Mathis."

"I have not seen either of them at the hospital or the station. I'll find them if you give me the name of the agency."

"Jack Burge's Agency."

"How did you happen to arrive just in time?"

"Melissa called me and told me she was followed home and she thought someone was trying to get into the condo. I told her to call 911 and beep the bodyguards and that I would be there as soon as possible. Traffic was terrible but I still made it in record time. Apparently Jones had to brag about his other hits and also spent some time enjoying his anticipated pleasure. That gave me time to get there before he killed her. When I reached the condo I noticed the glass in the door was shattered and the door was ajar.

When I entered, I heard the voice I will never forget and knew immediately what was happening. I went quickly to the bedroom and saw him. Both he and Melissa were naked. He was astride her and holding a large knife. I told him to put the knife down and get off her or I'd shoot him. I had bought the gun when we were threatened and kept it with me at all times. He said if I didn't put the gun down, he'd kill her right now. I shot him. He groaned and fell off the bed but reflexively stabbed Melissa in the left upper chest. Just at that time the police arrived and told me to drop the gun, which I did. They handcuffed me, but Melissa screamed at them that I had saved her life and I lived there with her. They freed me and I started trying to help Melissa. The paramedics arrived and commenced treatment on Melissa. They called for another unit to take care of Jones who was on the floor barely conscious. He had made no further attempt at resistance after he was shot."

Ladd, "That statement should clear you of any charges in the shooting. Incidentally, Jones is dead and he made a dying statement that he was hired to kill Melissa to keep her off the witness stand. You will have to come to the station tomorrow and give a formal statement of what you just told me."

CHAPTER 88

Sloanberg and McAllen had arrived just as Michael started his account of the happenings.

McAllen, "Where were Robin and Emily?"

Michael, "I haven't seen either of them since before our meeting at your office."

McAllen, "I'll call Jack Burge. In the meantime, Inspector can we keep a lid on this? It will prejudice the trial."

Ladd, "Obviously the media is going to be aware of the injury to Ms. Hailey and the death of Jones at the hands of the doctor."

Sloanberg, "I understand that, but can we leave out the reference to the other murders and the attempted intimidation of Melissa? Can we not treat this as a home invasion and attempted rape in which the doctor happened in and saved Melissa's life?"

"Yes, that's a good story. We can hold the details about the other murders and their relationship to the trial temporarily. In fact, that will help us, too. We have the persons who hired Jones in custody now and we want to find out who ordered those murders."

It had been a long night and the detectives left to try to get a little sleep before they started the interrogation of Nichols and Kurtz.

CHAPTER 89

Sloanberg, McAllen and Michael retired to the cafeteria to plan their strategy for their day in court.

Sloanberg, "We must petition for a recess until this mess is all straightened out. Do you have any objections?"

Michael, "I certainly need the time to get over the emotional trauma of seeing Melissa attacked and killing her assailant."

McAllen, "If we can get enough facts and find that one of the other parties to the suit is responsible for all of this mayhem, it would certainly help the doctors cause."

Sloanberg, "It's agreed then that you and I will go to the judge this morning and request a recess based upon Melissa's injury and the resulting emotional state of the doctor. I don't think we should tell her anything except the home invasion theory at this time. I do not want to tip our opponents that we are aware of their relationship to the other crimes and the real reason for the attack on Melissa.

CHAPTER 90

It was now 7:00 a.m and McAllen decided to call Jack Burge about Robin and Emily. He had always found Burge and his people reliable. Jack was already in his office when the call came in.

McAllen, "What happened to the bodyguards that I hired?"

Burge, "I have no idea. What are you talking about?"

McAllen, "Neither one of them has been seen by my clients in forty-eight hours and it almost cost Ms. Hailey her life."

Burge, "I'll find out and get back to you."

Jack called each of their homes without an answer. He then checked with the clinic and asked for them by their assumed names. They were not there. Finally, he called their rented condos in Melissa's building without any response. He then called on their cell phones and their beeper but there was no response. Having no further thoughts as to their location, he reported them to missing persons. He was concerned for their welfare.

CHAPTER 91

At 9:00 a.m, Sloanberg and McAllen arrived at the court and told the bailiff that they needed to speak with Judge Levine.

The attack and shooting had made the early morning news shows and the Judge was aware of the happenings.

Sloanberg, "Good morning, your Honor. I assume you have seen the television accounts of the attack on Melissa Hailey and Dr. Lawrence's heroics."

"Yes, I presume you want a recess until the dust settles."

Sloanberg, "Yes, your Honor. Ms. Hailey was to be my next witness and her testimony is vital to expose the negligence of the clinic and the HMO."

Judge, "Mr. McAllen?"

McAllen, "I agree, your Honor. She is vital to the defense of Dr. Lawrence."

Judge, "I understand she was seriously injured and underwent surgery. How long do you think it will be before she would be able to testify?"

McAllen, "I have no idea—probably a matter of weeks."

Judge, "We can't hold up the trial more than a few days. You will have to make your case without her. I'll give you up to a week but you must report in daily and as soon as you can resume, I'll expect you to do so."

Sloanberg, "Without Ms. Hailey, it will be difficult, but I'll try to make alternate plans."

Judge, "Bailiff, summon the defense attorneys so I can inform them of the recess."

Needless-to-say, both defense attorneys were upset about the recess but somewhat relieved that Melissa would be unable to testify. Their protests were mild, but fell on deaf ears. The recess would occur.

CHAPTER 92

Holmes and Ladd arrived at the station about 9:00 a.m. somewhat refreshed.

They planned to interrogate Nichols first since he seemed the most vulnerable to pressure. His lawyer was William Needham, a well-known criminal defense attorney. A court reporter was present to take his statement. While Nichols had been read his rights when arrested, that litany was repeated for the benefit of the attorney.

Nichols, "Why am I here? What have I done?"

Ladd, "All that in due time. Do you know a syndicate hitman by the name of Sam Jones?"

Nichols, "Of course not. I don't deal with those types any more. I am a legitimate private investigator."

Holmes, "Mr. Jones says he knows you.

Nichols, "Maybe I met him in prison but I don't remember."

Ladd, "Mr. Jones says you engaged his services."

Nichols, "What would I hire somebody like that for?"

Holmes, "To kill four people."

Nichols, "That's ..."

Needham, "Don't answer that."

Ladd, "Mr. Needham, we have a death bed confession of the murders of four people from Mr. Jones in which he names your client as the person who hired him."

Nichols, "I didn't hire him for anything."

Holmes, "Mr. Needham, perhaps it would speed things up if you explained to your client the legal ramifications of a deathbed statement and conspiracy to commit murder."

Needham, "May I have a few moments with Mr. Nichols?"

Ladd, "Of course."

Ladd and Holmes left the room.

Needham, "Do you know what they're talking about?"

Nichols, "I'm afraid so."

Needham, "Were you just a go-between?"

Nichols, "Yes."

Needham, "They're obviously more interested in the person who hired you then they are in you. The so called "deathbed confession" has the same standing as a witness in court. Conspiracy to commit murder is punishable just the same as if you had pulled the trigger. Do you want to try to deal?"

Nichols, "I'm scared. I think this is syndicate business."

Needham, "It all depends on who you're the most scared of."

Nichols, "Let's see what they offer."

Ladd and Holmes were summoned back to the interrogation room.

Needham, "My client would like to cooperate, if you can make it worth his while."

Ladd, "I think if your client would identify and testify against the person who hired him, the D.A. could be persuaded not to seek the death penalty."

Needham, "That's not enough. A jury probably wouldn't give death anyhow."

Ladd, "We'll have to speak with the D.A. before we could go any further. In the meantime, Mr. Nichols will be charged with conspiracy to commit murder, jailed and a search warrant issued for his home, car, office, bank accounts, etcetera."

With that the questioning was suspended and Nichols was returned to his private cell.

CHAPTER 93

Kurtz was taken to a separate area for questioning. His attorney was George Heinrick, a less well-known criminal attorney whose practice was made up primarily of immigrants, both legal and illegal whose legal problems frequently involved international law.

Ladd, "Mr. Kurtz, you are charged with suspicion of conspiracy to commit murder."

Heinrick, "That is ridiculous. Mr. Kurtz is a respectable private investigator whose clients are among some of the most prominent citizens of this community."

Holmes, "We have a statement implicating your client in a murder-for-hire scheme that has cost three innocent people their lives."

Heinrick, "A statement by whom?"

Ladd, "A statement by the individual hired to commit those murders."

Kurtz, "That's preposterous. I do not deal with those kind of people."

Holmes, "Does the name Sam Jones mean anything to you?"

Kurtz blanched slightly and denied knowing such a person. He and Nichols had been in solitary cells since early morning and had not seen the television coverage of the shooting of Jones. So he had no reason to expect a statement by him.

Ladd, "Mr. Jones was shot this morning during an attempted assault. Before he died, he made a statement concerning three murders that he claimed you hired him to do. Mr. Heinrick, perhaps you had better refresh your client's memory of the laws concerning deathbed confessions and conspiracy to commit murder. Should we leave while you do that?"

Heinrick, "Yes."

After the officers left the room, Heinrick asked Kurtz if he knew what they were talking about. Kurtz admitted that he did, but insisted he just introduced one of his clients to another private investigator who arranged for the hitman.

Heinrick, "Did you know what your client wanted to accomplish?"

"Yes."

"You're guilty of conspiracy to commit murder then."

"What about the statement?"

"It has the same standing in court as a live witness to the crime."

"What can I do?"

"They want the person who commissioned those murders. You need to try to deal."

"All right. Let's see what you can do."

Ladd and Holmes were invited back in.

"Mr. Kurtz does have some vague knowledge of the matters you mentioned and he would be willing to cooperate if you make it worthwhile."

Ladd, "I'm sure the D.A. could be talked out of seeking the death penalty."

Heinrick, "His knowledge of this incident is so remote that your D.A. certainly wouldn't seek a murder conviction."

Holmes, "Cut the b.s. We know what happened. There were three murders bought and paid for by your client with your knowledge."

Ladd, "Perhaps the D.A. might settle for a deportation."

That did it. No way did Kurtz want to be sent back to Germany where the justice system was far more swift and severe and where he would face charges that could keep him in prison for the rest of his life.

Kurtz, "I'll tell all of it."

Heinrick, "Are you sure?"

Kurtz, "Yes, get the reporter in here."

Ladd summoned Marilyn Horn to record his statement. Kurtz was duly sworn, identified himself, his address and business and began his statement.

"In late spring I was contacted by John Bailey, a lawyer for an HMO. He was involved in a lawsuit against his client for malpractice. He wanted three witnesses intimidated or silenced, if necessary. I had no such contacts so I called Ralph Nichols for help. He in turn contacted Sam Jones and the three of us met to work out the details. It was decided that the only way to keep these people off the stand was to execute them. Jones was a sadist and he relished his work. He suggested that the murders should be made to look like a psycho serial killings. It was agreed to pay him $50,000 for each person. Nichols was to be the contact person with Jones and to make the payments. Nichols and I were to receive $100,000 each for making the arrangements. That's about it."

Ladd, "Why did you and Nichols go to the funerals?"

Kurtz, "Morbid curiosity."

Ladd, "That was your second mistake. The first was agreeing to this scheme. Was Bailey the person you met with in Pomona?"

Kurtz, "Yes."

Ladd, "What was the purpose of that meeting?"

Kurtz, "To get paid."

Ladd, "That does it. You will be expected to testify in the trial of Nichols and Bailey. Agreed?"

Kurtz, "What happens now?"

Ladd, "You will be held, probably without bail and search warrants will be issued for your home, office and bank accounts. We will advise the D.A. of your cooperation and recommend that he take that into consideration."

CHAPTER 94

With that Ladd and Holmes decided to go back to Nichols with the information just obtained and see if there was anything further to be learned. Fortunately, Nichols lawyer was still present in the interrogation room.

Ladd, "Nichols, your co-conspirator just rolled over on you. He confirmed the statement of Jones and said he only put his client in touch with you and that you and Jones plotted to kill those witnesses. Does that jog your memory?"

Nichols, "That son-of-a-bitch!"

Needham, "What is on the table now if Mr. Nichols can help you?"

Ladd, "Nothing. You missed that train an hour ago."

Nichols, "Kurtz did contact me to find someone to deal with those witnesses. He is the one who had the client with the money to pay for this mission. The three of us were equally involved."

Ladd, "Will you sign a statement to that effect and testify."

Nichols, "Only if I have some consideration from the D.A. and protection."

Holmes, "Protection from whom?"

Nichols, "The syndicate. The lawyer indicated that he represented them and Jones was on their payroll."

Holmes, "How can that be? Jones, yes, but an HMO lawyer?"

Nichols, "I don't know. I'm just telling you what I was told."

Ladd, "Were any of the other lawyers in on this?"

Nichols, "Not that I know of."

CHAPTER 95

Sloanberg returned to his office to ponder his next move. Without Melissa his case was somewhat shaky. He needed to be able to use the information Jones statement supplied, but there was no way he could get that in unless the two private investigators had confirmed a conspiracy to tamper with witnesses.

He called Inspector Ladd and inquired as to his arrest and interviews of the private investigators. He was informed that they both had been arrested and had confirmed Jones statement. He made an appointment to meet with them today to discuss the details.

On arrival at the station, he was ushered into the CID offices where he met with both Ladd and Holmes. He was advised the information was confidential as neither man had been indicted yet. He agreed and was given a detailed summary of the statements by Jones, Nichols and Kurtz. Bailey's involvement came as a surprise to Sloanberg. The reference to the syndicate also seemed incredible.

It was obvious that neither of the suspects could be used as witnesses. They wouldn't agree. They would not be credible anyhow. Would Ladd or Holmes testify? Possibly if their prisoners were indicted. What about John Bailey? Was he going to be arrested now? Yes. There was enough evidence to bring him in for questioning at least. How would that influence the trial? What role did the syndicate play in this drama?

His conference with the detectives had posed more questions than it answered concerning the further conduct of the trial. After Bailey's arrest the Judge would have to be made privy to all of this information.

CHAPTER 96

He thanked the detectives, returned to his office and asked McAllen to meet with him. Sloanberg briefed McAllen who suggested that he approach his broker to investigate ownership of the HMO. It was a publicly owned corporation and he should be able to ferret out the identity of the stockholders. They decided to await Bailey's arrest before approaching the Judge. A new attorney would have to take over the defense for the HMO.

Ladd and Holmes wasted no time in arresting John Bailey. He was taken into custody that afternoon and was charged with conspiracy to commit murder, four counts. He was held without bail.

Questioning was begun shortly after he was booked. His protests were loud and frequent until he was told of the evidence against him. He found it incredible that Nichols and Kurtz had implicated him.

Ladd, "Do you want an attorney present?"

Bailey, "No. I'll act as my own attorney."

Holmes, "You're accused of conspiring with three individuals to commit murder. How do you respond?"

Bailey, "That is preposterous."

Ladd, "We have sworn statements of two private investigators that you hired them to find a hitman and participated in the planning of three murders. They indicated that you met with them and the hitman on two occasions for that explicit purpose. One of those meetings was also observed by an uninvolved witness."

Bailey, "Who is that?"

Holmes, "That will come out in the trial. You know the penalty for conspiracy to commit murder. Would you like to spread the blame?"

Bailey, "What's in it for me?"

Ladd, "If the information leads to the ultimate guilty party, we'll inform the D.A. of the value of your cooperation."

Realizing he was trapped, Bailey decided that he had nothing to gain by his silence and a lot more to lose. Bailey decided to talk.

"This whole plan was devised by William Blake, the CEO of the HMO. He was making an exorbitant amount of money from building the HMO and the various leverage buy-outs of clinics, hospitals, PPO's, and smaller HMO's so he could not allow the medical reputation and the method of doing business of the HMO to suffer from losing a malpractice suit. In addition, if the principle of lack of responsibility for the medical acts of physician employees was compromised by the loss of this very notorious suit, HMO's in general might be destroyed.

"The three witnesses targeted would be devistating to the defense of the clinic and the HMO. The nurse would have been the coop de gras because she saw the changes in medical practices from before the HMO took over to the present type of medical practice. She also was a witness to Dr. Shepard's cavalier handling of the patient and, as a result his threat to fire her unless she kept it to herself. Finally, in desperation, Jones was sent to the office to intimidate Dr. Lawrence and Ms. Hailey."

He hesitated, but with each word he saw his career and life going down the toilet. He was covered with perspiration and tears were flowing down his cheeks as he added the final devistating sentence. "My assignment from Blake was to facilitate all this cover-up."

Ladd, "Is your assistant attorney in this trial aware of all this?"

Bailey, "None of it."

Ladd, "Incredible."

Ladd and Holmes pondered what to tell the media and when to tell them. They knew Bailey's office would be screaming to the media about his arrest. The judge and the other attorneys would be frothing at the mouth about the turn of events. Ladd remembered his promise to Maria and planned to keep it. He also was concerned about the outcome of the trial which started all this. He decided to brief Maria and then meet with the attorneys to provide the information to them before conducting a media conference.

CHAPTER 97

After six months of no progress, the multiple murder case had been solved in less than twenty-four hours partially due to good police work and partially to luck. It was almost inconceivable that a medical malpractice case could have been responsible for so much havoc. This was more like a syndicate-inspired solution to a criminal trial than corporate tampering with a civil case. Three innocent people and their killer were dead. Another intended victim was recovering from chest surgery. A lawyer and two private investigators were in custody and the CEO of a large HMO was wanted for questioning.

It was time to inform the lawyers of the new evidence in the investigation as it would have a major impact on the remainder of the lawsuit. Even though no one had implicated Attorney Smith, Ladd decided to leave the decision about including him in the conference to the other attorneys for the present time.

Ladd notified Sloanberg and McAllen that he had initial information and made an appointment to brief them on the new developments. They met late in the afternoon and were given the results of the interrogations as well as John Bailey's admission of guilt and his implication of William Blake.

The attorneys were left amazed and to ponder their next move.

Ladd and Holmes day was far from done. They had to arrest and interrogate William Blake. They could only hope that he had not gotten wind of the day's happening and fled. The only source would be Bailey's office. His arrest would make bells go off along with the attack on Melissa and the death of Sam Jones.

On arrival at the HMO offices, the detectives were informed

that Mr. Blake was on an out-of-town business trip. They were given no more information. Apparently his departure had been sudden and unexpected and he left no instructions as to how he might be contacted. They inquired if his family might know his whereabouts and were informed that he had no family.

Ladd, "It sounds like Mr. Blake got the message and decided to run. We'll have to put out an A.P.B. It's probably too late to catch him at the airport, but we should try anyhow."

Holmes, "This appears to be a virtual admission of guilt."

As luck would have it, Blake's plane was late in departing and he was apprehended at the boarding gate of a Delta flight to Miami. Needless-to-say, he had a ticket for a continuation of his flight to the Cayman Islands. He also had bank documents which would give him access to the HMO account and bank vault. He was arrested and taken to the station for questioning.

While he was being booked, Ladd contacted Maria and summoned her to his office for a briefing of all that had happened since he last saw her at the hospital.

CHAPTER 98

Maria arrived at the police station late in the afternoon. Inspector Ladd ushered her into his office immediately and briefed her on the arrests of Nichols and Kurtz and their statements and their implication of Bailey and Blake, their arrests and Bailey's confession and accusation of Blake.

Maria, "Can I print all that?"

Ladd, "As far as I'm concerned, you can. We have not questioned Blake yet and I doubt if he'll be forthcoming as his partners in crime. He obviously was headed for the Cayman Bank where a large amount of cash was accessible to him and then to disappear. I would suggest you talk to the lawyers before you print this."

Maria called Sloanberg and made arrangements to meet with him. She went directly from the station to the lawyers office.

Maria, "We have not met, but I'm sure you've read my article Sunday."

Sloanberg, "Yes I did. What can I do for you?"

Maria, "Inspector Ladd just briefed me on the arrest of the two investigators, the defense attorney, and Mr. Blake. I understand you have been given the same information."

"Yes I have, but I was unaware that Blake had been arrested."

Maria, "I obviously want to break this story as soon as possible, but I do not wish to interfere with the trial. I have been working this story since the very beginning and really want to see the HMO destroyed. And so, how can I write this story without causing a mistrial?"

"If you can hold off until mid-morning, I can meet with the judge and ask her to sequester the jury."

"Will the inspector defer a general press briefing until you've had a chance to scoop the rest of the media?"

"I think he will. Not only did he promise me an exclusive, he wants to question Blake before any general press releases."

"All right, I'll meet with the judge and the other lawyers first thing in the morning and make a motion for her to sequester the jury."

CHAPTER 99

Maria hurried to her office and caught Tim Dougherty just as he was leaving.

"Have I got a story for you!"

"At this hour of the day, it better be good."

She detailed everything she had learned from the assault on Melissa, the shooting of Sam Jones and his deathbed statement; to the arrest of the two private investigators, the attorney and their revelations about the planning and commission of the murders and finally the arrest of the CEO for conspiracy and solicitation to commit murder.

Dougherty, "You have been a busy girl. Your hunches and tenacity have paid off. Write your story and we'll feature it in the morning edition with banner headlines."

"No, we can't print it until the noon edition. I made a promise to Mr. Sloanberg to hold off until he could get the jury sequestered. He plans to approach the judge first thing in the morning and the police briefing of the media won't be until our story is on the street."

"You're walking a very fine line, but I'll trust your judgment. Go write your story."

CHAPTER 100

Sloanberg and McAllen called Judge Levine at 8:00 a.m. and made an appointment to see her at 9:00 a.m. Attorney Smith was also invited to attend. Promptly at 9:00 a.m, the three attorneys were ushered into the Judges chambers. She was quite curious as to the reason for this meeting. She also asked about Mr. Bailey absence. Sloanberg explained that Bailey was in custody for questioning on a charge of conspiracy to commit murder.

Judge, "What in the hell did he do?"

Sloanberg, "That is part of a very long story." He began a more accurate account of the attack on Melissa, the reason for the gunshot death of Sam Jones by Dr. Lawrence, and the fact that the attack was not just a random act of violence, but an attempt to prevent her testimony. The judge was livid with rage that someone would try to influence the outcome of a trial in which she was the presiding judge by attempted murder on a critical witness.

Sloanberg, "It gets worse, Judge." He continued with a step-by-step involvement of the two private investigators, the HMO defense attorney and the CEO of the HMO.

Judge, "How could this happen?"

Sloanberg, "It appears that Blake is an unscrupulous individual driven by greed and the sanction of his stockholders. He was apprehended at the airport on his way to the Caymans, apparently to empty the vault and disappear into the oblivion of some foreign country."

Smith, "How does this affect my client?"

Sloanberg, "Apparently not at all. No one has implicated either you or your client."

Judge, "What do you propose?"

Sloanberg, "I would suggest that the malpractice trial be allowed to go to its conclusion. The jury must be sequestered. The Telegram will come out at noon today with the expose of everything I have just told you. About the same time, the police plan to hold a media briefing. By this time, everyone in Southern California, if not the world, would be privy to this information."

Judge, "How will you conclude your case? Will you use all this material?"

Sloanberg, "I have one more witness and my summary. My witness will testify to the stock ownership of the HMO. The summary will deal primarily with the medical facts of the case. I will use the deathbed statement of Sam Jones and describe the attempt on Ms. Hailey's life. The other statements are possibly too prejudicial and have no place in the trial."

Judge, "Mr. McAllen?"

"I'll just defend my client in my closing statement as I had planned. The other information has limited application to his defense."

Judge, "Mr. Smith?"

Smith, "I'll summarize the facts as they relate to the alleged malpractice only as long as no one accuses me or my client of complicity with the attempted coercion."

Judge, "Who will close for the HMO."

Sloanberg, "You should contact Scott Huddleston, the second chair attorney for the HMO and assure yourself that he has no knowledge of the tampering. He has not been implicated by anyone so far."

Judge, "The other alternative is to declare a mistrial and start all over. I'll have to hear Mr. Huddleston on that before I make my ruling."

Sloanberg, "If I may, Judge, you will have a much less likelihood of a prejudiced verdict with the present jury sequestered. After the media and the DA gets through with this case, there won't be a prospective juror in the country who will not be prejudiced by the murder indictments to be handed down against the principles. I doubt seriously if the HMO will remain a viable entity."

Judge, "I tend to agree with your logic. I'll still have to confer with Mr. Huddleston. But I'll sequester the jury immediately, as soon as I have made those arrangements I'll meet with Huddleston."

CHAPTER 101

At 11:30 a.m., the media congregated in the auditorium of the police station oblivious to the purpose of the briefing. The Sam Jones attack had been described as a home invasion and the statement he made before his death have remained confidential. The arrest of the private investigators had stirred little media curiosity. The arrest of Bailey and Blake had not been publicized. Even Bailey's law firm had not gone to the press. Ladd, Holmes and Dunbeck sat at a table in the front of the room anticipating questions. The DA was also present. Ladd began the briefing with the attack on Melissa Hailey, the death of Sam Jones and the statement he made which he read. He then summarized the statements of Nichols, Kurtz and Bailey. Blake's arrest was next mentioned along with the fact that he refused to make a statement claiming his fifth amendment rights.

Needless-to-say, the members of the media were both amazed and outraged at the information provided them.

"Why did you lie to us about the Hailey attack?"

"We didn't lie to you, we just kept part of the facts confidential in order to prevent the co-conspirators from fleeing. As a result, they were captured without incident and made statements which essentially solved three murders and one assault."

"How will this affect the trial?"

"I can't answer that. It's not our problem?"

"Will you seek the death penalty for any or all of these people?"

The D.A., "That has not been decided yet."

"Is everyone involved in this in custody?"

"To our knowledge, yes."

"Will the doctor be charged in the death of Jones?"

The D.A., "The case will go directly to the grand jury. Our recommendation will be justifiable homicide."

"Where did Jones come from? Is he a local or an imported hitman?"

Dunbeck, "He was a pro out of Detroit."

"Who was the mastermind of this scheme?"

"Apparently William Blake."

Ladd, "If there's nothing else, this meeting is adjourned."

On leaving the building, the media participants were confronted with kiosks containing the noon edition of the Telegram with banner headlines, "Bedpost Rapist Dead." This was followed by the story and confession of Sam Jones. Other related articles starting on the front page included, "Conspiracy to Disrupt Malpractice Trial," "HMO Defense Lawyer charged," photos on page 3. There were photos of Melissa, Dr. Lawrence, Bailey and some taken at the scene of the murders of the three women killed earlier.

Needless-to-say, the members of the media were outraged to have been scooped in such a underhanded manner. Someone had leaked the story and they resolved to determine who. Of course, the by-line was Maria Gonzales. She would be besieged by her colleagues as to the source of her story, to no avail. They could only guess and keep it in mind to retaliate against Maria and the police sometime in the future. Actually, it's all part of the game.

CHAPTER 102

Judge Levine met with Mr. Huddleston. By this time he had seen the story. The judge related the facts as she had been told and the implications to the completion of the trial. He, of course, demanded a mistrial based upon the media blitz. She assured him that the jury had been sequestered before any of these stories were made public. She pointed out that if a mistrial or even a continuance was granted, this jury or a jury impaneled for a new trial would be subjected to the information being circulated by the media. The best chance to avoid prejudice against the HMO would be to finish this trial with the jury which was sequestered. She therefore ruled against both mistrial and a continuance. He was advised that the trial would resume tomorrow. All parties were notified and ordered to be ready the next day.

CHAPTER 103

On rebuttal, Sloanberg's first witness was Inspector Ladd. He was duly sworn and the pertinent biographical information was placed on the record by the initial questions. Following those formalities, Sloanberg began his examination.

Sloanberg, "Inspector Ladd, you have headed a task force investigating the so-called "Bedpost Rapes.""

Huddleston, "Objection. This line of questioning is irrelevant to the facts of this trial."

Sloanberg, "Your Honor, if you will bear with me, I will be able to show the relevance."

Judge, "Objection overruled."

Sloanberg, "Your investigation of those crimes climaxed two nights ago. Is that correct?"

Ladd, "Yes."

Sloanberg, "Would you explain the circumstances."

"A Mr. Sam Jones was interrupted in the midst of a similar crime involving Ms. Melissa Hailey by a gunshot from Dr. Lawrence. That gunshot proved fatal to Jones, but prior to his demise, he confessed to three murders and implicated two private investigators, a lawyer and an executive."

Sloanberg, "Who were those individuals?"

Ladd, "Investigators Ralph Nichols and Andrew Kurtz, attorney John Bailey and the CEO of the defendant HMO, William Blake."

Sloanberg, "You said he implicated those people. What was the motive?"

Ladd, "Jones was hired to eliminate four potential witnesses in this trail."

Sloanberg, "Hired by whom?"

"By the CEO and the lawyer for the HMO."

Sloanberg, "And the purpose?"

Ladd, "To influence the outcome of this trial."

Sloanberg, "Do you have any evidence of that motive?"

"Yes, I have a deathbed statement of Jones and subsequent statements by Nichols, Kurtz and Bailey confirming what I stated. Mr. Blake is also in custody, but he has so far maintained his innocence."

Sloanberg, "You plan to indict these individuals?"

"Yes we do."

Sloanberg, "Thank you, Inspector. Your Honor, I would like to enter the statements mentioned into evidence."

Judge, "So ordered."

"Mr. Huddleston?"

Huddleston, "Inspector do you have any reason to believe that the conspiracy that you testified to involved any of the other officers or board directors of the HMO?"

"No sir."

"I have nothing further."

Judge, "Any other cross?" There was none. "Being none, Mr. Sloanberg, do you have any other witnesses?"

Sloanberg, "One more. Mr. George Williamson. Mr. Williamson, please state your business."

Williamson, "I'm a stockbroker."

Sloanberg again went through his qualifications to establish his credentials as an expert.

Sloanberg, "In your business, you buy, sell and rate stocks that are not on the New York, American or NASDAC exchanges, do you not?"

"Yes."

Sloanberg, "Are you familiar with the stock of the HMO which is a defendant in this trial?"

Williamson, "Yes."

Sloanberg, "Would you give us a brief history of the stock."

"Yes. It became an IPO approximately two years ago and came on the market at $5.00 a share. For about six months it did not appreciate. Suddenly it began to increase in value and prior to this lawsuit, it was trading at $35.00 a share."

Sloanberg, "Can you explain this sudden rise?"

Williamson, "Two things. The CEO was very aggressive in taking over other HMO's, clinics, hospitals and physician groups. This management style caught the eye of an investment club in Cleveland, Ohio, which poured large amounts of money into the stock until it had obtained a 65% ownership of the company."

Sloanberg, "Is there anything unusual about this 'investment club'?"

Williamson, "Yes, that club is a syndicate-owned and operated organization which is used to launder money."

Sloanberg, "I have nothing further."

Judge, "Any cross?"

The courtroom was in stunned silence. The other attorneys could think of nothing else to add or subtract.

Judge, "We'll recess until tomorrow at which time we'll start the summations. Mr. Sloanberg, you will go first followed by Mr. McAllen, Mr. Smith and Mr. Huddleston. The jury will remain sequestered until a verdict has been rendered.

CHAPTER 104

L.A.'s appetite for all the gory details was whetted by the revelations in today's court session and nearly everything else was crowded out of the media. It was equivalent to the riots, the Rodney King trial and the Simpson trial. The populace lived on sensationalism.

The people had been confined to their homes and offices for months now for fear of the bedpost rapist. The dramatic solution to these crimes had been like the sudden release of a whole city population from the imprisonment of fear. There was also a resentment that they could have been subjected to this mental and emotional stress due to the greed of one man and one company, a company that was supposed to take care of sick people.

The Telegram headline was, "Syndicate Owns Health Care Firm." The lead story summarized Williamson's testimony concerning the ownership of the HMO stock and the appreciation of the price of the shares. The clear message was that syndicate members were enriched at the expense of patients and employees of the HMO.

In a related story, Sam Jones' confession was printed in chilling detail, including the clear motive of influencing the verdict in the malpractice trial. Of course, the national media picked this up and featured it all over the country. "All trends start in L.A. and spread across the U.S."

The only group shielded from all this media hype was the jury and they heard it first hand in the courtroom.

CHAPTER 105

Summations were brief and anticlimactic. Sloanberg went first.

Sloanberg, "Your Honor, ladies and gentlemen of the jury, you have heard three weeks of testimony concerning the wrongful death of Alex Boomer and the ripple effects on his family, his company, four innocent people who just happened to stand in the way of justice and a health care system run amok. You have heard how a young doctor, conscientious and with good credentials caved in to the greed of his employer and allowed his judgment to be perverted by rules, regulations and procedures which he knew were wrong and that directly caused the wrongful death of Alex Boomer. You have heard the excuse that he used a tried-and-true heart drug as a test. That simply is not acceptable in this day and time.

"You've heard how the medical director of the clinic compounded that error by negligently condoning Dr. Lawrence's treatment regime without either discussing the case with Lawrence, examining the patient or even entering his conversation in the chart. That also is negligent. Finally, the ultimate responsibility for the wrongful death of the patient and the premeditated murder of three witnesses belongs to the HMO whose greed is ultimately responsible for this whole tragedy. I urge you to find them all guilty of malpractice and punish them each according to its ability to pay. Thank you."

The courtroom was hushed during Sloanberg's presentation. McAllen was next.

"Your Honor and ladies and gentlemen of the jury, you have indeed heard all the testimony Mr. Sloanberg referred to. Your job is to interpret that material and try to place blame appropriately. Dr. Lawrence's care of this patient adhered to well established principles, long accepted as standard care for angina. The tests and treatments mentioned which you were told should have been done are relatively new, dangerous and expensive. It is not standard practice to subject every middle-aged man with chest pain to those tests and treatments. Observation and drug treatment is a standard first step in the diagnosis and care of such patients.

"In this emerging era of managed care, it is acceptable to relegate such sophisticated treatment skills to a secondary role. Dr. Lawrence followed his training, skills, his conscience and the procedures required of him by his employers. That is within the standard of practice. Thank you."

Judge, "It's time for the morning recess. Mr. Smith will give his summation when we return in fifteen minutes."

McAllen and Lawrence retired to a deserted corner of the cafeteria for a cup of coffee.

Lawrence, "Sloanberg did not seem to be trying to help me."

McAllen, "He has to place blame on you in order to get to Shepard and the HMO."

Lawrence, "Do you think all the publicity and the police testimony will influence the outcome of this trial?"

McAllen, "There is no way that it can fail to. The HMO will try for mistrial or a dismissal but I don't think the judge will go along."

Lawrence, "It's time to go back."

Smith rose and started his presentation somewhat hesitantly.

"Your Honor and ladies and gentlemen of the jury, Dr. Shepard does not remember the conversation with the deceased. It seems obvious that it took place. Again, he felt that Dr. Lawrence's treatment was appropriate and he was confident that continuing that course was appropriate. His decision not to intervene was based on medical judgment which proved to be wrong in this case. However, he must be judged on his adherence to the standard of practice which the Judge will tell you is far different from medical judgment. Thank you."

Judge, "Mr. Huddleston."

"Your Honor and ladies and gentlemen of the jury, we have heard many disturbing things about my client. It would seem that the CEO is responsible for those violations of the law and medical ethics. The HMO is made up of many honorable and dedicated professionals in both the medical and business worlds. The actions of one man cannot be the sole basis of judgment of the organization. A criminal court will sort all of that out and punish the guilty. This is a civil trial to determine whether the HMO is responsible for the actions of the medical professional it is contracted with. You have heard witnesses from law and business tell you that the courts have upheld the principle that it does not control and therefore is not responsible for the negligence of those individuals with whom it contracts. Remember that and let criminal justice deal with those who have broken the law. Thank you."

Judge, "Mr. Sloanberg, do you have any rebuttals?"

"Thank you, Your Honor. I agree with Mr. Huddleston that the guilty will be dealt with by the criminal justice system. However, the veil of separation of HMO and clinic does not apply in this case. Remember, the reciprocal stock ownership. That completely abrogates the legal theory of separation of the HMO from the clinic. This HMO had a forty-nine percent ownership of the clinic and therefore is responsible for its actions. In this case, the principle alluded to is not relevant to this case. Thank you."

Judge, "We are adjourned until this afternoon at which time I will give my instructions to the jury. Since you are sequestered, I want you to have the case over the weekend. So you will not waste two days before beginning your deliberations.

CHAPTER 106

The court resumed at 2:00 p.m. The judge's instructions were simple. She first explained the difference between judgement and negligence, that is, a physician could make a judgement error without being guilty of negligence. Negligence was defined as doing or not doing something which did not conform to the acceptable standard of practice in the community.

She next explained that any or all of the defendants could be judged guilty or innocent. Finally she explained the principle of proportionate responsibility. Based on their judgment, the jury could determine and assign a percentage of liability to each of the defendants being judged guilty of malpractice. With that, she discharged the jury and sent them to begin deliberations.

CHAPTER 107

Michael left the courthouse with his beeper in place to visit with Melissa. They had hardly seen each other since the night of her injury. He brought her up to date on the conclusion of the trial, especially the testimony of Inspector Ladd and Mr. Williamson. He briefly recounted the summations.

Melissa was now out of ICU, free of all the tubes and able to be up in her room and walk in the halls. They were so happy to be together again and free of the fear of attack, they just held each other without speaking for a long time. Their love had been through one severe test after another, but now there was a dim light at the end of the tunnel.

When his beeper went off, they both shook with anxiety. The verdict could hardly be in so quickly. The call was from Nancy. She was in labor at another hospital and she wanted him present at the birth of his son. The vindictiveness seemed to have temporarily disappeared or maybe she just wanted to taunt him with the birth of his son. Never-the-less, it placed another obstacle over the relationship between Michael and Melissa. When he left, all the happiness had disappeared and Melissa was in tears.

On arrival at Cedars OB Pavilion, Michael was ushered into the delivery room to find Nancy in hard labor and with another man acting as her coach. This was awkward especially since Michael did not know the man and had no idea that Nancy was already in another relationship. No doubt his ego told him that even though he had discarded her, she would never replace him. Between pains, she introduced him as George Kindle, a senior law student interning in the office of her divorce attorney. He appeared to be very attentive, was quite handsome and at least five year younger than

Nancy. It was obvious she had summoned him there to embarrass him. She had succeeded.

Soon her labor grew more intense and she was taken to the delivery room and a six pound four ounce boy was delivered without incident. The baby was perfect in every respect and both Nancy and her "friend" seemed thrilled. Michael was so taken aback by this whole episode that he hardly noticed the baby and felt completely detached from the whole episode, including his son.

CHAPTER 108

The days ground on without a verdict. The lawyers were beginning to fear a mistrial. After all that had happened, nobody was willing to accept a failure to reach a verdict. The press continued to camp out at the courthouse and all the lawyers and participants were in suspended animation. In the meantime, the case against Blake, Bailey and the two private investigators were taken to the grand jury. Blake was indicting for first degree murder and the others for conspiracy to commit murder on all three counts.

The press kept up a continuous harangue of the story. L.A. settled back into its normal indifference. The fear had disappeared. Bars, clubs, restaurants and movies were again full to capacity. The natives had successfully weathered another crises. However, their curiosity was unquenchable concerning the characters in the drama. Everyone who ever knew any of them was interviewed on television, talk radio and the tabloids. The whole topic of medical care delivery became a subject of debate in the media, in medical circles and at cocktail parties. Medical personnel were sought out for their opinions and were happy to be able to say, "I told you so." Politicians who championed managed care were derided in editorials and letters to the editor. People had long ago accepted that the syndicate controlled the garbage collection, disposal business but were unable to comprehend this domination of their medical care.

CHAPTER 109

The first break in the deliberations came when the jury asked the judge more precisely the difference between negligence and judgment error as they applied to malpractice. The second came when she was asked the limits of punitive damages and actual monetary loss. The clan gathered at the courthouse sensing a possible blood bath. Two hours later, their appetite was satiated. The jury returned a unanimous verdict of guilt of all parties and the limit of two hundred fifty thousand dollars punitive damage of each defendant. That was only the beginning. Dr. Lawrence was assessed additional damages of $750,000; Dr. Shepard an additional two and a half million, the Clinic an additional five million, and the HMO five hundred million. This was clearly the largest malpractice verdict damages ever assessed.

The lawyers were stunned as was the media. The defense lawyers immediately appealed to the judge to reduce the awards. She refused stating that it was in the discression of the jury to levy whatever amounts they felt were justified. The potential earnings of Alex Boomer and the potential loss to his company made this huge award justifiable. She could not deny that the attempt to manipulate the trial by the brutal murders, intimidation and assault influenced the magnitude of the award. The jury clearly was sending a message.

Of course, all parties filed notice of appeal, but it seemed unlikely any would be granted.

Michael was stunned. He had anticipated that the jury bought into the theory of "the devil made me do it" and he would be found not guilty. He could only console himself with the knowledge that his malpractice insurance level had not been exceeded and he would not be responsible personally for any part of the one million dollars. For him, it was a mixed blessing. Just how mixed he would soon learn. Shepard and the Clinic would be bankrupted. Shepard might have to move to the Caymans, the Clinic would be sold to help pay off the award. With Blake and Bailey in jail, the HMO would have to call a meeting of directors and stockholders to determine their next move. Elizabeth Boomer and her children would be wealthy as they most certainly would have been had her husband lived. Eric Sloanberg would certainly be the premiere plaintiff attorney in Southern California and probably the nation. He would be the rightful heir to the title of, "King of Torts."

CHAPTER 110

Gary Gebhardt immediately filed liens on the Clinic, its real estate, bank accounts, equipment and accounts payable. He filed a similar lien on the HMO covering all assets. Dr. Shepard's assets did not escape. This was accomplished the day the verdict was rendered, giving none of the defendant parties time to react. As a result, the Clinic and the HMO were forced to cease operations immediately, leaving a large number of individuals devoid of medical care. This, of course, caused a health care crisis in every E.R., hospital and medical facility in the city reminiscent of the doctor's strike of the mid-70's. Several thousand medical personnel and support personnel were out of work and without the salary owed them.

There would be no Chapter 11 bankruptcy and no structured settlements. Because of the actions of the officers in attempting to sorbourne justice by the murder and assault of witnesses, the plaintiff attorneys and the court had no mercy on the Clinic and the HMO. Both filed bankruptcy and their assets were sold to pay off the judgments and other legitimate expenses. Other medical groups would eventually take up the slack in patient care.

This decision sent shock waves through the whole managed care industry. They no longer were immune to malpractice litigation. The whole concept would have to be rethought.

CHAPTER 111

No one had seen or heard from Robin and Emily since the Saturday before the attempt on Melissa's life. Jack Burge had exhausted all of his resources to find them, but to no avail. He had turned the problem over to missing persons and eventually the problem surfaced on Inspector Ladd's desk. He remembered Michael complaining that his and Melissa's bodyguards had not responded before and at the time of the assault on Melissa. This just seemed unusual since the Burge Agency had a good reputation with the P.D. and the public. He decided to requestion his prisoners about this subject. He started with Nichols and hit a stone wall. He got the same result from Blake who had admitted nothing. Since the revelation about syndicate ownership of the HMO, Blake had been kept in a private cell for his own protection. Ladd finally brought Kurtz into the interrogation area and enlisted the aid of Holmes to play good cop/bad cop with him. The promises of intervention with the D.A. brought no response. Holmes then again brought up deportation. This threat opened the flood gates.

Kurtz admitted that he had bribed Emily to keep him appraised of the activities of Michael and Melissa. This was done at the instigation of Bailey and probably Blake. As a result, Jones had them under surveillance continuously during the last week before the attempted murder. Emily's last report was on the Saturday when Michael and Melissa met at Sloanberg's office for a briefing. He related this information to Bailey who then ordered the murder of Melissa. He also ordered the murders of Robin and Emily to neutralize any protection of the potential victims. Kurtz notified Nichols who gave the order to Jones.

"This is the last any of us heard from the two women. Only

Jones knew what happened to them. No doubt he killed both and hid their bodies in some remote location. Ladd notified Jack Burge of his findings. Jack was horrified by both the betrayal of trust and the death of his agents. He called McAllen and apologized for the breach of confidence. His reception was quite cool. This incident might well destroy the reputation he had worked so hard to earn and maintain.

CHAPTER 112

Under the leadership of the new board chairman of ACME Electric, Elizabeth Boomer, it instigated a suit for civil damages against the Clinic and HMO. There was little hope of collecting any substantial amount of money but this would assure that neither entity would be able to recover. With a new president who was knowledgeable about the business, ACME was recovering nicely. Elizabeth was adapting to the business climate quite well and it was therapeutic for her.

CHAPTER 113

On the day Melissa was to be released from the hospital, Michael received a certified letter from BMQA informing him that his license to practice medicine was suspended pending further training. The size of the award in the malpractice case convinced the board that it was unsafe for him to practice without supervision until such time as he had obtained further training in the form of a residency or a preceptorship at a recognized teaching hospital.

His divorce had become final and Nancy had been awarded sole custody of their son, their home, child support, alimony and her legal fees. Now he couldn't work and earn a living. What could he do? He wasn't trained for anything but medicine. Residency pay would be a pittance with his obligations. He was too proud to live off Melissa, especially to expect her to pay his alimony and child support. He had no family and no friends, only Melissa. How long would he have her under the circumstances?

He seriously considered suicide. He got out his Glock revolver and was gazing at it with fascination.

At that instant the phone rang. He picked it up reflexly. It was the hospital and he was told to come immediately. No other information was given.

He put the gun down and rushed to the nurse's station from which the call had been made.

The nurse escorted him into a conference room and offered him a cup of coffee. She told him only that the doctor would be with him shortly. William Sumner appeared almost immediately. He was dressed in his scrub suit. His face was covered in perspiration and his scrub shirt was soaked through with blood. His expression was solemn.

He put his arm around Michael shoulder and with a voice breaking with emotion said, "Melissa is dead." Michael screamed, "How could that be?"

Somewhat more controlled, Sumner said, "She had gotten along exceedingly well considering what happened to her. She was getting dressed to go home. The nurse was with her, she coughed, let out a scream of surprise and pain, fainted and fell to the floor. A code was called immediately. The team was here in two minutes. When I saw her and heard the story, I assumed she had a massive pulmonary embolism. I opened her chest in the room and tried to suck out the clot which was sitting at the bifurcation of her pulmonary artery. She never responded even though we got it out and controlled the bleeding. I tried this only because I got there so soon and I had two previous successful resuscitation from similar situations. I am so sorry for your loss."

Michael was inconsolable. "How did you miss the clot in her leg? Didn't you check for this type of thing?"

"Every day I examined her legs because she was a prime candidate for this type of complication."

He was allowed to go into the room to see her. She was so beautiful, even in death. He had loved her more than life itself. In death, she had saved his life, but to what purpose.